SOMETHING BORROWED, SOMETHING BLUE AND MURDER

Book Twelve: The Fiona
Fleming Cozy Mysteries

PATTI LARSEN

Cover design by Christina Gaudet
www.castlekeepcreations.com

Thanks, Kirstin!

ISBN-13: 978-1-988700-96-0

CHAPTER ONE

Vivian's face was as icy cold as ever as she spoke, though I had to wonder if the Queen of Wheat turned mayor would be able to sustain that chilly exterior as the town fell apart around her. A big contrast to the cutesy Christmas decorations someone hung to attempt to make things look festive and not like the bleak wasteland of French formality and control hadn't taken hold of the cutest town in America and turned it into a police state. She certainly didn't have Olivia's penchant for thriving on stress, as far as I was concerned, and would likely fall to pieces in short order.

Speaking of stress. Hello there, pressure and anxiety tied to what was actually happening right now. When she focused that intense stare on me, I knew better than to think I was going to escape my share of the weight she was about to unload on my shoulders just because she was that kind of person, and I was right in front of her for no good reason I could come up with.

"Yet again we find ourselves embroiled in a murder investigation," Vivian said while the other council members muttered and nodded like this was my fault. Argh. I wish they understood how disconcerting it was to stumble over dead bodies. Not one of them got it, though, did they? All safely protected from the gruesome knowledge and nightmare-inducing memories of being in the presence of victims over and over again. Twelve and counting, go me.

Vivian wasn't done and I snapped my attention back to her while she stared down at the surface of her desk like she was trying to maintain her temper and composure, prim pink Grace Fiore dress as much her uniform as that of Deputy Jill Wagner who stood beside me, her face tight, jaw jumping, hands grasping her gun belt for dear life.

"Sheriff." Vivian didn't look up, her voice so low I saw more than one of the witnesses to this little unfolding performance strain forward to hear her. Her tone rose when she looked up, pale eyes snapping. "I expect you to step up and take care of this problem ASAP." Right, because a dead body was a problem, not a terrible end to someone's existence. "Or I'll be finding you a replacement. Are we clear?"

I swallowed hard, heart suddenly pounding,

knowing this was it. The end of this particular road, and I was surprised how upset I felt about it. I glanced around, knowing any backup I might have access to was long gone as the Reading's sheriff answered in a voice far steadier than I expected.

"Mayor French," I said. "I'll do my best."

And whoopsie doodle. I think I'm a bit ahead of myself, aren't I? You're lost and wondering what the heck and I'm rambling. So sorry, back up the train, Fleming. I didn't mean to leap ahead like that, to make this a bigger mess than, quite frankly, it already was.

You'll be patient with me, though, right? See, a lot happened in the twenty-four hours prior to me taking on the job my fiancé held the last four years. Since I'd known him, in fact. Confused? Yeah, you're in good company.

But I digress.

All things being equal, shall we start again so your brain doesn't randomly implode like I think mine might have…?

CHAPTER ONE
(for real this time, I promise)

A very short twenty-four hours ago in a cute and messed up town in Vermont...

How weird to stand in the foyer at Petunia's and not hear a peep. So quiet, so still, mid-December sunlight streaming in the windows, the peaceful emptiness of a place so rarely without occupants making me a bit nostalgic for my childhood.

I'd spent so many summers helping my grandmother here, Iris Fleming's particular way of doing things, her dry sense of humor, her careful and precise language, the way she taught me with the steady and powerful self-confidence of a woman who didn't care one whit what others thought of her ingrained far more deeply in me than I'd ever imagined. At least, until she passed away and I'd come home to Reading.

To Petunia's, the place she loved so very much.

I wanted to think Grandmother Iris would be excited by the prospect of my wedding here in this beautiful house. Mom's attempt to get Crew and me hitched at a more impressive venue—the annex, for one—was really one of the only lines I drew in the sand (who was I kidding, winter in Vermont meant lines in the snow) and my gorgeous fiancé agreed when I insisted.

The annex was lovely and amazing, and I adored it.

But Petunia's was home. And I wanted, more than anything in the world, to marry the love of my life here inside its amazing walls. Fitting, as far as I was concerned.

I turned in a slow circle, my high heel slipping easily over the entry carpet, as I enjoyed these final moments of silence in my beloved home. Any second now I'd be overwhelmed (in a good way, I kept telling myself) by the people who cared about me the most, by the organist and the soloist and the minister and my parents, my bestie, my darling Crew… yes, it was only the rehearsal, not the wedding day, but there was something final feeling about this afternoon and the events about to unfold in the bed and breakfast that had claimed my heart and soul as much as the man I loved.

I glanced down and spotted my pug following my

revolving turn, huffing as she made sure she kept up despite the fact I wasn't really going anywhere, just spinning in a circle. She'd been acting funny the last two days, since I checked out the last of the guests and got down to cleaning, Mom cracking the whip on Jill, Daisy and myself (bless them for their patience) as we scrubbed Petunia's main floor within an inch of our lives.

While I'd felt a bit like Cinderella with Mom firmly ensconced in the Evil Stepmother role despite the fact we looked enough alike we could have been sisters, I had to admit the final result left Petunia's sparkling, smelling like spring was around the corner instead of months away and ready, picture-perfect, for my wedding day.

It had taken some wrangling to get a week free, but I managed it, starting as soon as we'd chosen the date, funneling visitors toward the White Valley Lodge, or promising them discounts if they'd just let me tie the freaking knot already. We'd stayed hard-core busy, both here and at the annex, despite the turnover in mayors. I shouldn't have been surprised, and wasn't, when Vivian French, the Queen of Wheat herself, took over the helm of the cutest town in America, easily winning the November election and sweeping Olivia Walker aside. Despite the latter's impressive record up to that point keeping Reading on the map, as far as I was concerned. But Vivian had asked me to back her, to trust her and though I was still wondering why I should, ultimately, it had been clear that Vivian's landslide win wasn't going to be changed just because Fiona Fleming decided one way or the other.

Reading residents wanted a change and Vivian was their new darling.

Petunia followed me, her triangle black ears perked, as I crossed the foyer and headed for the dining room. It had been emptied of the tables and chairs, the long sideboard that normally housed the buffet-style offerings Mom had made Petunia's famous for, and the tall, wooden hutch that held Grandmother Iris's prized china. Now relocated (temporarily) to the kitchen, that left this long, narrow room ready for the two rows of chairs flanking the central aisle of deep red carpet Mom managed to find somewhere, Christmas red bows gracing each of the seats, the setup lavish and, according to my mother, almost done.

As far as I was concerned it looked perfect three layers of decorations ago, but I was just the bride, right? Mom had clearly lost her mind. Snort.

Petunia sat on my foot as if she could pin me to the ground, looking up at me with a huge yawn that ended in a meowing pug protest.

"I know," I said. "She's gone overboard. But what was I supposed to do? She's my mother. And this is the only wedding she's going to get." At least, that was my plan.

Petunia sighed and rubbed her nose with one paw, like she wasn't buying my argument about my mother, and I shrugged it off before turning to leave the room, heading for the kitchen. The pug grunted before plodding along with me, her claws ticking on the tile floor as I held the door for her and let her precede me.

I glanced out the window toward the annex, knowing it was still packed and as busy as ever, that the Christmas Lights Extravaganza Olivia had set up and was left in place was still in full swing. I'd strolled last night with Crew, arm in arm, and smiled at the excessively lit and gift wrapped houses and businesses of Reading as the whole town seemed to throw themselves into holiday frenzy. Was it guilt that this was Olivia's venture, the third annual, and they wanted to make sure it was bigger and sparklier than ever to, what? Honor the woman they betrayed? Or prove to her they could manage just fine without her?

From what I'd heard, Olivia herself had taken her loss in stride and was running a very successful online marketing company, but every time I tried to talk to her, she avoided me like the plague.

Okay then. Though what I did to deserve it was lost on me.

Looking at the annex made me pause and think about the way things used to be, back when I first moved home and took over Petunia's. Was it that sense of nostalgia that triggered the flashback to Peggy Munroe and her creepily silent little dog, Cookie, leaning over my fence to gossip? Or was it the fact the old woman who hated my guts and broke out of prison with her grandniece's assistance was still at large that gave me a faint shudder down my spine?

Well, she'd been out and on the run since September and there hadn't been a whisper about her, so I had forced myself to shelve my fears and chose to believe she'd run off to Florida or wherever old murderous ladies with vendettas went to hide from the law.

I heard a car pull into the driveway, knew there would be more soon. Listened to the door slam, the sound of voices, thought about the honeymoon suite upstairs, my dress spread out on the comforter in the garment bag, the jewelry, my shoes, all carefully displayed and ready for the morning. For my makeup and hair and getting dressed and photos and...

And. Endless everything until I got to say I do to the most amazing, handsome, charming, kind and loving man I'd ever met.

Endless would be worth it.

My pug huffed while I grinned down at her. "Happily ever after," I said. "Doesn't that just sound amazing, Petunia?"

She tilted her head and grinned, tongue lolling out and I took that as a huge yes.

CHAPTER TWO

"Fee, sweetheart!" I knew Mom's voice anywhere and hurried into the foyer to find her laden down with an armload of groceries. She beamed at me as I ran to assist, liberating her from two large, canvas bags brimming over with vegetables while Daisy slipped in behind her, her own giant smile as sunny as the day outside.

Mom shook a bit of snow from her boots before slipping out of them, Daisy setting aside the box of fresh bread she held and taking Mom's lovely cream wool coat before hanging her own tailored red one in the hall closet. I caught tears in my eyes and my breath as I looked at the two of them, wanting to weep suddenly even though I was happy, so happy. Mom rushed to me and embraced me, Daisy joining us with a low cry and the three of us broke into soft sobs and giggles while Dad, his own burdens filling his arms, tall, broad body blocking most of the doorway, shook his head at our antics.

"You'd think this was a funeral," he grumped in typical John Fleming fashion, though his beaming smile for me when I laughed and pulled out of the gorgeous women's embrace and lunged for him, making his breath oof out of his lungs when I squeezed extra hard told a totally different story from his words. "Love you, Fee," he whispered into my hair, unable to hug me back, the bags he balanced held out of the way so I could get some solid Dad contact.

"Love you, too." I sniffled and smiled up at him, though when I tried to lighten his load, he dodged me with a grin and a wink, his own eyes faintly moist and just as close to emotion as the three of us were, the old fraud.

"I got this," he said, skirting me and heading for the kitchen. "I'm not useless yet, you know."

I snorted. Like my tall, big-shouldered father who hadn't gained an ounce of fat on his body since high school would ever be anything but my hero. No, don't burst my bubble. I refused to believe even for a second this time in my life would slip away and I'd have to face my parents getting older, me, the farty pug at my feet who had a bit grayer in her muzzle these days, not quite as much spring in her step. Nope, not going there, not now, not ever, thank you very much.

Choke.

Mom was back into frenzy mode while I fought off the emotional rollercoaster that had been my existence the last few days, hurrying off to the kitchen after Dad with her load of goodies, Daisy following more slowly, hooking one arm through mine while she balanced the box of bread between us.

"You must be so excited, Fee." She'd only said that at least four times a day, every day, for the past three weeks and the answer was always the same. Yes. Yes, I freaking was. Daisy sighed that delightfully delicious sigh of hers, the one that was utterly devoid of any jealousy but brimming and fully stocked with all kinds of happy goodness one might attribute to her getting married, not me.

Not that she was, at least not yet. She'd been spending a lot of time with the handsome investor, Emile Reis, who seemed to be, in turn, taking his time going home to Luxemburg or Belgium or wherever it was he was from, lingering in Reading like a lost puppy dog looking for someone (Daisy) to adopt (love) him. There was a time I'd thought him intensely attractive in his tall and icy blond, piercingly unnaturally blue-eyed, broad jawed European royalty kind of way. Until I recalled how he'd made Daisy feel like she wasn't good enough by telling her she needed to leave Reading. The jerk. Only to discover she had, of course, misread what he'd said, thanks to her evil half-sister Rose who always made things worse whenever she was around (gifted like that, the witch with a capital "B"). Emile himself had told me not so long ago he'd encouraged Daisy to leave because he saw so much potential in her he hated to see her stay small.

Imagine. He wanted that particular flower to blossom. Well, I was with him in that plan. But Daisy? Leave me? Double choke.

He wasn't the creep I'd thought him to be when he'd left that fateful Valentine's party with Vivian French on his arm instead of my beautiful friend. Rather, she'd rejected him (thank you, Rose) and broken his heart (poor guy) while thinking he was the one at fault (how easily communication fell apart when we let ourselves think we weren't good enough and yes, I was looking at you again, Daisy). The fact he'd come back to Reading over and over (I'd failed to realize how many times in the past three years, but it was a lot, apparently) just to see Daisy…? How had I missed it?

Well, she'd been in her own whirlwind of doldrums and, as per Daisy's way, hated dumping her silly stuff on me, so she'd kept it all bottled up until recently.

I hugged her arm with mine as we passed together through the swinging door into the kitchen and caught my breath at the thought of her leaving. Because as she let me go, I noticed the gorgeous bracelet on her wrist, the string of expensively jeweled flowers of her namesake that skimmed her skin, a single diamond dangling from a thin chain at the clasp indication enough she'd decided to take steps with Emile that meant, more than likely, my days with my bestie at my side full time were numbered.

I didn't get to cry over that. Just didn't. She deserved to be happy, too. But damn it. What was I going to do without her?

"Fee." I felt my jaw set at the tone in Mom's voice, jerking me out of my sadness, at least, and back into the present rather than anticipation of a weepy future with no Daisy in it.

"Mom." I knew that my answering tone would trigger her own jaw jump but just couldn't help myself. We'd been back and forthing like this since she'd taken over my wedding (yes, a bit resentful of that, suck it) and I was tired, hella tired, of being made to feel like this was her wedding and I was a bystander/slave/employee who had better step up or ship out.

So, the whole "what am I going to do without Daisy" thing I was just mourning? Yup, case in point. With the practiced ease of a trained hostage negotiator and a politician paired with a justice of the peace all wrapped up in honey-blonde hair, gray eyes and a flowered dress that would never show a wrinkle no matter if she slept in it or not, my darling Day beamed at Mom and touched her arm, instantly diffusing my uptight mother and saving the (if you'll excuse the pun) day.

"Lucy, let's get these groceries sorted, then I'll help you assemble the hors d'oeuvres." She winked at me. "I know Fee will be so busy greeting our guests as they arrive."

Mom grumbled faintly but was already distracted, diving into the shopping bags while Dad breathed a theatrical—if silent—sigh of relief before grinning evilly at me and escaping the kitchen. I joined him in a hurry, Petunia left behind to wait for scraps, the swinging door sighing for me so I didn't have to as I returned to the foyer with only a hint of annoyance clinging.

Okay, more than a hint. And I know Dad saw it because he engulfed me in his strong arms, the scent of his shirt as familiar as my childhood (Mom hadn't changed her detergent or fabric softener ever).

"One more day, kid," he said. "She's been making herself crazy for this because she loves you. Give her one more day."

I grumbled something unflattering into his buttons before sighing for real. "I know," I said, pushing him away a fraction. "But if this is a prequel to kids? Dad, one of us won't survive and it's probably going to be me."

Dad chuckled and kissed my forehead before stepping away with a little frown. "You two will be fine," he said. "I'm the one who's suffering, after all." He took on an air of horrified angst and made me laugh while I swatted his arm to make him stop.

"Whatever." I glanced at the sideboard, the newspaper there making me pause, heart hurting suddenly. I'd missed out on Alicia and Jared's wedding, though I'd managed to sneak a peek at a few of the pictures, thanks to the occasional over-the-shoulder snooping I wrangled down at Sammy's Coffee. At least a few of the local residents were up for letting me peruse their phones for snippets of the joyous occasion that I'd spent stumbling over and then investigating the murder of the local equestrian riding coach. Not much of a trade-off, if you asked me, but my life, in a nutshell.

The fact that I'd missed their wedding was the past. I was (mostly) over it (yeah, right, Fee, keep telling yourself that if it makes you feel better). But the disappearance and lack of any kind of contact from *Reading Reader Gazette* newspaperwoman Pamela Shard troubled me deeply. I'd spent about two weeks after she vanished into thin air, abandoning the paper to the Pattersons (how expected that Geoffrey Jenkins's son, Christopher, became the reporter/managing editor/manipulator of truth at the helm of the *Gazette* three weeks into Pamela's gone poof) terrified I'd get a call from Dad or Crew or someone else that they'd stumbled on her body. Or, heaven forbid, that I'd find her, dead and tortured, abandoned somewhere hideous, laid low by the Patterson family.

Hey. Finding bodies was my gig. I had precedent and good reason to think such things. No judging.

The fact was, though, that this whole happiness thing I was living day-by-day, my wedding now one day out? Just a smokescreen, at this point, for the fact I was fooling myself into thinking my town wasn't going to erupt into some kind of craziness yet again, just like it always did. Still, as I turned to look up at

Dad, his own frown real this time, his gaze following mine from the paper and what had to be similar thoughts told me this particular redheaded coconut hadn't fallen far from the tall tree in front of her.

"Fee." He gently grasped my shoulders in his hands and shook me just slightly, enough to get my attention. "Don't let them win. Okay? We've faced everything they've thrown at us and made it out the other side stronger for it." I knew he meant the Pattersons, though maybe he was also talking about Reading in general. Not like the residents of this town weren't at least partially complicit to what was going on around them. I couldn't believe all of them were that intensely stupid. "We got this. I got you." He hugged me again and I hugged him back, whispering my agreement into his plaid shirt while my heart lurched in my chest and that uncomfortable feeling came back.

The one that wanted me to marry Crew right now, in this moment, waiting be damned. Just in case something happened that would keep me from him forever.

CHAPTER THREE

Footsteps and voices alerted us to new arrivals, in time for Dad to step away and turn me around, pushing me gently toward the door. I plastered on a smile just as the entry swung open, letting in a little swirl of fresh snow onto the protective mat covering the immediate stretch of hardwood. The two men who entered did so with alternating shows of respect. The younger, leaner and taller of the pair, his thin shoulders hunched under his dark blue pea coat, scuffed his feet on the plastic and rubber combo before sliding them free.

The other, arrogance shining from his face, pushed past his companion with a beaming smile, hand outstretched to—yup, you guessed it—my dad as he breezed by me and pumped my father's hand.

Tracking snow on my floor and carpet. Earning my growing wrath and annoyance as his bigger-than-life voice boomed in the quiet of the foyer.

"John, good to see you." Dominic Twigg finally swung toward me and squeezed my shoulder with one of his big hands, his dark hair swept back from his high forehead, silver temples making him look distinguished, wrinkles crinkling the corners of his hazel eyes. He'd have been labeled attractive by most, despite being in his mid-fifties, though I always found his pompous bearing irritating and detracted from any kind of handsome factor he might have earned himself by being born with looks. "Fiona. So excited for you and our sheriff, my dear." He didn't wait for me to comment, striding past and into the dining room. I followed behind, hands clenched at my side as Reading's choirmaster and church soloist who thought that made him some kind of celebrity seemed underwhelmed by the arrangements we'd created. "Not ideal, is it?" He picked at his lower lip with his index finger and thumb, frowning enough a deep crease between his eyebrows showed his age. "Rather a small crowd, then?" He shrugged it off, smiling at me though I could tell he wasn't happy. Whatever. My wedding, my guest list. "We'll make do. Small audience or big, I'll sing my heart out for you, dear Fiona."

Since he was Mom's choice and I would have been just as happy with my MP3 player and sound system, I held off commenting while Dad steered the singer out of the dining room and to the kitchen where, past the swinging door, the overly loud echo of Dominic's deep voice told me he'd seen Mom.

Lovely. She owed me so big for this.

The other man who'd slipped into Petunia's without much of a fuss stood in his wool socks at the entry to the room, hands tucked into the pockets of his corduroys, thin, brown hair long around his ears and swept occasionally off his forehead before he returned his long fingers to those pockets. I smiled at Ian Rudge, nodding and gesturing for him to enter the room and pointed out the small organ Mom procured for his use.

"Sorry it's nothing fancy," I said. "I really appreciate you doing this, Ian."

The young man shrugged, though he did flash me a real smile, before sitting down to turn the instrument on. A moment later he gently and almost reverently played a soft tune that made my heart ache and I finally thanked Mom (silently, in my head, and she'd never hear otherwise) for insisting on live music. Dominic might have been a bossy, overbearing ass, but Ian was a true artist, and I was lucky to have him.

"That was beautiful, Ian." Mom waited to interrupt until he was done, the last notes fading as she gushed and then hurried to join us. She ignored me completely, hugging him hard, almost knocking his glasses off and he muttered something softly before hugging her back.

"My p-p-pleasure, Mrs. F-F-Fleming. Fee." He bobbed a nod to both of us as I heard the front door open again, Daisy hurrying past the entry to the dining room en route so I didn't have to rush. "I think Andrew was c-c-coming to look at it, though. The tuning is a b-b-bit off."

"Right here." Andrew Isaac was obviously our new arrival, hadn't even shed his jacket, heading at a clip toward us with a big smile for me and one for Mom. She hugged him, too, the short man with the round belly and balding pate returning her embrace perfunctorily before shedding his coat and hunkering down on the floor with a toolbox. "I shouldn't be long. Just a few adjustments."

Since Andrew was the one who'd procured the organ for us in the first place, the furniture restorer/electrician/general handyman had every right to tinker with his own property, so I left him to it, Ian hovering like the older man was doing surgery on a small, vulnerable child while Dominic stood by, humming scales to himself.

If he was going to break into vocal exercises I needed to get out of there right now.

Mom hesitated, though when the door opened yet again and Vivian French, her tall slimness dressed in a snow-white coat trimmed in what looked like real fur stepped inside, Mom abandoned our other guests to greet her. Sure, I'd had my moments with Vivian lately and despite our past was learning to trust her. But seeing my mother gush over her still gave me pangs.

Jealousy, okay? I admit it. I was jealous. She was my mother, damn it. And while I knew I was being uncharitable since Vivian's dad was dead, her brother was dead, her mother had run off to who-knew-where and she was stuck in that big, white mansion with two old ladies, one of whom had advanced dementia, the fact that my mother was kind to her and treated her like a daughter should have gotten a pass from me. Because if anyone needed a little mothering it was Vivian French.

Still. Get your own amazing mom. Growl.

"Lucy." Vivian hugged her with gentle kindness before greeting me with her custom icy stare. "Fee."

Oh, seriously, could we drop the act? "Thanks for helping out, Viv," I said, hugging her myself on impulse. She stiffened when I did before gently patting my back and letting me go. "It means a lot. To Mom." I swallowed. "And to me."

Vivian just nodded as if she was as uncomfortable with this whole thing as I was. Likely. "My pleasure." She turned to Mom, now all business. "Daisy picked up the samples?"

That set Mom off into raptures as she grasped Vivian's arm and tugged her toward the kitchen. I took the Queen of Wheat's gorgeous coat (hey, I wasn't above admitting it was freaking stunning and likely another Grace Fiore, her favorite designer and an amazing woman I adored who sent a delightfully wrapped wedding gift I couldn't wait to open) and hung it next to Daisy's before following them into the kitchen.

I stayed out of the way the rest of the next half hour, Mom and Vivian talking cooking Greek while

Daisy attempted to translate, Petunia got underfoot and Andrew fiddled with the organ in the next room. Just another day in the life of Fiona Fleming.

Though, as I watched Mom and Vivian, their voices dropping as they carried on their conversation like no one else in the room mattered, I wondered at how my old frenemy had volunteered to assist. She was different, had since she decided to run for mayor, even more so now that she sat in that particular seat. There were times she seemed almost human to me, now, though I was positive the icy exterior still served her well and actually found I hoped she wasn't crushed underfoot by the politics and general mishandling of the cutest town in America.

Not my problem. And yet... she trusted me. So. Stupid conscience.

Maybe I would have pulled her aside and asked her a few questions. Perhaps I would have even had that chance if Mom could be distracted. But it wasn't meant to be. Not when the front door of Petunia's opened one more time and the unmistakable gravelly deliciousness of my fiancé's amazing voice reached me, paired with the deep laughter of his former partner and best woman.

Heart beating far too fast for my own good, it was my turn to abandon everyone and run into the arms of the love of my life.

CHAPTER FOUR

He was faster than me, making it to the kitchen door before I could push it open, almost nailing me with it, though we both laughed over the incident.

Mom didn't. You'd think he'd just assaulted me with a chain saw. The gasp she let out echoed in the now quiet room, even our giggling about the near-miss silenced as my mother shook her index finger at my fiancé.

"If you give her a black eye or break her nose, Crew Turner," she snapped.

He hugged me tight, kissing me before crossing the kitchen and, in an uncharacteristic show of good humor, heaved my mother off her feet and swung her around until she giggled and batted at his broad shoulders, her green eyes now sparkling with laughter instead of irritation.

"You put me down this instant." Except, when he complied, she accepted the firm and noisy kiss he placed on her cheek, hugging him again when he was done. "Silly boy," she whispered. Was she choked up again? Yes, yes, she was. And she wasn't alone, nope, nope.

"If you're done manhandling my wife," Dad said, dry enough I knew he was doing his best to keep said wife from breaking down into weeping, "maybe you and I and your best woman here," Dad slipped an arm around her shoulders as Special Agent Elizabeth Michaud winked at me like she knew where this was going, "should sample some of that scotch you had delivered for the reception."

"Johnathan Albert Campbell Fleming." Mom had pulled out all four names which meant she wasn't happy with his suggestion. Not even a little bit.

But Dad waved her off when Crew joined them, though I wasn't about to let him go so easily, winding one arm around his waist and leaning into him, the scent of him making me giddy, how his body heat warmed me up in ways that had nothing to do with temperature and everything to do with chemistry. He looked down at me, his blue eyes telling me he had zero intention of joining Dad and Liz if they went in search of a drink.

Best fiancé (and soon-to-be husband) ever.

When Crew looked up from my eyes, he cleared his throat and just as when Mom gasped, we all fell into total silence. As if we knew, in that moment,

went on. "For better or worse, this place is home, now." He nodded to Vivian who nodded back. "No matter what happens, I guess I'm about to become a Fleming."

I laughed at that through my tears, while Dad chuckled and Mom tsked. But knowing Reading? That was exactly what everyone would think.

Poor Crew.

Vivian's phone rang, breaking the spell in the room. With a creased and apologetic frown, she met my eyes and, with real regret, said, "I'm sorry. I have to take this."

I stepped aside as she left, but reached out on the way by, while she pressed the handset to her ear, and touched her arm. She hesitated a long moment, icy eyes locked on mine. When had she abandoned the fake contacts that made her eyes so unrealistically blue for the pale, almost translucent shade I remembered from childhood? And when had she morphed from the bitter, popular girl with her catty remarks and patented nastiness into a cold and collected adult? I tried to remember but failed at it as she finally left, head down, speaking low into her phone, and realized it was about the same time I figured out I kind of liked her.

Go figure.

Made me wonder how much I'd changed in her eyes since we were kids. And if the death of her brother was the reason we lost our friendship, as much as the reason we were coming together again. No, I hadn't shared with her the fact I was having nightmares about Victor's drowning. Still, knowing he'd died, that it changed us both, triggered empathy if nothing else.

Liz grinned at me and Crew, tossing her glossy dark ponytail over her shoulder as she winked at Dad. "You said something about scotch?"

Crew groaned and touched his stomach with a wince while I made a wry face at his former partner. But it was he who denied her, shaking his head.

"I think I'll stop drinking forever," he said while she eye-rolled.

"You're turning into a lightweight," she cracked.

"It took three days to recover from the bachelor party," he shot back.

"Like I said." Liz laughed and, to his shock, hugged us both. "You two," she said.

And now even the collected and superheroine FBI agent was choked up?

"Maybe I should have thrown you a party like that?" Leave it to Daisy to second guess. She'd invited Liz to my bachelorette, naturally, and the agent took delight in doing both. Mind you, we'd had manipedis and enjoyed much tamer entertainment than I'm sure Crew and Liz and his old FBI buddies engaged in (and I didn't want to know about, thanks). Though, it had been funny to see my teetotaler mother tipsy on wine.

"It was perfect," I said. "You're the perfect maid of honor, Day."

She beamed at me, fingers sliding over the bracelet at her wrist. Was she thinking ahead to her own future? If so, I hoped she'd invite me to return the favor and stand with her. My only sorrow? The fact Jill Wagner wasn't in the official wedding party, though she'd brushed off my offer in favor of the small wedding I wanted in exchange for an invite to the soiree for her and Matt and a role reading a lovely poem she'd chosen for the occasion.

Like I'd be leaving them off the guest list. I really had so few true friends here in Reading, despite the fact everyone seemed to love the Fleming family. At least, in theory. Until I found a dead body and poked my nose in where it wasn't wanted.

I had no illusions.

When I turned back toward Crew, the soft sound of his voice against my ear as he talked to Dad about the ceremony the next day, my gaze fell to the tattoo on his wrist. The compass, the center of which housed a skull and anchor at a jaunty angle, the symbol of his family as much as it was the Reading hoard. When I'd asked him for his list of invites to the wedding, he'd admitted that aside from Liz there was no one. I'd known that I suppose, in hindsight. Though his mother was still alive, he'd declined to invite her. That left Crew and I did my best not to feel sorry for him.

He was about to become part of my family and we had more than enough room for him.

Liz touched my arm, drawing me away from my fiancé and toward the back door. I hugged her and she embraced me back but when she released me, her expression was all special agent and long gone from friend excited to see us married.

"Bad timing," she said, "but I figured you'd want to know updates."

And just like that Peggy Munroe crashed my party. I drew a breath, squared myself and nodded.

"Nothing bad," she said, touching my arm. "In fact, nothing at all." I wanted to exhale relief when she shrugged. "Could be a good sign, but whatever the case, it looks like you'll at least be getting married without her showing up to ruin everything." And, just like that, she gasped, both hands over her mouth, eyes huge and gaping and, for the first time since I'd met her, looked like she wished she'd learned to keep her mouth shut. "Fee, I didn't mean, I'm sorry, it's not going to—" That look of horror? I'd worn it a few times myself, though the way Liz reacted to what she'd blurted this was a first for her. "I'm so sorry."

I laughed. Because, honestly, it was funny. "And I'm so glad he has you." There were the waterworks all over again.

Liz swallowed hard, looked away, hands in her pockets. "Is that why I brought this up?" She met my eyes. "Because I'm uncomfortable with all this feely stuff?"

Snort. "You're awesome and amazing and if you do decide to say yes to Dad," he hadn't mentioned the job offer in a bit, but I knew it hung over her, between them, still, "I'll be super excited to have you here."

Liz gaped at me a long moment before bursting into tears.

CHAPTER FIVE

By the time Crew joined us, Liz had pulled herself together, though he looked concerned enough she made an excuse, hurrying from the room when Jill and Matt arrived, creating the distraction she needed to escape. Likely to go check on her face. At least, that's what I'd do, though she still looked stunning when she cried, unlike my redheaded blotchy extravaganza of awesomeness.

I'd stopped judging myself a long time ago.

Maybe I was being super sensitive—I'd been having that kind of day, after all—but was there something off about Jill? She seemed uncomfortable, awkward, even unhappy if I was going to go that far and I wondered instantly if she and Matt had a fight. Even took a moment to tug her aside and hug her before offering a raised eyebrow of worry.

"I'm fine," she gushed when I hadn't even asked a question yet, telling me, no, in fact, she wasn't. She stepped away before I could prod her and I let her go, partly because it wasn't my business and partly because I was afraid I knew what was bothering her.

She and Matt had been dating longer than me and Crew, hadn't they? And there was no ring on her finger.

Sigh. Maybe I needed to talk to the clueless boy before he lost her.

Our last guests appeared in time to save Matt from that particular conversation. Crew and I made a point of greeting the final two together, fingers laced together, footsteps in time with one another. Thea Isaac, our local minister, beamed at us both as she entered Petunia's, her tiny body shivering in delight—or the cold, maybe—as she hugged first Crew, then me. I caught the faintest hint of something truly horrific, a whiff of chemical awful that had me whipping my head around, wondering when someone spilled some cleaning agent, before realizing it was coming from the living room. Or was it? Whatever the case, I nodded to Thea's stepdaughter, Katelyn, who bobbed a nod back, though she was barely looking at me.

Thea handed over her coat to Crew when he held out his hands, taking the absent-minded twenty-something's as well when she finally paid attention long enough to dump it into his possession. It was clear Katelyn and Thea weren't related, the tiny minister's close-cropped gray hair and light blue eyes open, engaging while her stepdaughter's top-heavy height and long, brown hair wasn't even a match to her small, round father in the next room.

"So delighted to be invited," Thea said, slurring slightly as she shook her head and coughed softly into one hand. "I'm so sorry, Fee," she said, "feeling a bit under the weather. I think I'm getting a cold, sore throat and all that." She held up both hands and laughed. "I promise I won't breathe on either of you."

Yikes, that was all I needed, to get sick for my wedding day.

"All the more reason you should let me do the ceremony." I'd missed the fact Alfred Welling stood behind Thea, his skinny, short frame lost in the energy that was the older female minister, cold or not. His thinning red hair and immense face full of freckles made me so glad I'd taken after the auburn side of our coloring and not the washed-out tone he sported. Didn't help his hazel eyes were framed with barely-there lashes or that if he somehow sported one more freckle his whole face would be engulfed. A soft potbelly and a fairly whiny tenor meant Alfred might have been only thirty, but he was well on his way to being a cranky old man.

Oh, Fee. No judging.

"Unless Fee and Crew say otherwise," Thea said, mild enough but with the kind of edge that told me she'd been having this "conversation" (read argument) with Alfred likely for the better part of the day if not longer, "I'll be conducting the ceremony."

He was her junior minister, so there. But to be honest, if I'd had my choice, neither of them would be officiating. This was all Mom's idea. So, if I got a cold from the ill minister who sipped at a large water bottle filled with some kind of juice, this was on Lucy Fleming.

Maybe I could use Thea's illness to my advantage. Lean on Mom, convince her to let someone else do the honors. From what I understood it didn't take much to be ordained online these days. Maybe Jill would do it.

Alfred's face tightened, his jealousy clear. Yes, I'd heard the rumors he'd thrown a tizzy when Thea and her family moved here a year ago, that he argued against her being named senior minister for the Reading United Methodist Church. How he'd gone to council, seriously, to protest that she was an outsider, and he was owed the position. Talk about sour grapes.

Which made me think about Crew and, naturally, do my very best to make Thea feel welcome in that moment. I slipped my arm around her shoulders and guided her toward the living room, nose wrinkling as I did.

"What is that smell?" As we passed into the space, I noted Andrew on his hands and knees with a small, clear bottle of liquid he was using to clean something with what looked like a cotton swab. He looked up apologetically, waving the damp mess at me.

"Sorry," he said, "rubbing alcohol. Just have to make sure the bolts are clean." He set his tools aside after adjusting one more then nodded to Ian who sat behind the organ. "Give that a try."

Ian obliged, the sound so much better even I noticed. The young organist nodded his happiness, though he didn't look happy, so much, keeping his head down. Poor kid. I knew for a fact that stutter of his wasn't just something that showed up today out of the blue. I'd heard it when we'd initially talked about his role. Mom had been so patient with him, and I'd done my best to ignore it, knowing that bringing attention to stuttering often just made things worse.

Whatever it was Ian had gone through that reduced his self-confidence to ashes, I felt for him.

I let Mom finish preparing the room, exiting and leaving Crew behind, knowing it would be another half hour or so before things got underway and wanting to just have a moment to myself. I slipped down into my apartment and sank to the stool at my kitchen island, heart suddenly beating far too fast and feeling an overwhelming need to cry.

Which I did, tucking into my bathroom and having a good one, you betcha. Not because I was sad or upset or worried. Because, honestly, I'd never, ever been this happy and I just didn't know how to deal with it. Weird, right?

He found me there, slipped into the small space, Petunia at his feet, sinking to the side of the tub next to me and hugging me, rocking me all over again while my pug whined softly and licked her lips. Crew didn't speak, just continued that gentle sway of love while I pulled myself together and finally blew my nose into the wad of toilet paper I'd spun off the roll.

"Fee," he said, voice soft and sad. "Are you having second thoughts?"

Oh god, what was I doing to him? I grabbed him and kissed him, breathing into him, pressing so close I was breathless when I let him go. "Don't for a second," I said, "ever even think such a thing. Not for one instant, Crew Turner."

He exhaled. Relief? "I'll never understand you," he said, but there was laughter in his voice.

"Me either," I said, slumping. "I'm so happy, Crew. Why does that make me cry like a baby?"

"You've been through a lot," he said. "And I've watched you more than survive, thrive on the kind of stress that's brought hardened FBI agents to their knees. Even Liz says it." He shook his head, fingers sliding into mine and locking in place. "The moment you're happy? You lose your crap." That made him laugh out loud. "I guess I shouldn't be surprised."

Smartypants gorgeous fiancé. "We should go back upstairs before Mom comes looking for us."

Crew stood, grinning, still holding my hand and helping me to my feet. "That won't end well for either of us."

I hugged him then, breathing him in. "What about you, Crew?" I hated to ask, but I did anyway because fair enough and insecurities and just generalized holy crap, I couldn't be this lucky, right?

"Any second thoughts?"

Crew kissed me then, the way only he could kiss me. Convincing me, once and for all, getting married was the only thing he wanted, being with me, now and forever.

As for me? Well, my mind went elsewhere, wishing the people who waited upstairs were anywhere but here and that we could take a few more minutes together, right? Just the two of us since the bedroom was nice and close and he was so damned delicious...

Crew let me go, blue eyes telling me yes, he was thinking the same thing and that we'd be finding a private moment or two before he was dragged, kicking and screaming (okay, I imagined he'd be protesting leaving me) away because of some stupid rule that said he couldn't see me before the wedding.

I followed him out of the bathroom, to the kitchen, the steps. And paused when he stopped, my (our!) pug at my feet, to the sound of whispering in the staircase that was the perfect distraction from where I really wanted to lead the gorgeous man in my company.

CHAPTER SIX

If there was ever a doubt Crew and I were perfect for each other, it died when the two of us stood there, heads down, ears straining in collective nosiness, to overhear the obviously heated whispered conversation going on at the top of my apartment steps. Shameless, the both of us, and we seemed to realize it at the same instant, though I'm positive he looked far more guilty about it than I ever would.

It was impossible to make out details, but as we both quietly mounted the stairs and headed toward the exit, the faint light from the mostly closed-over door cast illumination on both Ian's distraught expression and Thea's sad face. They noticed us at the same moment, Ian wiping at his eyes and turning away, clearly embarrassed, but before he could hurry up and out into the main foyer, Thea engulfed him in a huge hug. He froze, shock in his expression a mix of emotions I could barely register before he tugged free and fled.

Thea turned and nodded down to us while we joined her, me finally feeling a bit guilty despite the fact they'd chosen my private retreat for their little *tête-à-tête*.

"Apologies," Thea said, choked up herself, apparently, that horrible scent of the rubbing alcohol drifting toward us through the now open door and making me gag. "I didn't realize anyone was down here or I would have suggested Ian and I go outside for our chat." She exhaled softly, turning her head to look up into the light before coughing into her hand one more time. When the minister turned back, her cheeks were pink, eyes faintly glazed. "Poor child," she whispered.

I was really starting to worry about how she was feeling as she swayed just a little. Crew caught her elbow and, with a quick look to me that mirrored what I was thinking, gently guided her upstairs. I let Petunia go next, following with reluctance, now, just wanting this to be over.

Mom was waiting and didn't give us a chance to express our concerns about Thea's illness, immediately bustling us into the dining room turned wedding chapel and clapping her hands for attention. Thea smiled faintly at her, sipping from her juice bottle with aggressive determination on her face before that smile widened and she nodded to us.

"Crew," she said, "Fee. If you're ready?" I looked up at my fiancé who smiled down at me, his concern shunted aside while he held my hand and squeezed just a little. Were we ready? Mom's expression told me if I hesitated one more second in agreeing, I'd be disowned. I returned Thea's smile and she raised her chin and her arms, sounding cheery. "Shall we begin?"

I'd attended a few weddings in my lifetime—more than a few, okay? Yes, I was aware being over thirty and not married yet myself meant certain things in certain people's opinions, but they could shove it—so I was pretty familiar with how things were meant to go. The fact we'd chosen a private venue meant I didn't have to sit through all the formal stuff if I didn't want to, though, being a minister, we'd negotiated with Thea on the religious stuff, namely that she promised to keep the proceedings to about fifteen minutes.

Perfect. Mom didn't know it, but this was going to be a fast and furious wedding because I was done waiting, thank you very much.

Thea took a moment to explain what we could expect while I stared into those gorgeous blue eyes I'd fallen in love with and missed out on most of what she was saying. To the point Daisy had to prod me with a giggle to get my attention to which I flushed and grinned while Thea swayed, one hand pressed to her forehead. Alfred's pinched unhappiness made me all the more determined to support the older woman, though it was clear by the way she gulped at her drink she was quickly deteriorating from healthy to unwell and my heart was going out to her while my panicked insides begged the Universe and all that was holy to protect me from whatever was laying her low.

"I'm so sorry," she said, giggling then, while her pink cheeks deepened, eyes now slightly glazed over. "I'm not sure what's wrong with me. I'm feeling rather off."

Um. Wait a second. She didn't sound sick, not with that slurring in her voice deepening, making her harder to understand. Wait, was she... oh my god. Was she drunk?

I gave her the benefit of the doubt, thinking maybe she'd OD'd on cold meds. I'd done that myself a time or two, ended up pretty stoned in the process. But the way she drank that "juice" she had almost finished by the time we did our ten-minute run-through of the only slightly longer real thing— something that should have, in my opinion, flashed by in two or three—I had come to the realization that, cold or not, flu or not, Thea Isaac wasn't suffering from medicinal over application.

She was smashed.

"Thea." Alfred hissed at her when she stumbled, dropping her Bible, almost falling over when she tried to retrieve it while snort-laughing hysterically and slapping one thigh. "What is wrong with you?"

"I think that's pretty clear." Dominic's judgy sniff into the air with that turned-up nose was met by a heavy sigh from Katelyn and a frown of disbelief from her husband, Andrew.

But it was Jill's reaction to Dominic's comment that caught my attention the most. Why did she look like she wanted to punch him in the throat?

Mom rushed forward, clearly upset, but I grabbed for her arm and handed her off to Dad, determined to deal with this personally. I hadn't heard that Thea was an alcoholic but apparently, that was the case. And if even Mom didn't know, she must have been hiding it very well. Looked like, despite I wished otherwise, Alfred would be the better choice after all.

I was about to say as much, to ask Katelyn and Andrew to escort the inebriated minister home and sober her up, oddly not all that worked up because, again, this was my life we were talking about and why should my wedding go off without a hitch, when Thea caught herself suddenly and met my gaze with hers wide, her breath gurgling faintly in her throat.

Before her eyes rolled back into her head and she collapsed to the floor, out cold.

Crew moved before I did, hurrying to reach her side while everyone stared, and I did my best not to sigh in irritation. Except, as my fiancé took a moment, I watched the set of his shoulders, the way he tensed, his body tight and rigid even as Liz and Jill joined him in a quick move of matching policewomen, their heads down next to his.

Oh. Dear. Lord. No. Not today. Not here, in Petunia's, at my wedding rehearsal. Please, if there was a benevolent and loving Universe or God or whatever looking over me, could this not be what I thought—nay, what I knew—it was?

It only took one glance at Crew's face as he spun on the balls of his feet, still crouched over Thea, to tear a groan of despair from my lips. Because I knew that expression, that forehead vein, that tight jaw and faint tic under one eye. Had caused it many times, been the source and the soothing.

"Someone call Dr. Aberstock," he said. "Thea is dead."

CHAPTER SEVEN

Well, at least it wasn't just me on the hook this time. Nope, my whole freaking family, my closest friends and a few assorted sorta strangers got to take part in the fiasco of body discovery. Reminded me with a twinge of unhappy nostalgia this time about the afternoon Skip Anderson collapsed in my lap at the parade in his honor after pissing off the bulk of Reading's residents with a drunken tirade about how much our hometown sucked.

Yup, wasn't alone then, either. Just felt like I was.

Normally, I didn't get upset over dead bodies anymore. Not that it wasn't tragic and heartbreaking and all that stuff that typical people muttered behind their hands when they heard someone died. Sorry to be cynical and all, but this made twelve corpses for me, and I was so over it, I couldn't even.

Thing was, I did feel upset, and for obvious reasons that had zero to do with the poor, expired minister Dr. Aberstock examined, lying on the hardwood floor of my dining room. Was it wrong I was grateful she hadn't passed on anywhere near a carpet because scouring wood was so much easier than throwing out antique rugs? Yes, Fee. The answer is yes.

So wrong.

I'd accepted the doc's brief arm squeeze on his way by, though I'd done my best to stay out of the way when Robert arrived, the only remaining member of the Reading Sheriff's Department that wasn't at the wedding rehearsal (again for obvious reasons) sauntering into my bed and breakfast like this was just the best freaking thing that had ever happened to him. The smirk he tossed my way made my blood boil. A woman was dead, for goodness's sake. Sure, right, like I wasn't more focused on the fact this was going to delay my wedding, wasn't it, than on the simple truth Thea Isaac was no more.

Crew held me, one of those strong arms of his around my shoulders, the other stuffed deep into the pocket of his black dress pants, as Robert proceeded to make a total ass of himself.

"Only you, Fanny," Robert chuckled. "Killed off your own minister, huh?" His beady eyes narrowed, that hideous mustache of his now grown to handlebar status, though the effect wasn't benefiting his face in the least. "Guess that's a sign, right? Of how your marriage is going to turn out?" He guffawed, that ridiculous sound men made when they thought they were being funny, but they were just being awkward and jerkish. Maybe I should have been more offended, but I couldn't tear my eyes off that fur on his face. If anything, the long and disgusting bars of dark hair that now trailed down to his chin reminded me of melting asphalt mixed with old grass clippings.

Just gross.

I heard Crew's molars grind together, his jaw next to my ear, his reaction clearly doing the job for both of us. But Robert either didn't notice or didn't care or had absolutely no sense of self-preservation because he ignored his boss and kept his nasty focus on me as he tapped his open notebook with the stub of his pencil.

"So, want to tell me what happened this time?"

Wow, the trained ape had learned to write, had he? Oh, Fee. So petty.

"If I can interrupt before you get started?" Dr. Aberstock didn't know it, but he likely saved Robert's life and Crew from going to prison on the eve of our wedding. At least, if the way my handsome love's arm had begun a boa constrictor-like contraction around me was any indication of just how carefully he was holding himself in check. The moment the doc stood, coming between me and Robert and turning his back to the clearly annoyed deputy, Crew's arm relaxed and, as if only then realizing what he'd been doing, his big hand gently massaged where he'd just recently been cutting off the circulation to my upper body.

All good. The things we do for those we love when we want them to not murder people and stay out of jail.

Did Dr. Aberstock have an idea of what he'd interrupted? I'm sure he did. He might have looked like a jovial Santa Claus in a white disposable coverall, with eyes that twinkled and round, rosy cheeks and white beard and hair to match, but he was one smart cookie, our doc, and firmly in Camp Fleming. Um, Turner? Fleming-Turner?

Wait, Turner-Fleming?

Oh, dear.

"I don't have a cause of death yet," he said, completely cutting out Robert while addressing me, Crew, Dad, Jill and Liz like we were the only ones that mattered (um, yeah. Right?). "However, I am detecting a familiar scent on her breath." He wrinkled that button nose a moment, so adorable I wanted to boop it. Shock. Okay then, I was in shock. "It's reminiscent of the bittering agents used in rubbing alcohol."

Well now. Wasn't that interesting.

And well now. There was something clearly wrong with my brain that instead of horror I immediately reacted with interest.

Sigh.

"I caught the same scent from her water bottle." The doc gestured at the empty container near the body where she'd dropped it before collapsing.

"There's an excellent chance she was poisoned."

Wait a second. "Wouldn't she have tasted it?" The smell alone was eye-watering.

Andrew spoke before I could finish my thought, clearly distraught where he sat in a chair in the corner with Daisy rubbing his back and his daughter perched next to him.

"Thea couldn't smell," he said.

Dr. Aberstock refocused on the widow. "Ah," he said. "How severe was her anosmia?"

Andrew was shaking, but he pulled himself together, wiping at his eyes, averting his gaze after a quick glance at the sheet the doc had pulled over his wife's body after his examination. "Complete loss," he said. "She could barely detect bitterness. Which is why she loved grapefruit juice." He gestured with ineffectual despair at the bottle on the floor. "She drank it because she said it was one of the only things she could actually connect to her old sense of taste."

Dr. Aberstock nodded. "Thank you, Mr. Isaac," he said, that genuine and sweet-hearted bedside manner of his seeming to help. Andrew slumped into the chair and wept again, hands over his face, but without the choking sobs he'd been uttering until now, I realized.

I'd zoned out, apparently, all but my own needs. Nice going there, Fleming. Way to be selfish and all that.

Thank goodness for Daisy—and Mom, too, apparently—as they comforted the widow while Dr. Aberstock spoke again, a little more quietly.

"There's a chance she would have simply equated the bitterant additives with the acidic nature of the juice, if her anosmia was that severe," he said.

"She was complaining of a cold," I said. "Sore throat, coughed a lot." I flushed, knowing then I was watching the woman slowly die in front of me and had done nothing but worry she might get me sick, or Crew, or disrupt my wedding.

Holy crap. I really was a horrible person.

But the doc was nodding with enthusiasm, eyes bright again. "You may have nailed it, Fee," he said. "The additives they use in isopropanol would definitely have given her such symptoms while the quick inebriation effects would have lowered her ability to realize what was happening to her." He shook his head then, grim but oddly still adorably cherubic. "A terrible way to die, my friends."

"So, we're talking murder," Crew said.

Before Dr. Aberstock could respond, Robert cut in, one beefy hand on the doc's shoulder, tugging him back away from us while the normally sweet-faced old gentleman glared at the deputy like he'd rather it was my cousin's body under that sheet.

Nice to know he had that effect on everyone I considered quality.

"I'm running this investigation." Did Robert really just belly up to Crew and stick his bristling facial anomaly in my fiancé's vicinity? Yes, he did, and it was only by the (startling but hopefully not painful) pinch I gave to the back of his arm that kept my darling from punching that piece of wasted space right in the kisser.

I didn't want Crew to hurt his hand.

The sheriff knew when to back off, though it looked like doing so was agonizing. Maybe I should have let him hit Robert. We had a house full of witnesses I was positive would say my cousin fell into a doorway or something. That was until she sauntered in, and we lost our home-team advantage.

Wait, was that a badge clipped to Rose's belt?

Crew saw it the same moment I did, his reaction far more violent than my simple staring and swearing in my head.

"What the actual hell," he snarled, jabbing a finger at the other half of Rosebert who smirked and crossed her arms over her chest, "is *that?*"

No. Way. She had a *gun*. I glared at her, partially in fury that Robert was arrogant enough to deputize his girlfriend without telling anyone and partially because, quite frankly, I'd been deputized in September and my dear, darling friend Jill? Refused me a sidearm.

And I'd almost died, could have used said weapon when I'd been attacked by the murderer I'd cornered. Alphonse Brunbaugh wouldn't have gotten the drop on me, the British cad, if I'd had a good old six-shooter at my side.

So, how come Rose had one?

Crew didn't seem to care about the gun at all, spluttering while Robert watched with the sort of nasty darkness I'd become accustomed to. Was he waiting for my darling to lose it? Looked that way.

Another pinch, this one likely to leave a bruise (forgive me, my love), cut off Crew's spiral down into more punching and possible killing before he could go any further and give Robert what he wanted.

What he needed, I was then sure. To get his boss fired.

After all, there was no real love lost between Crew and the town council, was there? Dominated as it was by the Pattersons and their new agenda. Helmed by Vivian or not, I was positive all it would take would be one false move—reasonable or not— on Crew's part and it would be all over, sayonara, the fat lady gushing her heart out while he did a rapid exit stage left.

No way was I letting him go out that way. Not when there was a very good possibility the next sheriff of Reading would be none other than the craptastically disgusting douchebag standing in front of us.

Maybe I was overreacting. There was a possibility of that. Except, of course, when the door to Petunia's opened and three council members decided to poke their noses into my dining room, an active crime scene, none other than Geoffrey Jenkins at their head?

Yeah. Suspicions confirmed loud and clear.

"I take it you have things well in hand, Deputy Carlisle?" Geoffrey smiled his shark-like grin at Rose. "Deputy Norton?"

Rose simpered back at him, but Robert replied

before she could. She actually glared at her boyfriend when he cut off her attempt to bat her eyelashes at the married-to-the-Pattersons. Yuck. Although considering her taste in men to this point, I suppose I shouldn't have been surprised.

I was going to throw up.

As for the council members, I noted the discomfort and regret on Terri Jacob's face, her little wiggle of fingers at me like the owner of Jacob's Flowers would have rathered be anywhere but here at that moment. Not so for Sophia Bell, the owner of The Bride Boudoir. Sure, she'd been happy enough to sell me that overpriced white gown upstairs, but she didn't mind sniffing around the murder of my minister, did she? Like some kind of critter who cleaned up after the big predators had their way.

Speaking of which, Geoffrey looked far too delighted in his cold and murky way to be at the death of a Reading resident.

And they called me a busybody. Crew's body vibrated next to me, and I knew an explosion was imminent. He'd put up with a lot, being Reading's sheriff, including having to deal with me and Dad all this time. But he'd been trained by the FBI, and he had certain standards he'd done his best to uphold since I'd met him, even under very trying circumstances. And while visitors to a crime scene wasn't uncommon, the three council members appearing the way they did, after Rose's deputization and the fact that our wedding likely wasn't going to happen on schedule?

Crew was on a steady path to a meltdown.

Okay, so I didn't know that for sure and, in all fairness, he was his own person and had his own mind and I didn't know what he was thinking. And yet, I knew him very, very well.

So, intervention time, Fiona Fleming style.

CHAPTER EIGHT

"If you'll all excuse me," I said in my best bed and breakfast owner during check-in on a summer Sunday in July when the White Valley Lodge was overbooked voice, "thanks for coming, nothing to see here, time to move along." I left Crew's side and firmly and not-at-all politely headed right for Geoffrey and his two hangers-on. If he was offended to be herded out by my no-nonsense and definitely not taking his crap attitude, he didn't show it, that shark grin of his firmly affixed and not going anywhere while he tracked snow back toward the door and out into the December afternoon.

Were they all raised in a barn? Did no one have the common decency of taking off their damned boots?

"I'm sure everything will get sorted out in short order." Geoffrey's smirk told me otherwise. What, did he and Robert have some kind of plan up their sleeves I needed to know about? From the gleam of delight that made it to those cold, dead eyes, that was exactly the case. "The council was happy to approve the official inclusion of Deputy Norton to the roll call of the Reading Sheriff's Department. We're sure she'll be a fine addition during this trying time."

So, this had been a council move. Was that what had taken Vivian away earlier? But no, that would have meant they'd been planning this all along, maybe only using Thea's death as an excuse, Crew's distraction by our wedding, to swell the ranks of the department with their own brand of yuck.

Sounded accurate enough.

Rather than give Geoffrey any kind of satisfaction by commenting, I slammed the door on the three of them, ignoring Terri's attempt to smile her apology at me, and hustled back into the living room, passing Dad on the way by as he headed for the door.

Abandoning me? At a time like this? I could hear Robert's strident voice, Crew's rumbling retort, and knew I had to get back in there before my love lost his mind. But Dad? Really?

"Better places to be?" I stopped long enough to punch him in the arm.

He didn't even pretend to flinch, the mountain of my father hugging me tight before letting me go again and leaving me a little breathless. I spun and watched him heave on his coat, slipping into his big boots before he waved.

"Don't worry, kid," he growled. "I got this." And then, in his uber-typical John Fleming patented SecretiveDad™ fashion, he was gone.

Look, if he managed to sort things out in time for tomorrow? I'd forgive him. For now, I had other things to worry about. Namely the fact I'd left my agitated fiancé in the company of the one person on the planet I was positive he was capable of murdering and not feel a single scrap of guilt over.

I'd be helping him hide Robert's body, so there was that. I did love him, after all.

Thing was, the moment I re-entered the dining room with the intent of protecting my true love from the inevitable, I heard my deplorable cousin (why were we related again?) utter the words that signed his doom. And not from Crew.

"You'll just have to postpone the wedding."

Yup. I'd be murdering him personally.

I needn't have worried about me or Crew, to be honest, not with Lucy Fleming in shouting distance. Mom? She lost her mind.

"Robert Eustice Carlisle!" She'd grown fond of using full names these days, though I wasn't arguing her reasoning at the moment. I saw him flinch, visibly shrink from the diminutive redhead that was my incredible mother, knew then he was more afraid of Mom than he ever was of Dad. Or me. Like he was ever afraid of me. But my tiny little mother with her normally collected persona of sparkling kind goodness and caring understanding? Yup, he was ten years old again and she'd caught him stealing cookies from her kitchen.

Not that it ever happened, that I know of. Though, I wouldn't have put it past him.

"It's not my fault." He actually sounded contrite in the face of her anger. His sideways glance at Crew didn't last, Mom taking all of his focus as she stepped into Robert's space, her hands on her hips, lips tight and green eyes flashing. "This is a crime scene now, Aunt Lucy."

Wow. He rarely called Dad Uncle John anymore (though, hadn't he used that term when he spoke of my father to who I was guessing was Marie Patterson herself, just this past September?). I'd never actually heard him address Mom that way.

She didn't seem swayed by the familial label. "I don't care if the house is falling into a volcanic pit and we have ten minutes to vacate the premises," Mom snarled with a level of heat that told me she was the magma chamber, and he was the sacrifice at the top of said volcano stupid enough to throw himself at her mercy. "Fiona," she jabbed a perfectly pink manicured finger at me over his shoulder, "and Crew," that hand whipped sideways though her face remained locked on Robert's, aiming in my fiancé's now grinning direction, "are getting married." She made one final motion, that sharpened digit arrowing straight down toward her feet. "Here. At Petunia's. Tomorrow afternoon. And that's final."

I think if Robert had been alone, he would have caved. Even with the backing of the council, apparently, if he had been there without backup, I know he wouldn't have stood a chance.

Unfortunately, he had Rose. Argh. And she wasn't intimidated by my mother, not one little bit (though she should have been, because even I was and, from the hurried wiping of his grin from his face when Mom whipped around to glare at Crew, so was he).

"You will all vacate this place," Rose said it like Petunia's was some kind of flophouse and we were squatters, "while Deputy Carlisle and I conduct a thorough," she met my gaze with hers, tight smile on her face, "investigation."

There was the sign of dissent again in their ranks, the way Robert looked at her for the briefest of moments as if she'd stolen his thunder. He cleared his throat and shouldered her back behind him while she did her own staring in anger, arms crossing over her chest.

Robert ignored his unhappy girlfriend in favor of trying for official and ending up somewhere south of arrogantly ineffectual. "The wedding will have to wait. You are all suspects in a murder—"

"Ahem," Dr. Aberstock intervened, one finger held up much as Mom had only much more kindly, "suspected murder. I won't have that conclusion for you until I conduct my autopsy."

Robert snarled at him but went on as if the doc hadn't spoken. "—and, as such, you are to leave Petunia's and not return until this crime is solved."

Wait, what? "What the hell does that mean?" He

wasn't implying I couldn't come home until he solved the case? Because with Robert investigating, that could be never.

Suspicion sucked the air from my lungs as I glanced at Daisy and had a horrible thought. Why did they need to kick us out? All they had to do was sniff around the dining room, not the entirety of Petunia's.

So, if access to my B&B was what they were after, why was that? What were they looking for?

Nope, wasn't lost on me Daisy had told Rose about our treasure hunt. Nor was it a huge leap to think maybe the pair had gotten around to being curious enough to dig into what I might know. But no, wait. Why now? They'd had ages to do their own poking about. Why would that even be on their radar if it hadn't been up until now?

I was clearly jumping at shadows. Right?

Unless they'd found something themselves and were putting two and treasure together...

"This won't stand." Crew scowled at Robert but didn't bother trying to argue with him further, guiding me toward the living room door. He had me out and in the foyer, whispering in my ear before anyone could follow. "Are you thinking what I'm thinking?"

Oh, crap. "The treasure." I swallowed. "The music box is downstairs." Along with everything we had, except the frame the map had originally been housed in. That remained at Mom and Dad's.

Crew instantly steered me toward the apartment door, but Robert was faster, blocking my way down the steps to my place while we both stopped in our tracks.

"Out," he said with that oily smirk of his, the darkness surfacing fully in his eyes, that dangerous edge of breaking point Robert I knew lingered behind the grossness that he lived moment to moment. "Now."

That's how we found ourselves on the front step of Petunia's, staring at the door as it closed on me and Crew, my pug on her leash stuffed hastily into her harness. The asshat had allowed everyone else to stay, including Liz, my mom, Daisy. Ian and Andrew, Katelyn and Dominic. Even Jill and Matt. To question them, apparently. Only Crew and I had to go.

I turned to my fiancé, heart breaking, not even caring about Thea Isaac at the moment and knowing that made me a truly terrible person. Even as Crew's phone rang, and he answered it with a deep frown of anger.

He didn't speak, didn't move, his face tight and rigid. And then, with the barest nod, he hung up, thumb mashing the red hang-up button before he tucked his arm into mine and turned me toward the street.

"City council meeting," he said. "Our presence has been requested."

Was I the only one who didn't think such a summons boded well?

CHAPTER NINE

I stood off to one side, Crew front and center in the council room, the place eerily empty without a crowd of Reading residents at my back filling every nook and cranny just to find out what was up.

Nope, not this afternoon the en masse gaping of every soul that lived in our fine little town. Turned out this was a closed meeting despite being held in the huge room at the base of town hall more suited to mayoral debates and the odd craft sale. Multi-purpose? You betcha.

It was hard not to shuffle my feet, to clear my throat endlessly as my discomfort at being present when I had no idea why I was even here prodded me over and over to ask the obvious question. The problem being that from the moment we walked into said council hall and realized the full ensemble of Reading's fine elected members of government sat, rigid and watchful, Crew had gone silent, stubbornly so.

Vivian had taken her good old time, the only hold-out, joining us. When her assistant, Hugh (yes, I still thought of him as Olivia's assistant, so sue me) gestured for my sheriff fiancé to take the center position—standing—and motioned for me to join Jill and Rosebert—at least they weren't rifling through my house at the moment, one tiny saving grace—I'd stumbled my way to the aside without argument, though you can bet complaints and demands for answers were brewing the longer I stood there.

No one said a word to Crew, the jerks. I wanted to rejoin him, a show of solidarity, but when my body wavered, I felt Jill's hand grasp my wrist and caught her barely perceptible headshake.

Read, moving to his defense wouldn't do him any favors.

Fine. Then so be it. But this redhead's temper was riding the razor's edge, and I wasn't afraid to use it.

The side door opened, Vivian sweeping her elegant way into the chamber, all icy cold perfection and blank stares and blah, blah, blah. I shot her daggers with my own gaze, a fact she chose to ignore at her own peril, taking her seat in the center of the gathered councilors who perched so high and mighty over the rest of us while I simmered and bubbled and thought about Mom's lava references.

Mt. Fleming would erupt. When depended entirely on the pinched-faced and judging assembly before me.

"Crew Turner and deputies of the Reading Sheriff's Department." How hideously formal of her. Vivian's voice rang out as she spoke like we couldn't hear her. Oh, I was hearing her just fine.

"Excuse me," I interrupted, hand in the air, not caring even a tiny little fraction of a crap that Jill groaned softly next to me, that all eyes flickered in my direction and gave me focus, that Vivian's lips tightened just enough I knew cutting her off undermined her authority. Wicked. Let the good times roll. "I'm wondering what the hell it is I'm doing here," I said then, "on the eve of my wedding when I'm not even a deputy."

Vivian locked gazes with me and, with that same crisp and overly supported tone I wanted to shove down her throat so far it made wrinkles in her perfect dress, told me something I really didn't want to hear. "According to town records, Fiona Fleming," she said, still official, "you remain on the roster of deputies and have since you were granted that position in September."

I was *what*? "I handed in my badge." Okay, now I was off-center and spluttering and shaking my head, hating that I'd lost my strong stance and felt reduced to blithering idiot.

She shrugged, that tiny and dismissive gesture of hers that gave me the most angst and triggered my anger all over again.

"And yet," she said, sounding bored now, "you remain. For some reason."

That was it. If you'll pardon the pun? The Queen of Wheat was *toast*.

"Now then," she went on as if I hadn't spoken and wasn't even remotely interesting, "to the matter at hand. It has become increasingly apparent to this council the leadership of our sheriff's department has been sorely lacking from the moment the mantel was placed in the care of Crew Turner." Wow, Vivian, way to be a total and utter bitch. There was so much I wanted to say to that, but it was hard to focus with Jill pinching me in the exact spot I'd pinched Crew back at Petunia's. Damn it, was she going to let Vivian throw my love under a bus? I wasn't going to stand by and—

Vivian was far from done. "While leeway was allowed during the previous administration, it was decided upon my ascension to the mayoral seat that one more botched investigation during Mr. Turner's watch would result in immediate termination."

My heart thudded painfully in my chest. She'd called him Mr. Turner. And despite the fact I was fighting it tooth and nail inside my head, it was clear where this was going even if I wanted to shout out the reasons why they were all smug asshats who couldn't solve a crime if it presented a confession personally.

I know, I know. That made zero sense. I wasn't exactly in the frame of mind to string coherent thoughts together, so cut me some slack.

"Mr. Turner," Vivian went on, as coldly as I'd ever heard her, "your incompetence has known no limits and, over the past four years, you have left it up to private investigation and amateurs to deal with the crimes you, yourself, have been responsible to solve." The fact people died in town had nothing to do with Crew. This was ridiculous and Vivian had to be aware of it. Was using it as an excuse to get rid of him, they all were.

Not to mention the fact she did *not* just publically humiliate the man I loved. She wanted murder? I'd be happy to show her what it looked and felt like up close and personal. "It is this council's ruling—and mine, personally—that you have not been and, certainly, will never be, a suitable choice for sheriff of our department. And so, from this moment on, you are released from your employment and active duty." She frowned then, looking down at the papers in front of her before meeting his eyes. "To our deep disappointment."

Two things and two things alone saved Vivian from a sudden and painful end at my hands. The fact that Geoffrey was grinning beside her like he was enjoying the show, and, even more telling, Robert's reaction to the events and her proclamation.

"Finally!" My icky cousin stepped forward, shouldering Crew aside before my fiancé had a chance to respond, hands on his hips just under the roll-over of his growing belly. "I take it the perfect candidate for his replacement has been chosen?" Because Robert—poor deluded, ridiculous, idiot

Robert—clearly thought that was himself.

Thing was, despite knowing how absolutely farcical such a suggestion even was? This was Reading, wasn't it? And the likelihood he'd end up with Crew's job and office?

So real I could taste it like bile in the back of my throat.

And that, my friends, was the moment the Patterson's plan went... sideways. Because as Geoffrey opened his mouth, his smile firmly affixed, lazy hand wave at Robert a clear sign of agreement pending a verbal confirmation, Vivian spoke up.

Shutting everyone down.

"There are three deputies in Reading at the moment," she said, her tone unchanged, her challenge obvious as we all gaped at her—Robert the most shocked, since he obviously thought he'd been handed a golden ticket and was likely promised as much—Vivian went on. "A terrible tragedy has again struck our town." She shuffled her papers, the light catching the French manicure she always wore before her hands settled again, the only sign of her agitation. If it even was that. "It is my decision that in order to select the perfect new sheriff for Reading, we must endeavor to choose that deputy with the talent, skill and intuition necessary to not only solve this horrible crime but to do so quickly and with careful thought to the continuing good name of this place we call home." She looked up then, chin a bit higher than normal while Geoffrey stared at her, his blank expression telling me she was so off book by that point he was going to make sure she was punished for it.

Vivian didn't seem to care as she locked gazes with me. A gaze that told me a lot in a very short period of time. Things like, "I had no choice, Fee. Don't be angry with me. I had to fire Crew, they wouldn't allow for anything else. But I'm giving you the chance to make this work for you, for us. Don't screw it up."

All between one slow blink and the next.

"In the interim, I am appointing Fiona Fleming as acting sheriff," Vivian said while the collective council gasped softly. But there were enough smiles and nods in my direction I knew she'd made that choice with carefully weighted calculations. "Though, she, like Deputies Wagner and Carlisle—"

"And Norton," Rose piped up, like anyone wanted to hear from her.

"No," Vivian said, not even looking at the now furious woman. "Your position was appointed by another deputy, making your addition inadmissible."

Um, considering the fact Vivian was likely making this up as she went along, such a rule was kind of ridiculous, but no one argued, and Rose backed down, so yeah, I guess there was a new sheriff in town.

Dear god. That sheriff was me.

"The full-time, permanent position will be awarded to the deputy who solves this murder and brings proof to the council of said murderer." Wait, did she know for sure it was murder? I'd jumped the gun myself on many the occasion without knowing for sure.

"Dr. Aberstock hasn't confirmed that yet," I said, knowing I wasn't making her life any easier and not really caring.

Vivian froze, then nodded. "Agreed," she said. "Bring me confirmation, then, Sheriff Fleming." She stood, the council standing with her before she finished. "Yet again we find ourselves embroiled in a," she paused but pushed on anyway, "murder investigation," Vivian said while the other council members muttered and nodded like this was my fault. "Sheriff." Vivian didn't look up, her voice so low I saw more than one of the witnesses to this little unfolding performance strain forward to hear her. Her tone rose as she looked up, pale eyes snapping. "I expect you to step up and take care of this problem ASAP. Or I'll be finding you a replacement. Are we clear?"

Déjà vu, right? Remember our little leap ahead in time? Well, here we go again.

"Mayor French," I said, hating this meant betraying Crew, forcing myself to trust her when all I wanted to do was walk out of there and say screw it to her, to the council, to Reading as a whole. Instead, I nodded. "I'll do my best."

Vivian left, the council exiting after her, Terri waving at me with that same attempt at a smile I ignored yet again in favor of heading for Crew because no amount of pinching my arm was going to allow Jill to keep me from the man I loved.

He met my eyes, his own blue ones empty, calm. The phone call he'd received. Was it from Vivian? He seemed pretty collected, as if he'd known what was coming. Did she warn him in advance? And, if so, why didn't he warn me?

I was going to kick his very handsome butt if that was the case.

"Not here," he whispered. "You did the right thing." I almost choked on that. "Just handle assignments for the case and I'll meet you at home." He paused one more moment. "You got this, Fee." And then, with his head high, shoulders back, Crew turned and left the council room and I had to just stand there and watch him go.

Taking my breaking heart with him.

CHAPTER TEN

Jill's mournful expression wasn't helping any as I crossed to join her and Rosebert, those two closing ranks and glaring at me like this was my idea.

Let them. I had a job to do. And no way was I doing it with this crew. Ack. Bad choice of words. I whipped out my phone as I stopped beside Jill and dialed a familiar number, knowing there was a 50/50 chance he wouldn't answer if he was already distracted.

To my surprise, Dad picked up almost immediately. "I heard," he growled. "Grapevine. Viv made you sheriff?" Why did it sound like he was trying not to laugh?

"If you'd please get yourself to the sheriff's office," I ground out through clenched teeth,

"Deputy Fleming," let him chew on that a minute as Robert grunted like I'd kicked him somewhere it hurt a lot, "I'll brief you on the case."

It wasn't very often I got the drop on my father. From the brief silence on the other end of the line, I had a sudden worry I'd given him a stroke or some debilitating ailment from sheer shock. Instead, a breath later, he burst into laughter like this was the greatest joke in the history of hilarious missteps and comic timings.

"I'll see you shortly, Sheriff," he said around more laughter before hanging up on me.

Jill's wide eyes but barely-there smile told me she approved whole-heartedly of what I'd just done. As for Rosebert, they could screw off and go do whatever it was that kept them out of my way and from bungling this case completely before I could solve it.

Wait, I was going to solve it? And become sheriff for real? Nope, no way, not in a million years. And yet, that was Vivian's plan, apparently.

We'd just see about that. Especially considering the tall, broad-shouldered blonde in front of me who'd made a fine deputy under both my father and my fiancé deserved to wear the badge of honor, thank you very much. Not me.

So, we'd just have to make sure Jill shone, wouldn't we?

She stepped in, head down, but Robert was already muscling his way toward me, shoving her aside while I glared up at him like he hadn't just assaulted a fellow deputy.

"Don't even think about giving me orders," he blustered.

"You already have your orders, Deputy Carlisle," I said. "Go search Petunia's for whatever it is you think you can find and leave the real police work to those who have a chance in hell of solving this case."

He spluttered, he hummed and hawed, but it was Rose who grabbed his arm with a weasel-like slyness that told me she wanted to get her hands on my bed and breakfast and screw her boyfriend's chance at the sheriff's office.

"That's right," she said, tugging his arm, lips pursed as she spoke up at him like he was a dolt. Okay, so he was a dolt, fair enough. "We have a job to do, Robertkins. Remember?'

Could they be subtler? Doubted it. Dripping don't mind us, sleight of hand, what's behind that curtain while we slip out the back door.

Whatever.

It was a quiet walk to the station, Jill keeping her head down, me stomping my way through the skiff of snow that had fallen since this morning. I couldn't think about my wedding, about the fact my fiancé was now unemployed and that my dad, my grinning and chortling and childish father was standing on the steps emanating some kind of vindictive glee that made me want to smack him.

"Not funny, deputy," I snarled on my way by.

"If you say so, sheriff," he winked back, still chuckling.

Seriously. Dads.

Five minutes later, with his assistance and me swearing a few times at feeling awkward, Dad was officially a deputy in the Reading Sheriff's department. I winced when I thought about what Mom was going to say to me for recruiting my retired from the force father, though she'd stopped being angry with him over the investigation firm—finally—so maybe she'd cut me some slack knowing I didn't have a choice in the matter.

Things might have been slowly sliding downhill in a very large hand basket filled with my fading wedding plans, my commitment to my bed and breakfast and the fact I'd accepted my fiancé's job out from under him when a tiny sliver of light showed through the rapidly descending darkness.

And, wouldn't you know, that illumination came from Daisy, in the form of a text.

I could almost hear her giggling glee as it pinged and caught my grumpy attention.

Got the goods out, all clear. Her second message arrived shortly thereafter while I gaped and inhaled and realized she was talking about the treasure evidence. *Did I do good?*

DAY. I sent her a huge smiley face and a string of hearts. *Fast thinking, brilliant woman.*

Learned from the best, she sent, far too cheery for a text message to translate but I could see her face beaming over her phone screen so there was no mistaking it. *See you at your mom's.*

Okie doke.

That was one crisis averted. Let Robert and Rose waste their time tearing Petunia's apart looking for... well, who knew what. They certainly wouldn't be stumbling over anything to do with the hoard. But wait. What if they were after something else? Totally unrelated that I had, as yet, to suss out and really should have been far more concerned they might uncover?

Like what? Instead of making myself crazy over something I couldn't control and trusting that the people I loved and the life I lived wasn't about to go totally to the bottom of the toilet the Pattersons— yeah, blaming them, down to the ground—were making of my town, I chose to focus on the now and present and deal with the consequences of Vivian's shenanigans later.

The one person I was really worried about in this whole mess sauntered casually into the office, his handsome face smiling, a huge hug for me telling me that despite my lingering worries to the contrary Crew was perfectly fine with this state of affairs.

"We all know this was the only way Vivian was going to let things go." We tucked ourselves into his (my) office, Liz joining the party, and consulted on our next moves. "Fee, we also know I've been thinking about leaving anyway. So, she did me a favor."

"Like when she called you to warn you?" I did smack him then, a soft punch to the upper arm that he pretended hurt way more than it did. "You could have told me."

He nodded, jaw jumping. "I know," he said. "But Vivian said if it was going to work you had to be genuinely surprised." Crew touched my hair, my cheek, kissed my forehead. "I'm sorry, sweetheart."

I was terrible at hiding my feelings, so they had been right to keep it from me if Geoffrey in the dark was the goal. Still. Grumble.

"You two," Dad said, pointing between Crew and Liz while Jill hovered near the door, looking pale and uncomfortable, "are going to have to take over Fleming Investigations for the time being." They what? Dad looked down at me then, shrugged. "Conflict of interest, kid. You know it's going to come up. Might as well cut that viper's head off right now."

Wow. "You're rather blasé about giving up your business, John." Crew was grinning, eyes narrowed and gleaming wickedness. Even Liz chuckled, the pair of them worse than Dad if truth be told, all co-conspirators and about twelve years old to boot.

"Just keep the doors open," Dad sighed then like he realized he'd made a mistake. Before beaming at them and clapping his hands together before rubbing them with the faint sandpaper sound of his big mitts celebrating this victory of his. "Now I have you right where I want you, we can talk."

That knocked the childlike joy from the former partners, but not their enthusiasm.

"We'll have to sign paperwork of some kind," Dad said, "but for now, if you two would witness?" He nodded to me, to Jill. "I, John Fleming, owner of

Fleming Investigations…" He paused, grimaced. "Damn, this won't work." Those eyes met mine again. "We need another witness."

Right. Because I was co-owner of that outfit whether I'd agreed to it or not.

"Allow me." And there was Toby Miller, right on schedule, ducking into the office like she'd never left, the old receptionist back in her sheriff's department sweater vest, beaming a smile at me as if Dad hadn't poached her for his own office and left Crew bereft. She made a little apologetic moue at my fiancé. "Sorry, dear," she said, "but I go where John goes."

And just like that, with Toby and Jill witnessing, Dad and I divested our interests in Fleming Investigations over to Crew and Liz for a dollar.

My father groaned when Crew handed over the bill. "I'm coming back," he said. "And you can bet the paperwork will say Lucy is on the board of directors just to be safe."

Snicker. Didn't he know that was as dangerous a decision as letting Crew and Liz take over?

"We'll see." Liz laughed and winked at her former FBI compatriot. "What do you say, partner? Just like old times?"

Crew's smile lit up his whole face and for the first time in a while I really saw him. No stress, no worries, free and released from the pressures of this job I now occupied, the last four years of tolerating the likes of Reading's residents and politics gone from him. The only times I'd actually seen this side of Crew were when he talked about the hoard, about the treasure hunt. Now that he was free, would I be seeing more of him like this?

And would we still love each other the same way?

All my worries he wasn't the man I fell in love with, not really, dashed to pieces and turned to dust when he crossed to me in a rush and hugged me so hard, I groaned a little.

"I love you," he whispered in my ear. "Now and forever. This is the best thing that ever happened to us." He laughed then, releasing me just enough he could look down into my eyes. "Because murder has always been our strong suit."

He could say that again. Except... "We don't know it's murder," I said, echoed at the exact moment by Dad, Jill and Liz.

Great. Same page and all that. Though, hard to stay grumpy when I had the most amazing posse in the history of posses at my back.

"Time to find out if there's anything to investigate," I said, turning to Jill. "Shall we drop in on the good doctor, Deputy Wagner?"

She hesitated, glanced at Dad. "Are you sure you don't want to take Sheriff—" she paused, blushed, stammered, "sorry, Fee, Deputy Fleming with you?"

And then I saw it, her worry, but more so her hurt. That Vivian made me sheriff, overlooked her, was making her beg for scraps and the chance at the job that should have been hers, hands down, no question.

Dad had inhaled to respond but I was already moving, crossing to my friend and taking her hand.

"You're my first choice," I said. "You think I want to work with that?"

She tried a smile and nodded. "I won't let you down."

"Jill," I said, ever so softly, just between the two of us, "you never could."

Why wasn't she perking up? Oh well, I'd deal with it.

Instead of pursuing it with the others lingering, I turned and focused on the task at hand. "If you two don't mind," I said to Crew and Liz, "we have an investigation to undertake. I was thinking Fleming Investigations might like to log some research hours."

"We'll see what our booking schedule allows," Liz said instantly with a little frown, "and get back to you." Then, she laughed, a bell-like peal of pure delight. "I've always wanted to say that," she said.

Not funny. "Just get digging into the suspects, please, while Jill and I talk to the doc and Dad…" I waved one hand at him, "does what Dad does because he's not going to listen to me if I ask him to do something specific."

My father actually had the nerve to look hurt, one hand on his heart, though the glitter of amusement in his eyes told me he was anything but.

"I'm kinda busy, actually," he said, "but I'll see what I can do."

Smartass former sheriff fathers and their attempts at humor.

CHAPTER ELEVEN

As soon as we got in the car—Jill driving her deputy's cruiser while I took the passenger's seat—I started in on a fumbling attempt to reassure my friend that I had no intention whatsoever of actually keeping the sheriff's job.

I think I was making things worse, not better, as she stayed intensely quiet and withdrawn. I finally mumbled my way to a pathetic halt and fell silent, not sure what to do or say as she pulled into the parking lot at Curtis County General and turned off the ignition.

She sat there a long moment, staring out the windshield into the freshly fallen darkness, the lights from the emergency room door to the left of the morgue entry casting brilliance on her blonde ponytail, making her eyes translucent.

I jumped a bit when she spoke, holding my place and my breath until she did without realizing I'd stopped breathing when she'd parked the car.

"Fee," she said. Stopped. Started again. "It's okay." I opened my mouth to protest but she was already turning toward me, one hand on my arm, doing her level best to be a trooper about things and succeeding, darn her, when now I just wanted her to be angry at me or something. Anything but that hangdog expression of defeat and acceptance.

"It's not," I said.

Her ponytail bounced when she shook her head, reaching behind her for her hat and cramming it on her head. "We both know you're ten times the investigator I am, and you don't have any training." She paused then, not sounding bitter at all. I would have been bitter if that was where my brain took me after the day we'd both had. "You're the right choice. Vivian made the right decision."

"You listen to me," I shot back, angry now, for her if she wouldn't be for herself. "The only reason Vivian made me interim sheriff was to piss off the Pattersons and to ensure Robert didn't muscle his way into the role. She knew appointing me would be the only thing the council would accept." I knew it was true. "Despite the fact you were the only choice."

Jill sighed. "No, keeping Crew was the only choice. What were they thinking?" She met my eyes, hers wide and sad.

"Seriously? They've been trying to get rid of him for ages." I knew that was true, too, saw it so clearly now. "Throwing all that Not-A-Fleming garbage at him, making him doubt himself, feel like an outsider. It's a wonder he didn't pitch the badge ages ago."

She nodded then. "A solid testament to what a good man he is," she said. "You're lucky. And so is he."

That last wasn't an add-on, not in the least, to make me feel better. Which made me feel worse.

"We're going to win Vivian's little challenge, Deputy and soon to be Sheriff Wagner," I said, "and while I can't for the life of me understand why you'd ever want the job, I'm going to make sure you are the one who delivers the truth of what happened to Thea Isaac." Because the dead woman was dead, justice would still be served and Jill was my priority, so there.

Jill just stared at me, expressionless

"Stand up to Robert more visibly," I said. "And take authority from me, publically." She flinched but I shook my head in return. "Just do it, Jill. You deserve to be sheriff."

My friend exited the car, waiting for me to follow before locking it behind her. She was silent on our short walk to the morgue door, but at least that low-level hum of defeat was gone. Maybe she wasn't feeling optimistic but at least she wasn't beating herself up and thinking in terms of being a failure anymore.

At least, I hoped so. Because I was going to need

her to keep her head on straight if I was going to deliver on my promise to get her the job I didn't want for any longer than absolutely necessary.

As we strode through the door, Jill holding it for me, I had a surprised realization. I didn't want the job. Yes, yes, okay, I'd been saying that. But hadn't a tiny little secret part of me loved being a deputy, always wanted to be in law enforcement, loved hanging with Liz on the last case together, always wondered what it would have been like if I'd pursued this career after all?

Here I had the chance to really find out. I wasn't just playing at being a deputy to protect me from being arrested for B&E. I was the town freaking sheriff, legit, yo. Despite Crew's loss of a job (which he didn't care about and was, I truly believed now, delighted to have lost) and Dad's good humor about the whole thing and Jill's suffering and having to deal with Rosebert... I accepted the truth.

I loved poking my nose in where it wasn't wanted, being a busybody, uncovering truths other people tried to hide. But I didn't want to do it from behind a badge.

Okay then.

I was so wrapped up in my thoughts about what I actually did want to do—because it was clear running a bed and breakfast wasn't going to satisfy me forever, was it?—I failed to realize until I was partway into the main morgue through the stainless steel swinging doors that Dr. Aberstock wasn't alone.

Barry Clement was with him. No shocker there,

since he was the doc's assistant. But Barry himself had company, backup if you like. The last person I expected to see standing in the bright lights of the large space that always gave me the creepy crawlies thanks to the lingering odors of heavy-duty cleaners that couldn't quite mask the scent of death should have been the first, really, if I'd been thinking clearly. And with any kind of foresight.

Geoffrey Jenkins didn't even acknowledge me or Jill as he shot that shark grin of his at the doc, finishing what he'd clearly already started with a final sentence that told me everything I needed to know and put him on my murder list all over again.

"Now, if you'll kindly go home as requested, Dr. Aberstock," the slimy piece of work said, "Mr. Clement will be taking over your work until such time your permanent position with our town can be reviewed."

Only then did Geoffrey turn and meet my eyes. And winked.

He did not just effectively fire Dr. Aberstock. Did *not*.

And yet, as the doc scowled at Geoffrey, at Barry, he didn't argue. Instead, the sweet-faced old man who always had my back, who'd offered me lollipops when I was a little kid and he came personally to treat me because he still made house calls, the Santa Claus replica with the sunny disposition who never judged, who treated everyone fairly and always, always had the answers I needed stripped off his white coat, tossed it at Geoffrey and walked out of the morgue.

Past me. Head high, face red, but jaw set.

Damn it.

Maybe I should have stayed and dealt with Geoffrey, but I couldn't. Instead, I left Jill to deal with the mess behind me and instead spun and went after the doc. He didn't have much of a head start and he was barely taller than me, but he'd built up a head of steam and made it almost to the door at the end of the hall before I caught his arm and turned him around to face me.

"Leave it, Fee," he growled. "Just leave it."

"I can't." I felt like crying all of a sudden while he opened the door, stepped inside. I'd never been in his small office before, stood there ineffectually wringing my hands, watching him don his winter coat, his boots, looking down at his neat-as-a-pin desk as if he was wondering what he should do now because I know I was wondering.

What was I supposed to do without him?

"This is just a means to an end," Dr. Aberstock said then, jerking me out of my downward spiral into begging him to stand up for himself. When his head lifted, he met my eyes, his snapping the sort of anger I'd never seen in him before. "A chance to not only eliminate Crew," he raised one hand, shaking his head, "yes, I heard about Crew. Ridiculous. So, cut out the excellent sheriff, then remove your ability to investigate the murder properly by installing a coroner without care or proper training." The doc's white beard wiggled as he ground his jaw. "Our town is going to hell, Fee, and I'm starting to wonder why

I care."

I couldn't argue with him there. "This is about the Pattersons, isn't it?" It had to be. "What are they hiding?"

He inhaled, exhaled heavily. "I wish I knew." One hand rose and wiped across his forehead, weariness replacing his anger. "Fee, I really do. I would tell you everything. Your father and I spent years trying to find something, anything. But they sealed themselves up tight against anyone not related to them. After Fiona Doyle disappeared."

So, this was tied to Malcolm Murray and Siobhan Doyle's daughter then. But why? How?

Dr. Aberstock clearly didn't have anything to give me and, as he drew near, grabbing his doctor's bag on the way to me, he paused only to lay one warm hand on my shoulder, sympathy and frustration on his cherub face.

"I'm so sorry, Fee," he said. "Please, take care and be safe. The Pattersons own Barry, you know that. They have since day one. I have no idea what they are holding over that boy's head, but it's enough to control him. And any investigation he might be part of."

So, if Geoffrey couldn't have Robert as sheriff as intended, he'd circumvent Vivian's attempt to level the field by removing my chance to solve the case before my cousin.

"You're so well-loved," I said. "This won't stand."

He shrugged and sighed. "Maybe so. And maybe

not. Certainly, I can simply continue my private practice. Unless they decide to try to ruin me." Dr. Aberstock seemed suddenly very old and worn thin. "If they do, I'll be calling. If I can count on you?"

Like that was even in question. I hugged him then, impulsively, and accepted his warm hug in return, realizing he smelled like cinnamon and peppermints and seriously could the man be more like Santa, red suit and sleigh or not?

And then, with a final sigh but not looking back, Dr. Aberstock slipped past me and out his office door, leaving me to fume and try to wind my mind around the unfairness of all of this while knowing there was nothing I could do from here.

Except solve this damned case, get Jill the sheriff's office then do my very best to bring the Pattersons down. Because they may have gotten a pass up to now, a step aside and fine, live and let live. Until they started actively coming after the people I cared about.

Big mistake.

CHAPTER TWELVE

I didn't leave Dr. Aberstock's office for some minutes, collecting my cool so I didn't march into the morgue and add some bodies to the stockpile behind the stainless-steel hatches on those cold, cold slabs that would be a fitting end to Geoffrey and Barry right about now. The fact I relegated most people who irritated me down to the nub of my last nerve to an untimely end was not lost on me.

I'd been around murder too long, it seemed.

Much to my furthered annoyance, as I finally turned and exited the doorway, heading back toward the swinging doors and the morgue proper, I realized I'd timed it perfectly to come into solo contact with none other than the first person I would have gladly added to the funeral home's list of customers.

Geoffrey Jenkins stopped in his tracks when he saw me coming toward him, that smirk eternal, I think, doing nothing to hide the savage and heartless predator behind those pale blue eyes. I suppose if one were to objectively observe him, one might consider him conventionally attractive, clearly, a gym attendee and well-preserved for his age with the middle-class corporate white guy metrosexual look going for him. But I knew him, knew the darkness of his soul, had witnessed firsthand his manipulative nature, the way he played people against one another—or tried, at any rate—and would never, ever trust him let alone find him even remotely appealing.

Funny thing was, Geoffrey seemed to feel otherwise and had proven it at least once before, though the few other times I'd thought he'd been kind of sort of hitting on me I'd passed off as holy ew, no way, I was imagining things, please god, save me from my overactive participation in anything to do with thinking such a terrible thought.

Now, I didn't have solid proof, despite the creepy moments he'd taken, gone out of his way, in fact, to touch my hair (once, at Sammy's, in passing while claiming I had a flower petal in it), squeeze my upper arm (also once, at a council meeting I attended when he snuck up behind me and made me squeak in surprise, that touch lingering long enough I wanted a shower after), and once both touched me (my shoulder) and my hair (tucked a piece behind my ear, I recall) while getting so close his breath tickled my cheek. That one was the most outstanding, in my opinion, because it had happened during the investigation into Lester Patterson's murder—and he'd so much as offered me Crew's job that day on the steps of the sheriff's office.

I hadn't forgotten, though I'd wanted to. But when I came to a halt beside him, ready to blast the councilor while knowing it wouldn't do a scrap of good, he leaned into me, one arm sliding around my waist as he whispered in my ear.

Stunned, frozen in place by his boldness, I held still and listened.

"You're making a huge mistake marrying Turner." Geoffrey didn't rush, his hand tightening on my waist through my coat. "There are smarter moves to make, Fiona, partnerships and agreements that will promise your continuing success in Reading. And that of your family." And his hand slid down, down, stopped at the curve of my hip.

I could have hurt him. Considered it. I'd been taking self-defense from Jill, hadn't I? Learned three or four ways to take a man down and have him beg for mercy from this very position. I really, really wanted to. But I wasn't going to give him the satisfaction of getting me fired for assault when I had no witness to his.

Because this was assault of the very worst kind, in my opinion. Not only was he touching me without my permission (physical) he was implying sexual favors (okay, not super clear but close enough so I tagged on sexual, considering the placement of his hand) and threatening me and my family all in one go (I didn't know what kind of assault that was—mental? Emotional? But it felt like an attack so there had to be a law against it). It was the epitome of privileged white guy who thought he could get away with anything because I was just a woman.

The fact he was a married man and tied into the Pattersons through his own wedding vows? Just made him all the more disgusting to me.

While my furious mind weighed which of the moves Jill taught me would cause him the most pain, my logical brain slowly turned my head, my eyes meeting his, my entire being willing him to sense just exactly what it was I thought of him.

It took a second, but he got it. I watched it register in his gaze, in the downturn of his lips. I didn't scowl, didn't frown, even. Just stared, flat and empty and cold, a hunting lioness stalking a shark who'd found his way on land and really should go back to the ocean if he knew what was good for him.

To his credit, he held his ground, neither of us backing down. It took Jill emerging from the swinging door, poking her head out, to look for me apparently, to break our stalemate.

"Fee." Her low, tense voice told me she suspected something wasn't right, but she didn't sound worried, mostly just frustrated.

"I'll be right there." I didn't look away, waited for Geoffrey to leave.

Which he did, finally, nodding to me once, slowly, ceding defeat? I doubted that, though, honestly, was that regret on his face? Disappointment he slathered over with that smarmy grin before spinning and exiting out the main door, leaving me with the desperate need to scream at the top of my lungs and punch some(one)thing.

Jill joined me, quiet and still. "Are you okay?"

"No." I know that came out harsh, but I wasn't in the mood for tempering my tone. "If we fail, and Robert becomes sheriff, I'm moving."

She exhaled, nodded. "I think we'll all need to."

I'd been kind of joking but when I turned back to meet her eyes, I realized she'd been thinking it, too. Not really a surprise because Jill had almost left us once before, thanks to the nefarious whisperings of Rosebert. I got it, I really did, why she wanted to go back then. They'd undermined her confidence and left her a shell of herself.

This time, though, it wasn't about quitting, was it? "They won't let us stay."

Jill's shoulders rose and fell, in acceptance, though, not defeat. "So, let's solve this murder and move on," she said. "Because if one of the two of us becomes sheriff," at least she was considering the fact I was going to hold up my end of the bargain, "the first thing we're going to do—"

"Is fire Robert Carlisle." We said it together, in tandem, and there was no way in hell the Pattersons were going to prevent it.

I grinned at last, punching her gently in the shoulder. "All right, Deputy. Let's see what their puppet has to say about our body, shall we?"

That made her hesitate, hum and haw a bit before she squared herself, her body between me and the swinging doors. "Can I make a suggestion? Sheriff?" She added that with a grin of her own, though far more serious than good-humored.

"I'll consider your suggestion," I said, going for haughty as a joke and breathed a sigh of relief when it worked.

"Excellent," she said. "How kind of you." Jill laughed then. "I couldn't joke around with Crew."

I wanted to hug her but didn't want to ruin the mood. "Speak, trusty second in command. I'm breathily bated and all that."

She snorted, then sobered again. "Let me deal with Barry."

She was right, of course. It made the most sense. Because hadn't I just been thinking about cramming his useless body into one of the coolers and seeing how long it took for him to suffocate? Never mind the tiny pinch of ego that prodded me. Jill knew what she was doing, and I had to trust her completely.

After all, she was going to be the next sheriff of Reading.

"Okay," I said, keeping my voice down, "done. And." She nodded as I went on. "We need to find out what the Pattersons have on him." He'd mentioned money at one time, right? Was that when I was forced to work with him at the Black Woods Hunting and Fishing Retreat last November? Maybe. It was the first time I had any indication the weakling was on the Patterson's payroll.

Jill's blue-gray eyes sparked. "I love the doc," she said, anger making her voice vibrate just a little, "but I can keep my cool. So yeah. I'll deal with Barry, and you dig. Maybe he'll tell me things he wouldn't tell you?" She tucked her hands into her jacket pockets after patting the front of her coat. "I have his preliminaries, anyway, so we can go, if you want."

Meaning I didn't have to see Barry's face again today?

Awesome.

CHAPTER THIRTEEN

I sat behind Dad's/Crew's/my desk feeling awkward and uncomfortable and oddly giddy as I did my best not to let hysterical meandering fed by the itching between my shoulder blades that screamed FRAUD IN THE SHERIFF'S OFFICE! keep me from doing the job Vivian entrusted me with.

Instead, here I was, questioning a witness and doing my very best to hold it together while Andrew Isaac, still lost in grief, didn't seem to notice, thank goodness. Because any second now someone (likely Vivian) was going to storm through the door and demand I get my butt out of this chair that was surprisingly comfortable even considering the circumstances and stop playing at being someone who was supposed to be leading a criminal investigation.

Supposed criminal investigation.

Argh, times a million.

Shades of my father lecturing me and Crew giving me the third degree lingered in the ether as Andrew blew his nose into the tissue I'd offered him from the generic box on my (gulp) desk, slumped low in the wooden chair across from me.

What was proper procedure here? Get up and comfort the man? Stay where I was and do a Crew and Dad and just let him cry it out? Hug him? Sheesh, I had no idea, though common compassion and her sister, empathy, forced me up and out of my own chair and pushed me physically around the desk to sit on the edge, reaching out one hand to take Andrew's.

He seemed grateful, squeezing back just a bit before letting me go. "I'm sorry," he said. "I just can't believe this is happening."

Neither could I. Flickers of Crew grilling me about the death of Pete Wilkins mingled with chewing out sessions when I couldn't seem to mind my own business, crossing over memories of collaborating and then, finally, him breaking his office rule and kissing me right here, in this very spot...

Whoops. Andrew was looking at me expectantly and had (maybe?) asked me a question and I'd missed it. (Right?)

"I'm sorry, too," I said. "Did Thea wake up not feeling well?" So, I'd skimmed over his inquiry, let him figure that one out.

It didn't seem to bother him, so score. "No," he said. "It wasn't until she came back from the church. She had to get her Bible and the paperwork for you and Crew." He swallowed hard. "She said she started feeling ill shortly after she got there and had been drinking her grapefruit juice to try to ease her throat. It wasn't helping. I asked her to step aside, let Alfred do the service." He choked then, coughed to catch himself from sobbing. "If she wasn't so stubborn, maybe she'd be alive. She was always pushing herself, never happy with what she gave, keen to just give more and more. I kept telling her she would kill herself with her refusal to care for herself first, but she wouldn't listen." Andrew exhaled slowly, shakily. "Was I right? Does the doctor know what happened?"

I didn't respond to that. Not because he didn't deserve an answer, but because someone knocked on my door, Jill peeking in a moment later and gesturing for me to join her.

"Please, excuse me one minute." I left Andrew there, knowing the deputy would only have interrupted if it was important.

And was it. "Barry got back to me with the full autopsy," she whispered just outside my door as I eased it closed and nodded to her, peeking behind her to find Robert and Rose watching, scowling. They'd have the same info already, knowing Barry's Patterson connection. Whatever. His initial report told me nothing that Dr. Aberstock hadn't mentioned, including the scent of rubbing alcohol. No, it wasn't lost on me that her husband—the very man sitting in my office right now—was not only the prime suspect because the spouse was always top of the list, but because he'd been using the very stuff on the organ in front of the entire wedding party.

"And?" I didn't have to prod Jill who went on with that same soft tone that told me she'd had lots of practice, likely having to share things with Crew in exactly this manner to keep Robert out of the loop. Great workplace. Really inspired confidence and team building.

"He said that at one time it's clear Thea was an alcoholic," she said. "The damage to her liver isn't fully repaired. At one point she had cirrhosis, but it's improved, though he said the scar tissue would be with her forever. Likely she quit drinking in the last two or three years from the improvement in her condition." Huh. Interesting for a woman known around Reading for Bible-thumping (if you'll pardon the expression) about drinking and drugs. Though not uncommon in reformed addicts. "And she has old, fading needle marks indicating excessive drug use."

A junkie, too? Awesome.

Oh, Fee. No judging. We all had our addictions. The fact she'd seemed to kick hers spoke volumes about her. But it also made my intuition tingly. Even more so when Jill wrapped up her report.

"Forensics is testing the bottle," she said, "but Barry's analysis of her blood gave him an overdose of isopropanol."

Rubbing alcohol. The doc had been right. And an ironic way for a former alcoholic to die, right?

"Thanks, Jill," I said. "Anything further?"

She shook her head and backed off. "I'll keep you posted." My favorite deputy waved and turned back to her desk, pointedly ignoring Rosebert while they pointedly ignored her, and everything was rainbows and unicorn farts in HappySappyReadingLand.

Grunt.

Time to check in with hubby dearest on the state of Thea's soul, not to mention her habits.

But when I sat once again on the edge of the desk and very kindly asked him if Thea was drinking, his entire body rejected the idea. In fact, he almost leaped out of the chair with a horrified cry, and I found myself restraining Andrew with two firm hands on his shoulders before easing him back down into the seat.

"No way," he said, one hand chopping through the air, definitive. "Thea hated everything about alcohol." He cleared his throat. "I'm a reformed alcoholic myself," he said. "It's part of the reason we fell in love. Because we were both so dead set against drinking." He wiped at beads of sweat that had erupted from his upper lip. "The moment we set foot in Reading, she started the preteen and teen support groups at the church, to make sure local kids had what they needed to say no to drugs and alcohol." I'd heard that, too. "Why?"

"You know she used to be an alcoholic, too,

then?" I didn't bring up the track marks while he nodded.

"She never said as much, but it takes one to know one. And I didn't miss the old needle tracks, Fee, in case you're wondering about that." Figured. I nodded kindly for him to go on, feeling much more confident and like I was finally channeling the persona I needed to feel comfortable in this office, this position, as this suspect spilled his guts willingly.

Hey. Don't get cocky, Fleming.

"I didn't push her about it," he said. "And she didn't ask about my past, either. We came together in mutual need, and then in love. She was the best thing that ever happened to me." He burst into fresh tears, and I let him cry a moment before handing him the tissue box again.

"How long ago did you move to Reading?" I had a vague number, but I wanted specifics.

"Two years ago," he said, "next month." January. Okay. "From Montpelier." The capital? Interesting move, though for the chance at her own church, it would make sense for Thea to accept. "She wanted the opportunity." I was so smart. "And my daughter…" Andrew hesitated before looking hopeless. "Katelyn was struggling as a freshman at college. She's only twenty, lost her mom young, and had me to deal with her whole life." He sounded like he blamed himself for something. "They didn't get along very well." That was said softly, hesitant. "We hoped that the move would give her something to focus on."

"And how long had you and Thea been married?" I wasn't liking him for the murder, though this was only the first layer, wasn't it? There always seemed to be more digging to do.

"Three years." He flushed then, shook his head. "And we only knew each other two months before I asked her, and she said yes." Andrew's hand shook as he wiped his eyes with the rumpled tissue. "It was a whirlwind, part of the reason Katelyn struggled to accept Thea. But I loved her so much." He choked up one last time. "I can't believe she's gone."

"I'm sorry to have to ask you these questions so soon," I said.

Andrew reached out and took my hand this time. "I just want to know what happened," he said. "I'll do anything you need. And so will Katelyn." Sounded like on pain of massive punishment, so I let that go.

"And you know nothing at all about Thea's past?" Could this have been something that came back to haunt her from her days as an addict?

Andrew's hangdog expression was everything I needed to know. "I don't." He hesitated then, like he wanted to say more, but instead shook his head and looked down at his hands.

Whatever it was, I'd get it out of him eventually. For now, the man had been through enough. Maybe that was a terrible attitude for a sheriff investigating what she now knew was a murder, but it was a great one for a human being.

I chose human, thanks.

"Andrew," I said as I guided him to the door, "I need to speak to Katelyn next."

He nodded, more under control than he had been. "She's likely at the church," he said. "She was Thea's assistant, and I know she was planning to start packing her things."

A bit premature considering this was a murder investigation. I gestured for Toby who hurried toward me and gently led Andrew away while I spun back to my office door to fetch my coat.

Only to come face-to-face with Rose.

"You're not going to win," she hissed at me before scuttling away like the revolting eight-legged arachnid she reminded me of. Considering the web of lies and deceit the Pattersons (Marie, in my opinion) had woven around Reading, that meant Rose was in good company.

I couldn't wait to find a newspaper and squash her with it.

Damn it. Why did I have to go there, to use that metaphor, to tie Rose and the Pattersons and Pamela Shard all into one whirling ball of anxiety?

I didn't have time to worry about my missing friend at a time like this.

Did I?

CHAPTER FOURTEEN

Needless to say, I was in foul humor when I arrived at the Reading United Methodist Church. I huddled inside my coat, the chill air only getting colder, not typical for mid-December. I scowled at the front door, knowing I was supposed to be getting married tomorrow and that I was investigating a murder instead while now once again embroiled in a blame/fear/anger cycle surrounding the missing newspaperwoman I called my friend.

As I headed inside, the heavy door thudding shut behind me, I immediately spotted suspicious behavior in the whispered arguing of none other than Katelyn Isaac and Dominic Twigg. Unfortunately, the two of them were having their little hissing conversation in the foyer of the church so I missed out on the chance to eavesdrop, though from the guilty expression on the choir master's face and the dissatisfaction and frustration on the young woman's, it wasn't unfolding to either of their satisfaction.

Dominic nodded to me but didn't speak, exiting swiftly out the side door and down the stairs, presumably to the basement. Katelyn, her generous chest squeezed behind her crossed arms, glared at him as he ran off, her heavily made-up eyes finally meeting mine and her anger easing just a bit.

"What?" From pissed at Dominic to annoyed with me in about a half-second flat? Either hormones were involved, or she hadn't grown out of her teenage angst despite the digits in her birthday.

"I need to speak to you about your stepmother, Miss Isaac." If she was going to be a child, I was going to parent her in my best Dad, Sheriff Doomsday Fleming persona.

Sure, it didn't really work on me, but it did on her, surprisingly. Maybe that was why he cultivated it? I'd grown up with him and was far too much like him to let it get to me. But clearly, someone not raised by said John Fleming didn't have the wherewithal to counter it.

I could only imagine her own father, guilt over his alcoholism and the death of her birth mother influencing his choices, went far too soft on her in the beginning and that Thea's no-nonsense style of doing things must have rubbed Katelyn the wrong way.

First off, what twenty-year-old needed to wear

that much eye makeup? Or thick lipstick? Or dress like that for the curves she had?

Oh my god. I was turning into a fuddy-duddy. Maybe I needed to get out of Reading regardless of whether Robert became sheriff or not.

"You want to know about Thea?" Katelyn's attitude shifted, from annoyance to bitter resentment. "She was a nightmare. Dad didn't see her the way I saw her." She jabbed one perfectly manicured fingernail at her chest before crossing her arms again. She really needed to take care because the pushup bra she'd chosen wasn't up to the duty she was demanding of it, especially when she squeezed the girls together in such an aggressive fashion.

Nope, not a fuddy-duddy. A total and complete prude.

"Can you be more specific?" Don't let me down, Dad.

Katelyn bit her lower lip, leaving a red rim on her teeth as she pouted like a child. "She was horrible to me, treated me like a little kid." Um. Deep breath, Fee. "It wasn't fair, she made Dad take her side all the time. I hated her." That was hissed spitefully, you betcha. "I'm glad she's dead."

Oh, wow. Okay then. Hello, Suspect #1, so nice to make your acquaintance.

Time to let this petulant girl know the kind of trouble she just landed herself into. "Thea Isaac was murdered, Miss Isaac," I said. And waited.

Watched as her face tightened in shock, her eyes widened, pupils dilating before she inhaled sharply and covered her mouth with both hands. When she lowered them, she was shaking her head. "I didn't kill her," she said.

"And yet, you're glad she's dead." I freaking loved the Dad voice. Seriously. Why had I not used it to this level before? He had it going on. "And had access to your stepmother. And knew she had no sense of smell. Not to mention the murder weapon." I'd disclosed enough, kicked myself a bit for letting that last slip.

"What killed her?" Katelyn was that mix of horrified curiosity and morbid voyeurism that made me want to smack her.

"I can't share more details of an ongoing investigation," I said. "But my point remains, Miss Isaac." Now, did I think this bratty child without the foresight to not confess she wanted her own stepmother six feet under actually had the brains or the ability to put two-and-two together and find a clever way to murder Thea? Not really. But stranger things had happened, and I wasn't about to let her off the hook. Worst case scenario, she was my murderer. Best case, she learned a lesson and smarted the hell up.

Either way, it was a win-win in Fiona Fleming's books.

Katelyn burst into tears—crocodile, if you asked me—and ran off in the same direction Dominic Twigg had escaped not so long ago. I needed to talk to him, too, since he'd been at the rehearsal. But I was distracted by the sound of weeping coming from inside the doors to the nave and followed my gut.

I found Ian Rudge bent over the keyboard of the organ, sobbing, hugging and rocking himself. He started when he noticed me watching, wiping at his face and running nose with the cuff of his sleeve. I'd stuffed some tissues into my jacket pocket and shared them with him. He took them with hesitant anxiety, a rabbit in the snow trying to decide if I was a wolf wanting to make him my snack or a deer doing a good deed.

"Are you okay, Ian?" I sat down next to him on the bench, sliding him over with sheer determination and he gave way, nodding down at the wad of tissues in his slender hands, his thin shoulders shaking as he fought off further sobs.

"T-T-Thea." He managed her name before inhaling long and deep. "She m-m-meant so m-m-much to me, M-Miss Fleming." He seemed to have missed the memo I was sheriff now. Not on my list to alert him to the fact maybe he should ask for a lawyer list and I sat there and nodded and listened instead. "I was one of h-h-her kids." Ian managed a weak smile, slightly bulging eyes huge behind his glasses, face mottled with blotches from crying. Ouch, I felt him. When I cried it was a disaster of epic redheaded complexion issues. "I was l-l-living out of s-s-state with my m-mother. When she died, I couldn't l-l-live with it." He bowed in half like his spine had lost the ability to hold him upright and I found myself cradling him against me. "I dropped out of c-c-college, got into d-d-drugs. I finally came back to R-R-Reading to try to start over. And I m-m-met Thea." He pulled away from me, not out of offense, but so he could meet my eyes. "She saved m-m-my life." The crumpled wad of tissues made it to his mouth as fresh tears poured down his cheeks. "How could this hap-p-pen to someone so g-g-good?"

He deserved to know. "Thea was murdered, Ian," I said while he wailed his despair. "I promise, I'm going to find out who did it and bring them to justice."

Ian leaned into me again and though he had easily a foot on my height he was so slender he felt feather-light against me.

"Only a m-m-monster could kill s-s-someone like Thea Isaacs," he said in a cold, dead voice.

Wow. Poor kid. I just hoped he wouldn't fall back into drugs now that he'd lost his second mother figure.

Not my problem. Or was it?

Sigh. Can't save them all, Fee. As much as you'd like to try.

Ian stood abruptly and left in a hurry, still weeping and I let him go, staring at the multitude of keys in front of me, the organ a foreign object. The tall pipes stretched up behind me, and while I was tempted to poke a finger to see what would happen (grow up, Fleming, this was serious business) I resisted the temptation and stood, heading for the basement and my talk with Dominic Twigg.

The moment I set foot on the bottom step,

however, all thoughts of chasing down a killer flew out the window and, with a low cry of happiness, I rushed forward and hugged with great enthusiasm the two old ladies who instantly hugged me back.

"Fiona," Mary Jones said in her five-pack-a-day voice even though she didn't smoke, her silent sister Betty embracing me. "We're so glad you're here."

CHAPTER FIFTEEN

I hadn't seen the Jones sisters in what felt like forever and repressed instantly the guilt that I'd failed to pursue our relationship past the occasional bumping intos and run acrosses we'd managed over the last year or so. Neither of them seemed put off by the fact we'd been hanging out in different circles, the delighted beaming smiles where once only dour judgment lived was proof enough to me, they meant what Mary said.

"Ladies." I smiled right back, releasing them, for some reason feeling like I just walked through a breath of fresh air heavily oxygenated enough to make me giddy. "You look fantastic."

Betty blushed just a little while Mary poked me in the ribs. "Liar," she growled but she was still smiling.

"We're the same old brick houses you've always known, Fee. But we'll take the compliment, won't we, Bets?"

Her silent sister nodded shyly before pulling me in for a kiss on my cheek that made me giggle. How had I ever thought these two were horrible, negative old women who, in their sour dislike of me and my replacement of Grandmother Iris wished me ill? I'd spent two weeks when I'd first arrived back in Reading thinking they hated me. Only to discover they were both terrified I was going to fire them and replace them.

It had been a lesson for me, in leaping to conclusions and though I loved to jump when the opportunity presented, it was often with that particular bout of education in mind that tempered my judgments.

I had a million questions for them and was about to leap into the first on the list—namely what they were both doing at the church—when we were interrupted. He huffed his way to us, ignoring me completely, narrow nose in the air, skinny body tucked into a beige wool cardigan that did nothing for his washed-out redhead complexion dominated by far too many freckles.

"We don't pay you two to dilly dally," Alfred Welling pronounced in that type of arrogant tone that told me he was a small man in a position of power who had to push his weight around to feel worthy of that role. "I expect you to do your jobs, ladies. Miss Jones." He turned his snotty focus on

Mary who scowled back at him in that way I recognized from my first days at Petunia's. "The main bathroom upstairs needs cleaning. And Miss... Jones." He stammered over the repeat of the name, now speaking to Betty who took her cue from her sister and shared her expression, "I'd like to discuss the meal plan. There will be changes from now on."

Part of me wanted to kick him in the butt just for trying to bully the Jones sisters. After all, they were seniors, elderly and wasn't this some kind of abuse? And yet, as I stood there and watched them both stare at him with their perfectly matched glares of discontent, I almost laughed.

He wasn't going to survive. Just saying.

Alfred looked back and forth between them as the silence grew long and heavy, then longer and heavier, until he seemed to crumple under it, a faint sheen of sweat standing out on his forehead. "I expect you to do what's required or you will be replaced."

Oh, he did *not* just present them with an ultimatum. Damn, where was a microwave when I needed one? I wanted to make popcorn for the show.

"Have we failed in some way up to now?" Mary didn't even bother to address him by his name, just bluntly hit him with the question. "Either of us?"

He spluttered a moment then shook his head. "I'm merely informing you that with the change of guard there will be a firmer hand at the helm of this church."

"The next time you decide my sister and me are in need of that kind of talk," Mary said, turning her back on him and facing me, "we'll be leaving, and you can find someone else to put up with your smart mouth, Alfred Welling." She shook her head as Betty firmly turned to me, too, cutting the young, now discombobulated minister out of our conversation so effectively I almost felt sorry for him. "I knew his grandmother, changed his diapers when he was a wee tot." Mary's growling voice didn't change inflection, factual despite the flash of anger in her eyes. "Imagine trying to tell someone who's wiped your dirty bottom what to do."

His pale lashes fluttered while he hovered there, fish lipping as if not sure what to do from here. I chose to ignore him, to do the ladies that service as I talked to them instead.

"Have you been here long?" When had they started working for the church? When they'd left me, they told me they were retiring. I fretted then, worrying they needed the money, but Mary shrugged as Betty stepped in a bit closer, iron-gray hair matching her sister's.

"We got bored," Mary said. "Figured some light work for the both of us would keep us young." She grinned at Betty. "And off each other's backs, right, Bets?"

Betty smiled back before ducking her head.

"We heard your Crew got canned," Mary said, voice dropping a bit. "This town, Fee, it's going to hell, and it doesn't need a handbasket to get it there.

More like it's taking a rocket ship." Betty nodded emphatically along with her sister's words. "We know you're sheriff now." Mary beamed a bit, Betty, too. "We're darned proud of you, missy." Well now, that was… wow. Sniff. "Your Grandmother Iris would have thought this was the funniest joke ever told." I eye-rolled as Mary wheezed out a laugh. "And we think we might have some information to help."

"Please," I said, grinning in turn. "I'm certain nothing makes it past you two." I glanced over Mary's shoulder, surprised to see Alfred still hovering. Was he trying to make up his mind about leaving or looking for a way to regain (well, gain, since he never had it in the first place) control of the conversation or was he just awkward and didn't know when he should exit quietly and cut his losses? Regardless, he lingered, and I was okay with that because since he was here? I didn't have to chase down my next interview, did I?

Meanwhile, Mary and Betty exchanged a look. "Betty saw Thea and Dominic Twigg fighting yesterday," she said, her sister's hands clasping each other tightly, big eyes locked on me as if begging me to believe her while the only one vocal of the two went on. "Something to do with Katelyn, right?"

Betty bobbed another nod.

"Why didn't you tell me about this?" There it was, Alfred's attempt to intervene. Mary ignored him, though she did address the question.

"Just because you're head minister now," she said, "doesn't make you God, Alfred. Hush while your elders finish their conversation."

Whoops. I'd never seen a redhead go that particular shade of purple under freckles before. Not attractive. Or conducive to continuing heart health.

"Thank you, Mary, Betty," I said before meeting Alfred's eyes, speaking to him directly before he could blow his gasket. "Tell me, Mr. Welling," what did one call a minister officially? I didn't know, so I went with the usual prefix and forged on, "about your relationship with Thea Isaac?"

He flinched then, shook his head. "I don't have to talk to you without a lawyer present." He swallowed like that was final.

"True," I said, just as Mary spun around and smacked him hard across the arm. He yelped and grasped for the hurt spot, eyes bulging as he stared at her in shock.

"Don't be a smart mouth, Alfred," she growled. "Tell the sheriff what she needs to know. Now."

His head dropped, all semblance of his attempt at control vanishing in the face of the older woman who wouldn't accept his nonsense for a single second. Smart boy. "I wasn't in favor of her taking her position. Are you happy now?" He snapped that last before flinching as if expecting Mary to strike him again. But when he met my eyes his were defensive and sullen and his weak chin retreated further, making him appear petulant rather than anyone I would want running a garbage dump, let alone the religious base of Reading's population. "I was next in line for the job. She was an outsider, an unnecessary addition." He inhaled, shoulders going back, dropping his hand from his arm and trying, again, to pull his composure out of thin air. "But I am a man of God, Sheriff Fleming. Despite my protests to council I would never commit murder."

Right, like I hadn't heard anyone hand me that line before.

For now, I had a sense of him and that was what I needed. "I'll be in touch for a more formal interview," I said. "Down at the station." I smiled then, knowing it would grate on him and wondering why I was feeling so petty. "I'll expect you to make yourself available."

He dropped his gaze and nodded, finally lurching away while I let regret surface. I'd just bullied him, hadn't I? And privately laughed while the Jones sisters did the same. Okay, just Mary, but still.

Guilty as sin in a church basement? Time to go before lightning struck.

I said my goodbyes to the Jones sisters, with hugs and promises to catch up, knowing I'd likely lose track of them again and sighing as I exited the church after a search for Dominic Twigg turned up nada.

Instead of chasing him down (while chasing my tail), I headed back to the office in the late afternoon sunset, since home was out of the question still. I was just climbing behind the wheel of my car, looking up from a message I'd sent to Jill about my chats with suspects/witnesses when I spotted Vivian French driving by in her crystal white SUV. She traded in her sporty red convertible every November for the flashy giant monstrosity she favored for snowy roads. Not that I blamed her, we lived in the mountains, and that beast was much more practical in winter conditions. But it wasn't the sight of the vehicle itself that caught my eye, but the fact Vivian wasn't alone in the front seat.

A woman sat in the passenger's side, a blonde who spoke with great enthusiasm if her hand gestures were any indication.

Curious. And, like I needed another mystery to solve, telling myself I needed to talk to Vivian about making me sheriff, I made an impulse decision and followed her. All the way to her big, white house. By the time I parked in the curve of her circular driveway, Vivian and her guest were already inside, the door closing on their heels. I hesitated only a moment before heaving myself out of my car and trudging through the skiff of snow to the steps, the front door, pressing the bell and listening to the chime go off inside while I asked myself several times why the hell I was even here.

Vivian wasn't going to talk to me. This was useless. I really should have just gone back to the office or Crew's or Mom and Dad's. Instead of standing in the chill evening air on the Queen of Wheat's front step shivering from more than just the cold.

The door whipped open and, after a surprised moment, the woman on the other side beamed at me, pulling me into a hug, closing the way behind me as she kissed my cheek.

"Darling Fiona," Clara French said in her faint British accent that reminded me I still needed to talk to Dominic Twigg. "How lovely to see you again."

I hugged Vivian's aunt in return, just as happy to see her. She and Vivian's grandmother had not only been friendly to me the last time I'd been here, the latter had, in a moment of dementia, called me Iris and asked me about the doubloon. Telling me she knew about the treasure. I'd never had the opportunity to question her or find out what she knew. Vivian kept the older ladies too cloistered. For their protection? Maybe. Whatever her reasons, it meant the only way I could question Martha French was to sneak into Vivian's house.

Well, she'd finally given me a reason to come here, a legit one that had nothing to do with the treasure and everything to do with the position she'd put us both in. So there.

Yes. I could justify anything.

I opened my mouth to respond in kind, but someone's high-pitched, "Whoo-whoo!" and clickity-clack of heels on the marble floor of the foyer silenced me. I stared in surprise, knowing I had to look shocked, as an older and carefully preserved version of Vivian tottered toward me on shoes far too tall for comfort, her body elegantly sheathed in a dress tailored to the last itty-bitty detail as if she'd been sewn into its deep blue fabric.

"Oh, my goodness gracious and all the stars in the sky," she practically sang as she hurried to me and air-kissed both of my cheeks, her augmented lips shining, makeup carefully applied to hide her age but doing little at such close proximity. "This can't be dear little Fiona Fleming?"

And I knew in that instant exactly who this was, even before Vivian appeared, fury barely contained behind her icy glare. Not aimed at me. Nope.

"Rachelle," I breathed. The woman simpered, twirled, then patted my cheek like I was some sweet pet she'd forgotten all about until now.

Vivian was unamused.

"That's enough, Mother," she said.

CHAPTER SIXTEEN

I could tell Vivian was going to try to shut things down and kick me out of the house, but her mother was a force to be reckoned with, apparently. Even as the Queen of Wheat inhaled to either a) tell me to leave or b) deliver some kind of scathing comment about her mother (if her disdainful and angry expression that overwhelmed the typical tight control she was famous for was any indicator) or c) explode/implode/lose her marbles, Rachelle French, her overgrown fingernails biting into my arm despite the thickness of my coat, grasped firmly onto my person and practically dragged me through the fancy foyer and into the faintly rose-scented sitting room, her mouth running the entire time.

I shrugged an apology I didn't mean at Vivian on

the way by, propelled by the chatty and, from the martini in her hand, alcohol-fueled passion of the mayor's formerly estranged mother.

"Do come in, Fiona dear, how lovely of you to visit, and how is that darling and adorable mother of yours? And your father, still a handsome and dashing devil, I bet. And I hear you're getting married yourself, how lovely, my dear, Vivian, sweetness, Fiona's getting married, isn't that delightful?" Rachelle finally paused for a breath—and a sip of her martini—before rushing on as she planted me in a wingback chair in the stuffy sitting room despite the massive ceilings and towering windows, all shielded from the outside world by thick, velvet curtains in a remarkable shade of blue. "I'm certain you'll be having wee little Flemings before long, Fiona, my love, and they'll just be adorable with that lovely red hair of yours and I hear your fiancé is quite the dashing and yummy young man himself, I just bet he is." Her eyes, pale amber instead of Vivian's ice blue, twinkled at me over the rim of her glass, her lips twitching as her gaze flickered to her daughter. Vivian sat, rigid and clearly unhappy, across from me, hands firmly folded in her lap, ankles crossed, her perfect poise all the indication I need she was on the edge of her temper as much as she was her seat. And I recognized, in that chattering ramble of words her mother tossed out so casually there were clear and present barbs aimed directly at her daughter, cuts so thin as to go unnoticed to the casual ear, but more than likely only reopening wounds unhealed and flayed wide through time and careful application of pressure.

Vivian was unmarried, with no prospects that I knew of, and unlikely to have kids at this point. And that was just for starters, bits and pieces I was able to personally glean from all the commentary. What else was hidden inside what I now could only guess wasn't a trackless ramble but a deliberate attack that had history so long and well seeded it was no wonder Vivian was the way she was.

I'd felt empathy for her before, especially after I realized she'd lost Victor, and that we'd been friends once. But this was the first time I actually felt real and honest compassion, that I wanted to defend her, to tell her holding onto beautiful on the outside but hideous on the inside mother to shut up already.

Rachelle snapped her fingers at her sister-in-law. "Fiona, will you have a martini with me? Clara, fetch one, be a dear."

I shook my head while Clara hesitantly started to rise. Since when was her sister-in-law relegated to being Rachelle's servant? "I'm fine, thank you. I'm on duty."

"Duty?" Rachelle made a big deal of that word, lips twisting as she leaned back. "Don't tell me you're actually sheriff after all, dear. My heavens, how horribly pedestrian. Vivian, darling, how could you foist such a terrible job off on this lovely girl." Rachelle leaned toward me, whispering though everyone could hear her, including Martha who sat with a quilt over her, watching me. "Honestly, Fiona, what dreadful business, all that death and aren't you just frantic you'll have nightmares?"

I didn't bother telling her this was my twelfth victim, shrugging instead. "Daughter of a sheriff," I said. "I'm actually here to talk to Vivian." I half-rose, meeting her eyes. Was that gratitude there?

But before she could stand and take the out I offered, Rachelle's hand grasped my arm and jerked me down into my seat again. She didn't seem to do so with spite in her intent, but she started talking again and I found myself grinding my teeth at her incessant speech giving, wondering how anyone could put up with her for any length of time and what, exactly, had led her back to Reading.

If she was here to spend Christmas with her family, and I was Vivian, I'd be switching religions.

"Surely such terrible business is more suited to a male officer." Wow, she didn't actually say that out loud, did she? "I always left anything that meant disruption to Ranier. He took care of all the details, so I didn't have to." She said it so casually as if her departed husband was going to be home any minute and I wondered if part of her act was a ruse to hide her grief. Except Vivian's reaction to her mother's comment told me otherwise. Nope, just another way to torment her only remaining child, apparently. "You know, I often thought he would have made an excellent lawyer or secret agent or something of that nature, all dashing and tuxedo-wearing, you know. The spy type." She winked at me. "He was so handsome and such a gentleman and I just know

Victor would have turned out to be the spitting image of his father. Just like Vivian did of her mother. Isn't that right, darling?"

So, there are definitive moments in our lives when things come into crystal clarity. The type of events that seem to have giant flashing signs built around them, huge billboards of THE TRUTH that were impossible to unsee and kind of took your breath away.

This was one of those moments. Never in my life had I seen anyone as clearly as I did Rachelle French. The vindictive, spite-filled and empty shell of a woman who had zero redemption available to her. She might have had a chance to rebound once, but she'd chosen hate, embraced it, wallowed in it and allowed it to suck out her soul and slither into its place, her disguise a razor-thin skim of scum over a seething black pond of sludge ready to destroy anyone who allowed it the tiniest opening.

She was evil incarnate. With all of that nastiness aimed at the one person she hated the most in the world, likely because she only really had her daughter left to blame.

Vivian surged to her feet as the image flashed out and I was simply staring at Rachelle French again. The mayor grasped her mother's hand and, as the older woman squealed in protest over spilling her martini, dragged the elder French out of the room.

I sat there a moment, swallowing bile, stomach churning from what I'd seen. When I met Clara's eyes, she looked sad, worried, then leaped up and ran from the room the way Vivian had gone.

Leaving me alone with Martha.

The old woman had held still the entire time I'd been there, silent with half-lidded eyes and a rather vacant expression that made me worry something horrible had happened to her since I saw her last. I knew she suffered from dementia, perhaps even full-on Alzheimer's at this point. But the moment Clara ran from the room, Vivian's grandmother surged forward, shedding her quilt, and almost leaping on me. Her rock-hard fingernails left half-moon indentations in the back of my hand when I squeaked protest at her quick return to mobility.

"Iris." She hissed my grandmother's name, winking and grinning, old lips wrinkled, moisture creeping into the lines around her mouth, her faded blue eyes sparking with some old secret while my heart pounded, and I nodded.

Going to hell myself, apparently.

"Take it." She stuffed something into my hand before settling back into her seat again. "I can't use it, not now. And I know he would want you to have it. All of it."

"Who?" I didn't dare look at what she'd given me. The old lady was cracked, that much was obvious. Okay, not a nice way to talk about someone who had an illness that would claim her life at some point, as it had clearly taken her mind.

Martha giggled like a girl, hands covering her mouth before she winked at me.

"You know who," she said. "Alistair."

Wait. What? "Alistair Markham?"

She inhaled quickly. "You know he always had a thing for you, Iris. Why do you think he worked so hard to find the..." she leaned in again before hissing, "*you know?*"

This was almost too much. Was Crew's grandfather in love with my grandmother? And, as my mind skimmed over possibilities, did that mean I needed to somehow be worried about my marriage? But no, I knew my grandfather, right? And Dad looked just like him, didn't he? I swallowed more bile, panic subsiding while I wriggled with discomfort in my chair.

Please, don't let Crew be my half-cousin or something equally creepy or I'd seriously be finding a nunnery and joining the cloister.

"Doesn't matter now," Martha sighed, leaning back once more. I fetched her quilt and draped it over her legs, tucking the soft bundle she gave me into my coat pocket. "He's married, you're married, unrequited love is a bitch." She cackled a laugh then and I exhaled in shaky relief just as she caught my hand and brought me so close to her, that I could smell the stale peppermints on her breath. "He gave it to me to give to you, but I was jealous." Tears stood in her eyes then. "We all wanted him for ourselves, even Marie." She shook her head. "But he loved you, Daniel loved you. They all did." She seemed to fade then, lips parting as she stared at the floor and sighed. "Now you have what you need, and I'm done with it, Iris."

I wanted to ask her specific questions, so many, but she was clearly worn out, suddenly unresponsive for real and, as I sat back in my chair, hand going to my pocket and whatever it was she gave me, I heard the side door slam open and stood to find Vivian storming toward me.

"Come with me," she snapped. "Now." And kept moving, back toward the foyer exit.

I knew where this was going, had been ushered out in the past. Not like this wasn't what I'd been expecting. Except, as I paused to touch Martha's cheek, she looked up at me and smiled, squeezing my fingers.

"Hello, Iris," she said in a little girl's voice. "I didn't know you were here, dear. Would you like to play with my dolls?"

I left her there, picking at the hem of her quilt, humming softly to herself an old nursery rhyme while I felt my heart constrict and begged the powers that were out there in the wild beyond to please take me long before I could become like her.

CHAPTER SEVENTEEN

I was surprised, then, when Vivian didn't stop at
the front door after all but kept going, leading me
past the exit and toward the other side of the grand
main entry. She opened a tall, elaborate doorway and
stepped through, leaving it open for me to follow
and I found myself, a moment later, standing on
thick, dark carpeting in the midst of a huge study
with a roaring fire in the massive fireplace. Books
lined the walls, more library than office, though the
giant leather wingbacks and the tall portrait of a
handsome man over the mantel told me this had to
be Ranier's room once upon a time.

Vivian was clearly using it as her own space, with
files and recent documentation piled on the desk next
to what looked like one of her handbags. She hadn't

redecorated, the dark interior more masculine than her typical off-white designs, so her father still meant something to her, didn't he? I guess I was getting good at this detective thing after all.

She stopped beside one of the chairs but didn't sit, one hand resting on the back, and I wondered if that was Ranier's seat, if she somehow drew strength from being in her father's space. Okay, now I was just ascribing fantasies, but still. It wasn't hard to do so, not when it was obvious she chose this room for a reason.

"What are you really doing here?" She didn't meet my eyes. I shut the door behind me and closed the gap, enjoying the heat of the fire for about thirty seconds before feeling myself start to sweat inside my winter coat and boots.

"Nosy," I said, admitting to it.

She looked up then, and a faint smile pulled at her lips. I guess my honesty caught her off guard.

"I told you to trust me," she said. "You don't have to be here or ask me questions. I'm handling things. As long as you take care of your end."

"That's really obnoxiously obtuse," I said, knowing I'd matched her dry tone perfectly. Again with the lip twist. She didn't argue so I went on. "Thing is, it's a two-way street, Viv. I'll trust you the second you start to trust me."

She physically flinched like I'd hurt her. "I *am* trusting you," she said, her instant look of hurt smothered by an attempt to hide it. "Why else would I have made you sheriff against the Pattersons?"

So, I'd been right, not a big shocker. "Geoffrey wasn't very happy with you. You tipped your hand, Viv. Are you ready for the consequences?" Like I even knew what I was talking about. But it felt like the right thing to say and, as she nodded slowly, sinking at last into her father's chair—it had to be—grasping the arms in both hands, leaning forward like a Medieval queen about to have me killed or sent on a quest.

Quest. Please, let it be a quest.

"I wasn't ready," she whispered, voice shaking just a little. "I only needed a few more weeks, maybe a month. But then Thea died, and they used it against him and I..." she looked up at me then, anguish on her face. "I had no choice. And then I only had one."

Me. "What are you looking for, Viv?"

She shook her head, biting her lower lip. "I can't, Fee. Not yet." Vivian sank back into the chair, hugging herself. "I don't have proof and until I do... you'll think me mad."

I laughed. Couldn't help it. And sat next to her in the other seat while she met my eyes, her own open, vulnerable.

"That's the last of your worries at this point," I said. "This whole town has gone mad. Driven there by the puppeteer who runs the Patterson family." I paused, stared into the fire, wondered how much I should bring up. And plunged in because it was the only thing I could say that might convince her to finally share what she knew. "I've been having nightmares," I said. "About that day, Vivian." I turned to her again, watched her face register understanding, then the kind of grief that could cripple, then fury so powerful I knew she was in danger of losing herself the way her mother had. I couldn't let that happen. "Dr. Aberstock says I repressed the memories for a long time. But almost drowning triggered it, Vivian. And I started to remember."

She sat there, silent, watchful, lost in the past.

"The day Victor died." I worried she might lose it, but she didn't, no reaction, so I went on. "Do you remember, Vivian?"

Tears trickled down her cheeks, pale, so pale, and a trembling hand rose to wipe them away. "I remember," she choked.

"Do you remember who was there?" This was important. Because maybe my buried memories were playing tricks on me, and I didn't have things right. Except I knew I did. Was positive of it, that it was Robert who stood by and watched Victor drown before running away.

Whatever progress I'd made, whatever opening into Vivian's psyche slammed shut with that question. She surged to her feet and shook her head, lips tight, anger a visible fist around her entire body.

"No," she said. "Not now. We can't do this now, Fee."

I stood too. "Why?" What time like the present?

"Because." She swayed slightly. "I have so much to do, and I can't fall apart." That came out in a faint wail only to be smothered by the shutters closing on her eyes, her being. "I refuse to fail. I've come too far. I will see this through. And then those responsible will pay, Fee. I will make certain of that."

Did she have any idea how freaking scary she was in that moment? I doubted it. But even I wouldn't have crossed her just then.

Except she'd dragged me into this with her, hadn't she? And left me in the dark. "Fine," I snapped, not meaning to lose my temper, too, but not knowing how to get through to her. "I've backed you for the last time. The next call? You're on your own." I didn't mean it, of course, I didn't, but it drove an iron rod through her spine and put a giant gash between us wider than any chasm.

Rather than wait for more excuses from her, I left of my own accord, abandoning her to her loneliness and grief in the room that was her father's while I stormed out of her big, white, perfect prison with a self-righteous chip on my shoulder and a need to hurt someone.

As I exited Vivian's, the only thing I wanted to do was go home to Petunia's, curl up on the couch in my jammies, eat popcorn and copious amounts of chocolate and bury myself in a rom-com with Crew on one side of me and my pug on the other. Like, the perfect retreat from anything resembling Reading, Vermont's ridiculously complex and insanity-inducing politics.

Except, as I climbed behind the wheel and headed for home, I remembered with a painful flash that I couldn't. That I was banned from my own business and my apartment and the life I was used to living thanks to Rosebert and murder.

It's not that I wasn't used to stress, pressure, the devolution of my life on a regular basis. I'd been through this sort of unhappy experience multiple times in the past, so it wasn't like I didn't have precedents set or coping mechanisms in place or even escape plans unhealthy at the time but that beat sitting in my cold, dark car and crying my eyes out.

Yeah. But every other time I had home to go to, didn't I? A place to hide that was my own. I wasn't expecting the pileup of incidents and disappointment to hit me so hard, and I think that's why it took me a solid ten minutes of sobbing into a handful of old fast-food napkins I scrounged out of the side panel of my door to get myself back under control.

Did Vivian wonder why I hadn't left yet? Who cared, really. I was past giving a crap what anyone thought. All I wanted was to marry the man I loved and that wasn't going to happen tomorrow, not at this rate. And that only seeded more doubt, the sneaking, nasty whisper from deep inside that had tried its best the last few days to convince me this joyful existence I'd been living the last little while was all a smokescreen of deception meant to set me up for the most tragic failure of all time.

Fleming, Fiona. Pity party for one.

As I inhaled a shaking breath and wiped away the last of my tears, blowing my nose on the harsh paper, shivering from the cold since I'd failed to even turn on my car, I texted Jill on the off chance I might be able to go home after all.

They are still at it, she sent back. *Sorry, Fee. I'll keep you posted.*

Craptastic. I glared at my screen, reaching for my old friend, anger, hoping to at least warm myself up from the inside with a surge of heat. No such luck. Despair and the dull acceptance of apathy had come to roost.

Well, I could always go to the annex. Daisy would have gone home by now. I could tuck myself into the living room there and try to create some semblance of normalcy. Except the house was full of guests, so I'd likely be interrupted multiple times. And the last thing I wanted was to come in contact with other human beings.

At least, human beings who didn't know me. So, how about Mom and Dad's? Could I handle my mother's freak out over the delay of the wedding, or my father's attempts to calm her down? Grunt. No way, not with the mood I was in at present.

Silly girl. There was only one destination for me. Why then was I hesitating to go to Crew's house? He had everything I needed in his possession, really, from his own awesomeness to the pug we both adored. Bless him for taking her home with him so I didn't neglect her.

Took me a bit to admit it, but I finally accepted it as I started my car and pulled out of Vivian's circular driveway, heading for downtown and my true love. I was terrified. What if something did happen? What if this was all a dream and I'd been lying to myself, and

I never got to marry him, and we fell apart and he left town and married someone else—

Okay. Deep breath, you psycho.

I couldn't go to his place like this, not in the state of desperate need to know he still loved me. No way was I dumping all my fears and worries and insanity on the man who adored and wanted to take care of me for the rest of my life. I needed some perspective.

Instead of going right to his house, I parked at Petunia's, avoiding looking through the windows, keeping my head down and, hands in my pockets because I'd forgotten my mittens, set out at a brisk pace to Crew's.

Much better. I needed the exercise and the fresh air to clear my head. By the time I turned the corner and the home stretch to his street, I was inhaling giant gulps of chilled mountain freshness, perking me up like nothing else could.

We'd be fine. This was a setback, nothing more. Of course, he loved me, and we'd be getting married, and I'd be spending the rest of my life with the most amazing man I'd ever met. I really needed someone to shake me from time to time. How had I let myself spiral so badly when I had so very much to be thankful for?

I paused on the sidewalk and smiled up at the clear sky, the sparkling stars, the full moon rising over the lip of the mountains as early evening descended on Reading. There were Christmas lights on the next street over, lighting the center of town with their magical glow and finishing off what the walk had started. Optimism returned in a heady rush as I chose to release all of the crap and just trust everything was going to work out exactly as it was supposed to.

So. Awesome. I was grinning when I took one last deep breath. Just as tires squealed behind me, the sound of a car engine revving up, flashing headlights so brilliant that, when I turned in surprise to see what was going on, I had to raise my arm to shield my eyes from the glare.

And couldn't move, simply couldn't comprehend anything as those brilliant lights headed right for me.

CHAPTER EIGHTEEN

Self-preservation is a funny thing, isn't it? I don't even remember moving, telling my brain to fire, my muscles to work, my body to act. In fact, if I'm going to be totally honest, I should have been dead about two seconds after the headlights hit my gaze. Because if I had been in total control of me without instincts or a fight or flight guidance system? I'd have been a hood ornament on the front of that big, terrifying car hurtling toward me.

Instead, I came to from a sort of muddy haze, shaking snow out of my hair from the bank I'd thrown myself into, hands frozen where they braced me deep in the icy stuff, heart pounding, body shaking while the car peeled away out of sight.

Gone too fast for me to catch the license plate,

even if I'd had the wherewithal to notice such a detail. I panted my terror out into the freezing air, giant puffs of white exiting my lips, sitting in the snow and trembling as I pulled myself together yet again.

No one came out of the house whose yard I used to escape certain death, and my ever-ridiculous mind was grateful there weren't any witnesses to my clearly ungraceful leap into the snow, not to mention my struggled recovery. And, when I finally stood, brushing clumps of white from my coat, my hair, shivering as some of it made it down inside my collar, I fought for calm.

First assumption? Someone tried to kill me just now. I looked down with hesitant concern and noted the tire tracks on the sidewalk where I'd been standing. Yup, there they were, not my imagination.

Second assumption? It came on the tail of the first, that the driver had simply lost control of their car and it wasn't an attempt on my life and I was really being very silly, wasn't I? Making it all about me like that, typical Fiona Fleming.

Yeah, guess which one won?

My knees were weak, my whole body wobbly, while I set off the last block to Crew's. By the time I reached his door, I was mostly better, though I knew I was likely in shock, especially when my hand didn't seem to want to unclench from a fist after I knocked on his door.

First off, I hadn't knocked in about a year. Second, he had a doorbell. And third...

There was a third, right? Apparently, when I was worked up, I liked to list things in numerical sequence. Coping mechanisms I had in spades.

Crew's surprise when he opened his door just made things worse. With a low cry that told me my walk might have helped to a point but almost being run over trumped everything, I threw myself into his arms.

It wasn't long before I was installed on his couch with a beer, his arms around me yet again, Petunia happily leaning into my thigh with her wrinkled head in my lap and big, brown eyes staring up at me with that adoration she shared with everyone. I stroked her soft, black ears, telling Crew about everything that happened. Except.

I knew better than to fill him in about the car just now. He'd lose his mind and I'd lose my freedom and I really needed my freedom. I'd be more careful, watch my back. Whoever it was behind the wheel of that car, whether it was an accident or a murder attempt, I was pretty sure informing Crew about it would lead to Dad knowing and my existence as I knew it reduced to the office handcuffed to the desk.

I know, I know. It was a dumb decision to keep it from my fiancé. But he had more than enough to mull over so what he didn't know wouldn't kill him. Never mind I was aware it might kill me.

When I was done talking, Crew kissed me before resting his cheek on my hair, my nose pressed into that soft hollow at the curve of his collarbone that I loved so much. I closed my eyes and inhaled deeply of him, feeling everything melt away to the sound of his beating heart, the soft circles his big hands made on my back, the scent of him filling my existence with Crew and nothing but Crew.

The doorbell jerked me out of the sweet moment, my fiancé's regret clear on his face. But he stood, went to answer it, didn't make it as it opened of its own accord and Liz walked through, stomping snow from her boots.

"Fee make it home?" She waved to me, hanging her coat in his small entry, kicking off her shoes and joining us, accepting the beer Crew fetched from the fridge. It was only then I noticed the scent of lasagna cooking, realized he had a stack of plates out on the counter. He was expecting company?

Liz collapsed next to me, petting Petunia before clinking her bottle with mine. "Hell of a day," she said. "Best wedding rehearsal ever."

I snorted, then laughed, hopeless and helpless but the puzzle piece I needed to return to mostly me. I hugged her quickly before standing to help Crew who was taking the casserole dish out of the oven.

"I was about to text you," he said. "I thought it might be a good idea to have everyone over for dinner. Kind of regroup so we can decide what to do from here." His blue eyes looked worried. "Fee, it's going to be okay, sweetheart. I promise."

I suddenly wasn't anxious anymore. His arms were warm around me when I circled the counter and embraced him, kissing the side of his neck, his cheek, before smiling up at him. How had I doubted

I'd be marrying this amazing man? Nothing would or could keep us from each other. Just let Reading throw its worst at us. We had this.

Oh, Fee. Be careful what you wish for.

Mom and Dad arrived as I let my fiancé go, Daisy on their heels with a bright smile for all of us before she hugged and rocked me and whispered to me how much she loved me. She had no idea why my eyes stung with further tears, though she likely thought I was upset over the delay in my wedding.

Nope, not why I wanted to cry. Her support meant everything.

We sat down in a surprisingly cheerful mood, even Mom's jittery angst subdued enough she was able to smile and converse like a normal person while I sat back and watched the people I loved the most in the world bring light to each other, to me. This was why everything was going to be okay. I had these amazing, brilliant, supportive souls who loved me and had my back and nothing and no one would come between us.

"Do you think your cousin was looking for the treasure evidence?" Liz had been filled in on the hoard a few months ago, shortly after she helped me solve the death of Melina Canty at the Marie Patterson Olympic Equestrian Center (say that three times fast). With zero objections from any of the interested parties, Liz had been drawn into our inner circle and, her delight and fascination as clear as ours, had vowed to help in any way she could to uncover the truth.

Leave it to her to change the subject from Dad chattering on about his new snowblower to one of the tasks at hand.

I shrugged, still on the fence but leaning. "No proof of that," I said.

"Except they know about it," Daisy said, her misery obvious. "I messed up." She blushed deeply, her shame so clear I reached out and grabbed her hand, Mom doing the same, everyone else murmuring denial.

"Day, stop that right now." I released her while Mom continued her comfort. "Without you, we wouldn't have the music box." She'd known the secret to opening it. "Without you, we wouldn't have the letters clue that led us to Crew's grandfather and the book." Daisy perked with each point I now ticked off on my fingers. "We need you. And we all make mistakes."

She nodded, honey curls bobbing. "Speaking of which." She stood and went to the door where she'd left her bag, returning to the table. Mom cleared a space in the center and my bestie deposited the music box there for us all to see. I opened it, the chime of the familiar song ringing, the secret compartment popping loose. I retrieved the pieces of the map, the doubloon, and spread them out as Dad and Crew cleared the rest of the dishes.

Which made me think about Martha French and the thing she'd pressed on me at Vivian's. I'd mentioned it to Crew, but not the others, so I filled them in on my visit to the mayor while I went to my coat and retrieved the prize the old lady had given me.

I set the small, crocheted bundle on the table, not sure what to think, when Mom squealed and lunged for it, her fingers exploring it while she grinned.

"I haven't seen one of these in ages," she said. "We used to make them when we were little girls. There's a pocket here," she tugged on a single thread that pulled back a layer of the crocheted creation, revealing a gap and, inside, something that looked like paper. Mom gingerly retrieved the item and unfolded the now-familiar parchment, the edges crackling just faintly as she smoothed it out and my heart leaped.

This was the biggest slice we'd seen, easily half of the map and more than enough for us to piece together what we already had.

"John, the frame." Mom didn't exactly snap her fingers, but she didn't have to. Dad was on his feet, heading outside without his coat, feet shuffling barely into his boots. He was back a moment later while I perused the mountain range, the edge of Cutter Lake, the area where Reading now was, all still clear if faded slightly from age.

Dad set the frame upright on his chair and, with Mom's help, the pair of them pinned the existing pieces together while I bounced a bit and watched the image take shape.

"Almost," my father grunted with the growling delight of a bear elbow deep in a honey pot. He pointed to the bottom right corner, still missing, but so close, so very close to complete I had to wonder if we had what we needed to find the treasure.

Except there was no X marks the spot, was there? The red line I'd assumed (hoped) was an X when we'd first found it was actually just that a line that went nowhere and didn't seem to have a reason for being. Could it have been added there later, some kind of error or damage? But red, why red if it wasn't important?

Dad looked up from studying the map and his eyes fell to the music box with its delicate ballerina holding her perfect pose. His frown caught my attention, and I followed his gaze, noting the butterfly clips nestled in the main section, red velvet a contrast to the pretty blue of the costume pieces.

I'd recovered one of them from the nursing home when I retrieved Grandmother Iris's things, ever and long ago and found the other right there where it rested. Did he recognize them as his mother's? Likely. Made me wonder what memories they brought back for him.

He didn't comment, though, not while speculations flew, and Crew and Liz started throwing out ideas about what the map showed us.

For me, as I observed it, looking for clues, I had to admit there was nothing the new piece gave us except for one step closer to the full assembly. So, was this a wild goose chase? An old map of Reading and nothing more? Well, that would suck, surely, and yet we were having so much fun, weren't we? Could it be anything but awesome when this mystery had brought us together the way it did, regardless of the ultimate outcome?

Not in my books.

My phone pinged and I checked it instantly, seeing Jill's number and sighing in relief over her text.

They're done, she sent. *You can go home.*

Finally. I looked up to find everyone looking at me and smiled. "Petunia's is mine again."

I wasn't expecting everyone to come along for the ride home but was grateful when Crew harnessed my pug, Liz and Mom laughing over something they whispered about, wicked smiles on their faces, Daisy tucking her arm through mine as, en masse, we walked through the gently falling snow—the clouds had moved in quickly, moon obscured and still night air beautiful, fresh, inviting. More hope, more love, more gratitude for the people around me as we all went together to the place where we'd started.

Maybe this meant we could get married tomorrow after all. If Robert released Petunia's to me… yes, we'd lost a lot of time and the person who was going to do the ceremony and everyone else attached to the wedding (aside from my loved ones) were murder suspects, but.

But. Maybe.

That whispered sweetness? Crushed, dashed, destroyed the moment I walked through my unlocked front door and stopped, shock taking my breath, at the sight unfolding in front of me as I fought more tears, a faint wail building in the back of my throat, as I realized it wasn't the treasure after all Robert was after.

My foyer was trashed.

CHAPTER NINETEEN

Oh, and not just the foyer, with all my paperwork scattered around the floor, the carpet pulled up and bunched into a corner, the sitting room furniture tipped over, some of the upholstery torn away and a lamp on its side, the old ceramic shattered. No, as I moved into the disaster of my front entry, I caught a glimpse into the dining room, of the wedding decorations shredded, the side table tipped over, the red strip I was to use as my walk down the aisle torn and discarded like trash.

No one said a word as we toured the house together, the kitchen the only place that garnered a response, from Mom, her cooking tools spread out over the floor, the fridge door left wide open, food spilling out onto the tile, her aprons ground underfoot with old coffee grinds, from the looks of things, dug out of the garbage worked into the fabric by clearly defined shoe imprints.

Mom gurgled. That was all. It was enough.

I'd cried so much already today, there was no way I had more tears in me, right? Except they leaked out, endlessly streaming and I did nothing to stop them, hope turned to hopelessness, my inability to process what I was seeing just another symptom of shock. Because I'd likely been in shock all day, now that I thought about it. Hadn't I thought so, on a regular basis? Detached myself from the unfolding mess and destruction and accepted while clinical logic took over and saved me from hurt. At least long enough I could make it through the tour of the rest of the house without losing my mind.

Total vindictiveness, that was all this was. Robert lashed out at me the only way he knew how, by destroying what I loved.

Could he have known, though, as I completed my tour—the bedrooms upstairs in that state of disarray that could only have come from the deepest, darkest anger of a bitter and hateful soul—instead of collapsing into a heap of my own fury and descent into a need for vengeance, I felt a liberation like I'd never experienced before? If he had, it would have been the sweetest revenge. Because I caught myself shrugging, sighing, at the sight of my apartment kitchen overturned, my bedroom in broken disarray.

The only thing that stung? My wedding dress. Once secured in the heavy garment bag, spread out on the bed in the Green Room, my favorite, now sunk to the bottom of the claw-foot bathtub, soaked and stained with food coloring from the kitchen.

Unsalvageable. Like Robert's soul.

Someone had righted the sofa in the sitting room, everyone kind of wandered off on their own to make an attempt to put things right while I sank into the cushions and patted my legs, inviting my pug to join me. She did, heaving herself up and throwing herself down next to me, the whites of her eyes showing, faint whine escaping her. She knew, didn't she, how badly things had gone? That our home had been violated beyond anything I'd expected from Robert, despite knowing how far down the path of darkness he'd walked? But how much did she comprehend?

I stroked her ears, rubbed her ruff until she moaned softly and closed her eyes. "It's going to be okay, pug," I said. And believed it.

Dad settled next to me, his tall shadow blocking the light from the foyer for a moment before his arm went around me and he sighed, a pat for Petunia preceding a swipe over his face from one big, strong hand. I looked up at him, feeling nothing, really, as he met my eyes with a sad smile.

"She wouldn't have cared about this, any of it. It's just stuff, she'd say." I nodded. "Your grandmother adored you, did you know that?" He chuckled then, shoulders slumping a little, weariness in them, on his face. He looked around, with that sorrow releasing. "She was so proud of you, kid." He swallowed. "So am I."

What prompted me to tell Dad about the day Victor French died? What was it about that quiet moment, sitting in the wreck of Petunia's, thinking about my grandmother and my life that brought up the day that lingered like an old toothache?

I don't think I'll ever know, and it didn't matter. I told him everything, all the nightmares, the increasing return of memories, how, in the end, I realized the shadow that let Victor die was my father's nephew. Dad didn't say a word, his arm tucked around me, head down, ear near my lips as I felt like a little girl confessing a terrible secret to her loving Daddy who would do everything and anything to keep her safe.

When I was done, Dad didn't say a word, just shook his head, his face flat, troubled. I wanted him to tell me what happened, if I was remembering the day right, but I didn't get to wait for him to speak.

Crew appeared, interrupted. "Fee, let's stay at my place tonight, okay? We'll tackle this in the morning." He sounded sad, too, frustrated, but sweet. My darling.

Dad hugged me swiftly and stood, leaving us alone, with a quick squeeze for Crew's shoulder on the way by. My fiancé raised an eyebrow, and I shook my head. What could I say? Nothing mattered right now. And he was right.

I wasn't going to sleep at Petunia's tonight.

We assembled in the foyer then, no one speaking. I don't think I could have borne it, if one of them had said something about Robert, about revenge, about payback or complaining to council. Not then.

Not yet. It was too soon, and I knew, in my heart, that no matter what came of this mess, Robert would pay in ways that had nothing to do with the law.

I joked at times I was going to hell. He was already living in it.

We left together, as a group, though I was the last to go. I stood one long, final moment in the foyer of my home and felt the heartache surface, just for a single beat. Enough to chase me out before it consumed me.

I locked the door behind me and followed Crew home.

Jill arrived the next morning as Crew was making breakfast, her expression telling me she knew what happened, what Rosebert had done. From my fiancé? Or were they boasting about the destruction? Didn't matter.

She chose not to bring it up, though, setting a file in front of me that I glanced at as she spoke. "Confirmed murder from the forensics lab," she said. "Not that we needed it, but nice to have." She waved off Crew's offer of an omelet, setting her hat on the counter as she sat on a stool and took the cup of coffee he slid in front of her. "Eight ounces or so of isopropanol is lethal," she said, "though it could have taken less, considering Thea's size and history with alcohol abuse." She sipped the java before going on.

"Symptoms are just like excessive consumption of normal alcohol, ending in depression of the nervous system and death." She set her mug down. "Access to the murder weapon is a problem. It's a pretty common item, used for any variety of reasons."

"Including fixing an old organ," I said. "Andrew Isaac had some with him yesterday when he was here."

Jill grunted faintly. "It's used by doctors, sometimes as a cleaning agent." My deputy friend stared down into her cup. "Not sure it's going to be much help, but at least we have a definitive on what killed her."

The fact she was happy about the forensics report told me she wasn't trusting Barry's word any more than I was. "He giving you any trouble?"

No need to identify who I was talking about, apparently. "No," she said, forcing a smile that told me he was, but she had it handled, and I trusted her to do so.

"Might I make a suggestion," Crew said, looking back and forth between us. "Just as an outside observer with a certain set of skills?"

We both nodded in turn.

"He may not have anything to add," the former sheriff of Reading said in that graveled voice, "but he's been a huge help in the past and I'd wager Lloyd Aberstock might be a valuable resource." He sipped his own coffee. "Off the record, like."

I grinned at my fiancé and winked at Jill. "Feel like sticking it to the man?"

She laughed. "As long as that man is Geoffrey Jenkins."

Boo-yah.

CHAPTER TWENTY

Bernice Aberstock looked as much like Mrs. Claus with her round cheeks and white hair, her round body and sweet smile as her husband did the man in the red suit. Adorable, the pair of them, really, and no less so as she kindly beamed at me and Jill before ushering us inside their large two-story.

"Fiona, Jillian, how lovely to see you both." The (fittingly) red-clad woman closed the door behind us, rubbing her little hands together. "So chilly for this time of year, isn't it?" She held out her arms to us. "I can take your coats. I'm sure you're here to see Lloyd, aren't you?"

I nodded to her, almost wanting to apologize to her for the state of affairs but she simply hung up my coat, taking Jill's and her hat all the while chattering away like a five-foot-nothing bundle of Christmas cheer.

"Now, you two just go on into his study and I'll be along with coffee. Or would you prefer hot chocolate, girls?" She giggled then, hands over her mouth. "I'm sorry, I know you're not girls."

I grinned back. "I'd love hot chocolate, thanks, Bernice."

Jill seconded the request and followed me as our hostess disappeared at a clip, her slippered feet silent on the floor, deeper into the house, waving at a door at the far end of the hall.

I peeked inside, spotting the doc behind a big desk, bookcases behind him making him look very official, though when he looked up from his reading and noticed the two of us hovering at his door, that smile of his lit the room.

"Fee!" He stood, closing the hardcover with a thud, standing to wave us inside. "And Jill, how wonderful to see you both." As if we were here for a social call and he hadn't been basically fired from the job he'd held for ages.

"Hey, Doc," I said, sitting in one of the overstuffed easy chairs that made up a reading nook on the far side of his office. Jill hesitated before perching on the edge of her own, though the doc didn't seem uncomfortable with our presence at all, dropping himself into a third, the small coffee table between us not so much a barrier as it was a meeting space. Dr. Aberstock exhaled happily, folding his hands over the slight paunch of his tummy, his wedding band shining on his ring finger. I'd never noticed before, but it seemed embedded in his skin, as if he'd worn it for so long it had become a part of him and I caught myself twisting my engagement ring, thinking about Crew and the wedding and not wanting to wander down that mental and emotional road at the moment.

"We're sorry to intrude, Dr. Aberstock." Jill sounded as uncomfortable as she looked, cheeks pinking just a little while Bernice hustled into the room with a tray, the mugs rattling as she set it down on the coffee table.

"Not at all, Jill," he said while his sweet wife handed me a mug, dropping a scoop of mini marshmallows into my hot chocolate when I nodded at her silent offer. Jill did the same, though the doc waved them off, chuckling and patting that same rounded stomach. "Bernice has me watching my sugar."

I laughed at that while she rolled her eyes. "Mom tries that with Dad," I said to our hostess who sighed like it was a constant battle she knew she'd never win.

And when they met each other's eyes and that spark of love flew? The same one I saw between my parents? My wedding worries went away again. Because I knew that look, the feeling that went along with it and understood that what I had with Crew would end up just like this one day, teasing one another about who knew what—didn't matter, but there would be something—while his wedding band became part of him, and I adored him like the moment we met.

How awesome was that?

I half expected Bernice to leave us then, as she doled out a round of fresh chocolate chip cookies onto little plates we balanced on our knees. And yes, despite his teasing of her, she handed him one while I grinned around a bite of mine, though I was feeling a bit like a traitor. Mom's baking? Stellar, amazing, the best in the world. But Bernice Aberstock's cookies?

I honestly thought I'd die of the yum.

When she was done serving, she instead took a seat on the arm of her husband's chair with her own mug and sweet, clearly intending to be part of whatever conversation was to come. Not that I would ever ask otherwise. I was used to my parents, after all, and knowing these two were as inseparable... made my day.

Two cookies later—yes, I did take the offer of more, since my wedding dress was ruined anyway so I didn't have to worry I wouldn't be able to zip it up after indulging and besides two freaking cookies wasn't going to hurt me, thanks for the attempt to make me feel bad about myself, bridal magazines—I sat back with a contented sigh and addressed the white elephant in the room.

"Crew suggested we talk to you, Doc," I said. "About the case."

He nodded, smile fading, hands clasped around his bright red mug. He stared into the froth of chocolate at the top, the good mood in the room not completely gone, but dampened. "I assumed as much," he said. "Nice of him to do so. Considering he's in the same position I am, these days."

How much had they supported each other over the four years Crew was sheriff? Did they have each other's backs? I could only assume that was the case. I knew a little bit about what Crew went through as sheriff, the constant undermining of his authority, how he was tormented over the fact he wasn't a Fleming, wasn't Dad. Dealing with Robert, with being stonewalled by the Pattersons, my intrusions on his investigations, Olivia continually twisting events to the benefit of tourism and often to the detriment of his job. He'd shared some of it, but I could only guess, knowing him as well as I did, that I was seeing the tip of the proverbial iceberg. I hated that he didn't feel he could share, knowing he needed someone he could talk to.

Was Dr. Aberstock that someone?

"He's happy to be free of the job," I said before glancing at Jill who nodded, not surprised. "They honestly saved him the trouble of quitting."

The doc sighed heavily, nodded too. "I know, Fee," he said. "I can't tell you how many times I told that young man of yours he was better than this place, than how they treated him. I often thought he would quit, leave. But Crew Turner has a stubborn streak about as wide as yours, my dear." He laughed then, blue eyes twinkling. "I think the pair of you are in for an interesting life together."

Bernice giggled and slapped his shoulder. "They're perfect for each other," she said.

Okay, they had to stop staring into each other's eyes like they'd just fallen in love yesterday instead of... how long ago?

"Barry warned me," I said, wishing I didn't have to ruin the mood, "about my meddling. That it was making people's lives harder than they needed to be."

The doc waved that off, Bernice tsking and patting her husband's shoulder. "Nonsense," he said. "I would rather be fired, Fee, than carry on one more case in a position where I could be asked to do something that goes against my ethics."

Jill shifted in her seat. "Have you been asked to in the past, Dr. Aberstock?"

He hesitated while Bernice's face fell.

"Just tell them, dear," she finally whispered.

"Yes," he said, firm and determined, one hand thudding on the free arm of his chair. "And I've refused every single time." He met my eyes. "So, don't for a moment blame yourself for this, Fee. They've been looking for a way to replace me and you're just an excuse. I wouldn't have traded a single moment, not to mention the fact thanks to you and Crew we've put some truly horrible people away for reprehensible crimes." Not that I was taking myself totally off the hook, but it was good to know. "I've always been curious myself, not a suggested way of being when one has dealings at all with the Pattersons."

"What are they after?" Someone had to know.

Someone willing to talk, that was.

But Dr. Aberstock was shaking his head, with that same tired look he had in his office. "I wish I knew, Fee. I'd love to find a way to make sure they never, ever achieve it."

Well, now, who could have known Santa was so vindictive?

"Lloyd." Bernice poked him. "Tell the girls. About your suspicions."

He looked uncomfortable then, Jill on alert, while I waited it out. It didn't take Dr. Aberstock long to cave, to grunt softly and shrug.

"I don't have solid proof. I was trying to find some, to give to Crew. Probably the reason they fired me, ultimately. They must have found out I was suspicious." He set his mug down, voice deep and serious, the most serious I'd ever heard him. "I have reason to believe our local hospital is being used to funnel illegal prescriptions into the black market."

Wow. That was huge. "No proof?"

"Not yet." Dr. Aberstock's frustration was clear on his face. Those two cherry points on his round cheeks had nothing to do with cold or good cheer and everything to do with anger. "I've been hearing rumors, though, for months and when I went snooping, Barry caught me. Acted very suspicious."

"As if he knew about it," I said.

The doc nodded heavily. "I'm positive he's in on it, Fee. And might even be the one who is physically transporting the misappropriated drugs out of the hospital to wherever they are going."

"Is the prescription drug market a big one?" I glanced at Jill who nodded.

"In the billions," she said simply. "Doc, you need to be really careful." She met my eyes, hers worried. "The black market is huge, and the people selling fake and misappropriated opioids are as dangerous as any organized crime outfit."

He shifted in his seat while Bernice looked uncomfortable at last.

"I know, Jill," he said. "But I couldn't just let it happen under my nose. This is my home, my town and I won't let the Pattersons turn it into some kind of shiny on the outside, black as the pit of despair on the inside cesspool."

He might have been too late for that, but I admired his determination.

"This changes things." Surely this had nothing to do with the murder, or did it? "Let's talk about Thea Isaac. She had old track marks on her body, Doc. Which means she was a recovered addict."

He perked at that. "I didn't get to examine her that closely," he said. "Thea was certainly an enthusiastic supporter of drug and alcohol programs aimed at young people."

"Could she have found out about the trafficking and was killed for what she knew?" I was reaching, wasn't I? And yet, stranger things had happened in my cesspool.

Dr. Aberstock stroked his white beard a moment. "I don't know, Fee," he finally said. "I honestly didn't have enough contact with her to tell you. But it's possible, I suppose, she somehow found out because of her past and was killed for it."

"Much more likely," I answered my own question, "it was someone in her life, someone close to her. But thanks for the info anyway." One more mark against the Pattersons I could maybe, hopefully, use against them when the time came.

I had a momentary start of concern, though, when I flashed back suddenly to the car that swerved at me last night. Was I closer to the illegal drug laundering scheme than made Reading's ruling family comfortable?

"I can tell you," the doc said, "I ran across an awful lot of letterhead lately that had nothing to do with the hospital, and everything to do with that corporation that's been poking around Reading." My body chilled, my skin prickling. I knew what he was going to say before he said it and held my breath as he did. "Blackstone."

So, the friendly neighborhood corporation no one seemed to be able to pin down not only ruined towns and bought up property to do it, they sponsored golf tournaments, provided security for weddings (I was sure those black-ops boys at Alicia and Jared's nuptials were Blackstone) and, apparently, were dabbling in funneling prescription medications into the black market.

Awesome.

"Was I right about the murder weapon?" He seemed eager for an answer, and I let Jill tell him what Barry and the lab uncovered while I sank into my own head and felt the slow spin of my crazy, obsessive brain take me down paths I could do nothing about, all leading to a black background and a giant gold B.

I returned to the conversation when Jill fell silent, finding Dr. Aberstock focused on me, anxious expression making me sit up a little taller.

"Please be careful," he said then, a slight catch in his voice while Bernice patted his shoulder. "Both of you." He swallowed. "All of you, that includes Crew, your folks. Fee." He met his wife's eyes for a moment before returning his attention to me. "Something has changed, kick-started a shift. Almost like they've been sleeping, their plans on hold. Whatever's happening now, it feels like we're coming to some kind of reckoning."

Oh, there would be a reckoning, all right. I'd take the Pattersons down or die trying.

Whoops, terrible choice of words.

CHAPTER TWENTY-ONE

Jill and I left the Aberstocks with thanks, hugs and the firm assurance we'd do everything we could to reinstate the doc as soon as possible.

Neither of them commented on it, though as I climbed into Jill's cruiser, I couldn't help but feel like they only humored me, that they didn't believe I could follow through. I just hoped they were wrong because I had to have him back in the morgue.

I needed all the allies I could get.

Why did Jill have to take the route past Petunia's and make me think about what I didn't want to think about? Namely, how much work lay ahead to get my house sorted, make sure Robert paid for what he'd done in the most painful way possible (hello, vengeance, there you were, I missed you), let alone the delay in my wedding. Crew and I hadn't decided last night what we were going to do, and Mom had been oddly silent on the issue despite her previous spiral into control freaking over every detail, so our pending marriage was up in the air for now. Maybe it was better to wait until this investigation was over...

"Do you mind dropping me off?" It would be so much easier if I had my own car.

"Sure." Jill pulled into the parking lot between Petunia's and the annex, reaching out for my hand before I could get out. "I'm sorry," she said. "I heard what happened. I have no idea how someone like him can just get away with what he did. What he does." Jill swallowed hard, stared out her window a moment. "It's like we're living in some kind of alternate reality or bubble where normal doesn't apply, you know? And yet, we've normalized it." She turned to face me, then, grim and angry and looking like she was ready to take some kind of action she would likely live to regret. "We've made it okay to look the other way, to shrug off events because we've been led to, by inches, until it seems as if there's nothing we can do about it so why bother fighting anymore." Okay, Jill was going deep, and I considered stopping her but didn't, let her run on in the hope she'd expend the energy she'd held pent up (for how long exactly?) on this conversation and have nothing left to use in, say, shooting someone in the face. "But it's not right, Fee." She tightened her grip. Did she know she was grinding the bones of my wrist together? I doubted it and hissed softly at the pain. Jill let me go immediately, face full of regret now, but she wasn't done. "Someone has to do something. Don't you think?"

She had to ask me that question, point-blank and all. "We *are* doing something," I said. "Jill, promise me you won't try some stupid plan and sacrifice yourself or another ridiculous idea that might get you fired." I didn't say "or worse, killed" because, frankly, after the talk we'd just had with Dr. Aberstock, I felt like that was implied, thanks. And didn't need to be spoken just in case.

I'd have hated to think I jinxed someone I cared about.

Jill sagged but let me go and I left her there, shivering while I climbed into my own car, pulling out behind her, heading for the sheriff's office. Maybe I should have stayed with her and left my vehicle home. Maybe I should have stayed at Petunia's and tackled the mess. And maybe I should have stopped second-guessing every single detail of every single decision I was making lately and just trust things were going to work out.

I was really tired of doubt.

Despite the age-old town parking ban, I pulled up in front of the office and left my car there. Just let Robert try to ticket the sheriff. I'd love that. As I stepped out and slammed my door, I heard my phone ping, incoming text. When I checked it, I was surprised by the sender, though I supposed I shouldn't have been because it had been that kind of day.

Need to see you ASAP. Malcolm Murray's typing might have come out in flat English, but I read it with his Irish accent lilting each syllable.

Argh. I didn't have time for him right now and was about to send a brushoff text when the door to the office opened and two people descended the steps to the sidewalk, totally shattering my calm, cool collection into a million jagged pieces I hoped they choked on.

It was the matching smirks on Rosebert's faces that did it. I might have been able to ignore them and soldier on like a good Fleming if it hadn't been for their smug disdain and hideous amusement. Obvious why they were feeling oh so superior, wasn't it? Their attitude told me everything I needed to know. How assured they were there would be zero consequences, that they had the support of those who could smooth things over, that their actions, destructive and vindictive, would stand and I couldn't do a thing about it aside from shout empty threats and fume.

The frustration of having to tolerate what they'd done, that they would have an excuse for their actions, that it would be my insurance footing the bill and that the Reading Sheriff's Department might get a light slap on the wrist if I was lucky? Intolerable in a wave so sudden and hurtful I choked on it.

I knew they had to be expecting a blow-up, public and messy, for what they'd done to Petunia's. And the fact they'd exited the office together, in tandem, struck me as on purpose, with purpose. The fact I was alone, Jill as yet not returned to the station, only had to make their glee all the more fulfilling. Like a pair of jackals circling a wounded lioness.

Well, they were about to see despite my injuries I still had claws and teeth and the ability to bring them both a world of hurt.

So, what unfolded next? I'm not proud of it. Nor do I remember most of the details, to be completely honest. I know I launched into a tirade about Petunia's that devolved into firing them both multiple times while they stood their ground and yelled back at me. All the while the lovely townsfolk and tourists visiting our darling little berg stared and avoided us and whispered. How do I know? I didn't even have to guess. This was Reading, Vermont. Of course, they were staring and whispering.

Jill's arrival was the undoing of the messy public display that might have ended in me shrieking like a banshee while the pair of despicable human wasteicles wandered off and my deputy held me back, talking low and fast to keep me from rupturing a blood vessel in my brain.

How did Crew do it? My love's level patience was lost on me, his ability to contain his rage to the pulsing vein in his forehead and the tic under one blue eye. Me? Totally unable to keep my crap together though, when they were out of sight and Jill had me back inside the station, I panted myself into some semblance of control while Toby stood behind her desk with both hands over her mouth and her eyes huge and staring at me.

Like I was dangerous or something and might

attack at any moment. Well, I *was* dangerous, damn it. Just try me.

A quick drink of hot coffee and a few pacing circles around my office and I was ready to take the reprimand Jill was definitely going to hand me. I'd lost my cool at the worst possible moment with the two people who I needed to keep my crap together around and made a public idiot of myself all for what? A mess at Petunia's. Big deal.

"Only it is a big deal, Jill." I snapped that out, forgetting I had been running a conversation in my head she couldn't hear with her side and mine already underway. She didn't seem to mind I'd clearly lost all my wits and nodded as I raged on. "It's a big deal because it's not just Petunia's. It's all of it. Crew's job, the Pattersons, my wedding." I choked on that last. "Dr. Aberstock and Blackstone and, and…" I wanted to throw the coffee mug in my hand across the room and restrained myself with the ultimate effort that left me shaking. Instead, I set it very firmly and carefully on the top of the desk before turning my back on it like it represented everything that had ever done me harm and hurt, including this latest assault on my heart and soul. "I'm this close to done." Fingers pinched together created a clear illustration. "And so, so close to just quitting."

Jill sighed. "Didn't we have this conversation?"

Damn it. Only it had been her—infinitely more under control though she hadn't had Rosebert in her face, so I gave myself a pass while, ironically, also kicking myself for being such an idiot—talking and me listening. Whatever.

"Can I make a suggestion to both of us?" Jill held out a file to me and I stared at it, for a brief moment having trouble even registering what it was. I snapped out of my fugue and took it from her as she went on, taking my acceptance of the papers as my willingness to try it her way. "Let's focus on the case and deal with everything else later."

Ah, the good old bait and switch, deflect and distract. Perfect. I flipped the cover of the file open and read a bit about isopropanol while Jill spoke again.

"According to research, it has a variety of uses," she said. "And several of our suspects had access."

"We already know about Andrew," I said.

"He uses it in his business," Jill confirmed. "Cleaning and restoring old electronics, wood furniture, that sort of thing. And, according to the supplier he uses, he just bought a fresh case a week ago."

"So, lots of access to what he needed," I said. "Traceable?"

"Not sure," she said. "Forensics said if we can get them the exact bottle the poison came from, they should be able to match the chemistry."

"So, we confiscate all of Andrew's supplies," I said, "and go through his trash." Because it was likely he'd tossed the bottle after the fact. Crap, when was garbage day? Would the evidence be long gone at the dump by now? Or incinerated?

Only one way to find out.

CHAPTER TWENTY-TWO

As it happened, Andrew was in the middle of cleaning a wooden table when we arrived at his small shop. He'd converted part of their garage into his own space. Tidy but cluttered, stacked with old electronics, real wood furniture and a variety of tools, it reeked of the nasty concoction that had killed Thea.

"Katelyn told me you think it was murder." Whoops, I guess I'd failed to mention that to him though, in all fairness, I hadn't had absolute confirmation until after I spoke to him. He wiped aggressively at the surface of the small table he was refinishing, a bottle of rubbing alcohol beside him, pale blue latex gloves protecting his hands.

"We believe she was poisoned," I said, "with

that." I gestured at the bottle beside him, and he flinched, staring at me with wide eyes as he took in my meaning and the long pause after.

"I didn't kill my wife." Now he was angry, really angry. "I can't believe you'd even think it."

The door to the house opened and Katelyn stood at the top of the steps to what looked like the kitchen, arms crossed over her chest again (did she know what it did to her abundance, and did she use it for a purpose?), glaring at us as we questioned her father in the faint chill of his workspace.

"Please believe we are pursuing every avenue, Andrew," I said. "We're doing our jobs. We have to ask. You must know that if only to eliminate you as a suspect."

Katelyn huffed softly and slammed the door. I nodded to Jill as subtly as possible and she nodded back before heading for the house door, leaving me alone with the grieving widow.

"I have no idea how this," he jabbed his rag at the bottle beside him, "could have ended up anywhere near Thea."

"It was in her juice bottle," I said.

He blanched. "She didn't have a cold, did she, or the flu?"

I shook my head. "I'm sorry, no. It was a physical reaction to the additives they put in the rubbing alcohol to keep people from drinking it. Even a small amount is toxic."

Andrew sank suddenly and heavily to the surface of the table, sitting on it with so much pressure it tipped slightly but didn't go over. "I can't believe this is happening." He met my eyes again, tears returned as he tossed his rag aside and wiped at his nose with the back of one glove. "Thea kept her juice at the church," he said. "Katelyn hates the smell of citrus, so Thea had a small fridge installed in her office and that's where she kept her bottle, too."

Good to know. "May I please take a sample from your supply?"

He grabbed the top and the bottle and sealed it before handing it to me. "Take it," he said, voice cracking. "Take it all."

Okay, then.

"Who else knew Thea had no sense of smell, Andrew?" And had a grudge against her, but that would come later, once I had a chance to stop being so freaking distracted and could sit with Crew, Dad and Liz and find out what they'd dug up on the suspects. Because everyone was still a suspect at this point, as far as I was concerned.

"Everyone," he shrugged. "It was common knowledge."

The house door opened, Jill returning, while I refocused my questioning.

"Can you tell me what Thea and Dominic Twigg might have been fighting about?" I still needed to have a chat with the choirmaster.

Andrew seemed confused. "No idea," he said. "You'll have to ask Dominic."

This wasn't getting me anywhere, though from the tightening around Jill's eyes and lips she had something that might shed some light on my last question.

We left with a brief thanks to Andrew, this time taking my car, Jill in the passenger's seat while I drove.

"Well?" I glanced at her when I came to a stop at the end of the street and waited for two kids on snowmobiles to illegally cross the main road before tearing off toward the tree line. "What do you know?"

Jill's hesitation only lasted another moment and then broke in a flood of words. "I might know what their fight could have been about. Dominic has a… reputation." Her jaw jumped. "He enjoys the company of… young women."

Um, ew. He was what, in his mid-fifties? I tried not to judge, but how young?

"No one's done anything about it?" Growl. I wondered if Crew knew.

That look on Jill's face? Told me I shouldn't have jumped to conclusions and maybe should have instead kept my mouth shut because there was suddenly a sick feeling in the pit of my stomach as my friend finally spoke again.

"I might have some experience with his interest," she said, soft and level. "I sang for him when I was in high school." Wait, what? Here in Reading? "In Montpelier." Ah, right, she wasn't from here, I knew that. "He was younger then, of course, but I was only seventeen, Fee." Jill's hands clenched in her lap. "He didn't make it far, but far enough." Wow, we all had our secrets, didn't we? This totally explained her discomfort the day of the murder, though. Clear as a bell now, her awkwardness. I'd chalked it up to her and Matt, a possible fight or even her wanting to get married herself. I had no idea Dominic's presence was making her upset.

She'd held it in this long? I refused to pity her, just held space and listened as she confessed to the fact she'd been abused as a teenager by someone she trusted. "I managed to convince him to look elsewhere. And he moved away, left my school, not long after. But the fact I didn't do anything about it... still weighs on me. That I didn't stop him say something, try to keep him from making someone else a victim." She unwound slowly, but not relaxing, more like an uncoiling weapon waiting to strike. "It's part of the reason I became a deputy. So, I could keep men like him from doing things like that to girls like me." She shrugged but it didn't fix it, nope. "When I moved to Reading and discovered him here..." Jill's whole body shivered. "I have, and had, no proof, though. My word against his. And you know this town." Did I. Dealt with it daily. "Anyway, I doubt he's changed his ways since I was one of his students. It could be he was preying on Katelyn, Fee. If so, if Thea found out and threatened to expose him..."

Right. Because while a young girl's voice might not be listened to, that of a respected minister would be.

"Giving Dominic motive for murder." I headed

left instead of right and back toward the office as I'd planned. Nope, going to the church and a confrontation with Dominic Twigg. "Let's have a chat with our choirmaster," I said. "I'd love for you to run the interrogation."

She looked shocked and then wickedly delighted. "I'll do my very best for you, sheriff."

He was in for a world of hurt.

CHAPTER TWENTY-THREE

Jill's suggestion we try his house first turned up a darkened residence with no car in the driveway.

"If he did it, he could have cut town by now." She sounded anxious enough I drove a little faster than normal on my way to the church. When we pulled into the parking lot, the tall, white steeple overhead, shaded maple trees stark and bare in the December mid-morning, my deputy friend sighed at the sight of a few cars in the lot, one of which she pointed out specifically.

"He's here," she said.

I didn't ask Jill how it was she knew what kind of car Dominic drove, assigning it, instead, to good police work and an excellent memory on her behalf. However, it did worry me a little, the grim expression on her face, and I started to wonder if letting her question him was a good idea after all.

I peeked in the nave and instantly noticed Ian at the organ yet again. Jill was already stalking toward the basement door and the choir room downstairs, so I let her go, especially when the familiar nasty scent of rubbing alcohol reached me.

Ian was rubbing at the front of the organ with a white rag in slow, loving strokes. It was very clear he adored the old instrument, and its care was a labor of love. Wasn't lost on me, though, that the bottle he was dabbing against his cloth had the tell-tale scent and label of the murder weapon.

"Hi, Ian." He turned with a start, one hand covering his heart, nose wrinkling as the other, rag still clutched tight, came too close to his nose. "Sorry for startling you."

He shook his head, clearly more under control now, though the redness around his eyes told me he'd been crying lately. "I was j-j-just lost in thought." He turned toward me, setting the rag aside, capping the bottle. "Can I h-h-help you with s-s-something, Sheriff?"

I gestured at the clear plastic container. "I guess I should inform you the murderer used that exact product mixed with Thea's grapefruit juice as the means to poison her."

He blanched and set it aside almost like he'd somehow found himself in possession of a venomous snake. "That's h-h-horrible," he said, eyes sparking anger behind his glasses which he pushed up his narrow nose with one thin index finger. "She was so ag-g-gainst alcohol. Whoever did this, d-d-do you think they had some kind of m-m-motive connected to her ideals?"

I didn't respond to that, nor tell him I couldn't discuss an ongoing investigation. Instead, I held out one hand. "May I?" I took the bottle when he instantly offered it, not bothering with gloves considering he'd been handling it and, if it were the murder weapon, the fact it had *CHURCH PROPERTY* written across the label in thick, red marker told me anyone likely had access.

"I'm n-n-not the only one who uses that b-b-bottle," he said so horridly he might have been reading my mind. "I've seen the c-c-cleaner, Mary Jones, using it as w-w-well. To polish the s-s-silver."

As I suspected. "I'm going to have to take it regardless," I said with enough regret in my voice he didn't argue, just gestured for me to do so.

"W-w-whatever you n-n-need to do to find the m-m-monster responsible." He shook all over again, thin body quivering.

"Where is this kept, Ian?" I looked down at the label again, but nothing stood out to me. I'd have to wait until forensics checked it against the type that killed Thea. Looked to me, in the 16oz. bottle, more than half was missing, though. So, it was possible the 8oz. used to poison her had come from it.

"The m-m-main cleaning closet," he said, pointing down the aisle toward the entry. "Downstairs next to the choir room. And Thea's office."

Interesting. I wondered if Jill had Dominic nicely softened up by now and nodded my thanks to Ian before leaving him in pursuit of the choirmaster.

I found her standing outside his office door, shaking. Not in fear, but in fury, and it was clear she hadn't talked to him yet because she blushed as she met my eyes, whispering to me.

"I worried I might hurt him," she said. "So, I waited for you."

I handed her the bottle of rubbing alcohol, grateful to have something to give her as a distraction. "Turns out everyone had access to this stuff," I said. "Cleaning closet." I pointed at the small, narrow door just past Thea's office. "Unless forensics can identify the exact brand, we're no further along on means when it comes to the murder weapon."

She sighed, bounced the bottle in her hand, before fishing out a plastic evidence bag from inside her jacket, her focus on the container and, as I'd hoped, off Dominic Twigg. "I'll take care of it," she said. "Might even deliver it to the lab personally."

And leave Barry Clement out of it? Nice.

"It's unfortunate this narrows nothing down," I said, keeping my voice down as she had. "Each of our suspects not only knew about Thea's impairment, they all knew where her office was." I crossed to the door, tried the handle, shook my head as it snicked softly open. "And looks like she didn't lock her door, either."

"Which means anyone could have spiked her juice," Jill said. "You're right. Very unfortunate. We'll just have to keep looking for motive. And pin down alibis."

"That's going to be hard," I said. "We don't know when the poison could have been added to her juice. It might have been in the main bottle for days. Or added directly to hers yesterday morning."

"Let's test the main bottles," Jill said, slipping into Thea's office and heading for her bar fridge. "That could give us a better idea of timeline."

Smart thinking. And yes, I'm not an idiot. I'd thought of that. I was trying to keep her occupied and out of the wretched state I'd found her in not so long ago.

Jill turned slowly from her crouch and looked up at me, eyes narrowed slightly when she, a trained investigator, after all, put it together herself in a visible jigsaw assembly that crossed her beautiful face. "You're distracting me by getting me to collect evidence we both know is obvious."

I shrugged. "It's working," I said. "I'll be right back."

With that, I left her to finish up, crossing the hall and, rather than bothering to knock, pushed my way through the door into Dominic Twigg's office.

He had a few things to answer for.

Trouble was when I entered, there was no one there and, while I frowned around the empty space, I heard the tell-tale thud of the front door upstairs and knew my prey had bolted.

Damn it.

I returned to the hall when my phone vibrated, my tangled thoughts blaming me for not leaping on the chance to question the choirmaster, that I'd let him sneak past me while I did my best to help my friend regain her composure. Then again, Jill was worth it and so much more important to me. I'd track Dominic down, never fear. And just let him try to run. The state troopers would be happy to put a BOLO out for his smarmy ass.

I checked the text, this one from Dad, inviting me to the Fleming Investigations office. Maybe they'd made more progress than we had. Jill joined me in the hall, arms full of bottles, scowling when I told her what happened.

"Let's see what Dad and his new partners found out," I said, heading for the exit. "If they have corroborating evidence about Mr. Twigg, maybe we can bring him down for indecent assault or something related to that, even if he didn't commit murder."

Jill didn't seem to think that would pan out, but she kept her mouth shut, bless her.

It was a short drive to the office, Jill locking the evidence in the trunk though she fretted over the security of leaving it there, chain of possession making her uncomfortable.

"Stand in the doorway if you want," I said, pointing at the glass as we entered. "Keep an eye on the car. That's good enough." Considering how things happened in Reading? More than good

179

enough.

She shrugged, instead, heading down the long, narrow office to the back of the room where Dad's desk was now Crew's, apparently, my fiancé sitting behind it with his feet up, Liz perched on the edge, my true love grinning at my dad who scowled a little.

My, how the tables had turned.

"Sheriff Fleming," Crew said, "I've been poking my nose into your murder investigation. Want to know what I've uncovered you missed along the way?"

Okay, that was going to be annoying, and I totally earned it. When he rose and came to me with an evil chuckle, kissing me softly, I smacked his hip with one hand.

"No kissing in the office," I growled.

I would have loved to hear what he had to say to that, the bratski, except the ringing of the entry bell caught all of our attention, more so when a booming voice cut through the air like a grenade going off.

"By order of town council," Geoffrey Jenkins said as he strode toward us, coming to a halt with that shark expression firmly in place, "Fleming Investigations is required to cease and desist their interference in the murder of Thea Isaac or be arrested for impeding a criminal investigation."

He did *not*.

CHAPTER TWENTY-FOUR

Vivian looked utterly delighted to see us. I could tell by the chilly, downright frosty greeting she gave, the way Hugh eye-rolled at me on the way by and mouthed, "She's in a mood," to which I shrugged. He was used to temperamental and volatile Olivia Walker and her hard-hitting, dedicated and often chaotic way of doing things. Vivian French, on the other hand? Might as well try to sort out the feelings of an ice sculpture.

Okay, so not entirely fair because I'd seen that soft side of her that she hid so carefully from the rest of the world. And yet, I could see while someone like Hugh would be struggling to connect to his new boss and wondered if she was as much a nasty witch to him as she seemed to be to the rest of the world.

Aside from my mother. Go figure.

I crowded into the mayor's personal space with Dad, Crew, Jill and Liz all behind me, Geoffrey and Robert, Rose tucked into the dark patch that was my cousin's shadow, the three of them against the five of us. No way were they going to win.

Trouble was, the second we arrived the shouting started, and the accusations flew while I inhaled, exhaled and kept out of it.

Vivian let it go on for a moment before one of her hands came down on the surface of her desk with a loud bang. That shut up everyone, including—surprising me and him, too, if the widening of his eyes was an indicator—Geoffrey.

"I've had enough," she said, not a hint of snark in sight, an ice queen in a pink pencil dress with her hair in a French tuck, lips frosty with gloss. Going for a theme, Vivs? "Sheriff Fleming." She addressed me and ignored everyone else. "What exactly is the problem and why are you in my office sharing it with me when you're supposed to be out there solving a murder?"

She did not just smack me in the face with that kind of sarcastic disdain.

"The Reading Sheriff's Department has, in the past, utilized the research skills of Fleming Investigations for their background checks on victims and suspects in previous murders." I had tons of precedent, so there.

Dad grunted. "Olivia hired me all the time, Vivian," he said.

And instantly I knew that was the exact wrong thing to say while, from the expression on my father's face, so did he. Likely, he spent the next few minutes kicking himself as the Queen of Wheat turned fearless leader of the cutest town in America positively froze us all with her response and what, exactly, she thought of that state of affairs.

"I am *not*," she said, teeth barely clenched, tone deeper than usual, eyes narrow and tight, "Olivia Walker, Deputy Fleming," at least she remembered I'd made him a part of the department again, "nor would I want to be." She turned her attention to Geoffrey. "I take it this is the source of this invasion of my office? You're protesting, at length, knowing you, Geoffrey, the use of an available resource in the investigation of a crime I'd really like solved as soon as possible?" Wow, backhanded and absolutely smooth all in one go.

Geoffrey chose to ignore the fact she'd just taken a chunk out of his argument and pressed on. "If the Reading Sheriff's Department, as it stands with its present leadership," oh, now who was being backhanded, "can't handle a simple murder," seriously, the dude was on his very last tiptoe with me, "perhaps choosing another sheriff would be prudent now instead."

Vivian's eyes flickered to me. No way was she blaming me for this. I was doing my damned job, thank you very much, the job she'd forced me into, by the way, and never was I told I couldn't use Fleming Investigations, and this was ridiculous and unfair and I ran on and on in my head while she responded to him.

"Fine," Vivian said, "if this will get you out of my office and let me get back to work, Geoffrey, you can have half of what you want." She turned then to Crew and Liz. "Please turn over what you've uncovered to Deputy Carlisle and divest yourselves of any further investigations into the murder."

Crew looked furious but Liz handed off the file. Instead of giving it to Robert, however, she set it on Vivian's desk, right in front of the mayor, with a pointed look that clearly said you give it to him because no way was the FBI agent doing so.

The mayor's mouth twisted just barely, enough Vivian had to know what Liz's act of rebellion meant. Considering she didn't work for Reading and honestly could have come into the investigation if she so chose to make it an FBI matter (and could find a way to do so), Vivian should have been grateful that Liz was being so compliant.

Yeah, she looked grateful.

Robert crossed to her and, I kid you *not*, snapped his fingers at her for the file.

And the whole room went silent. Dead. Silent.

I almost laughed. I was this close to erupting into hysteria and cheering Vivian on because it was clear to me—to everyone in the room—that he was about to die a painful, agonizing, horrible death at the mental command of the Queen of Wheat. The look she aimed at him could have alternately frozen magma and liquefied diamonds. Did he notice? I have no idea if the stunned bag of hammers (and that's an insult to hammers, frankly, that have a very important job to do, after all, while he did nothing of value ever, if you asked me) noticed or not. Couldn't care less. Instead, I stood there, breathless in anticipation of his demise, vibrating with my silent shrieking for her to crush him like a bug.

Oh, how she disappointed me when she used one slim index finger to slide the file toward him about half an inch before waiting with her expression never changing for him to do the rest. Which he did with a grumbling mumble under his breath that turned into something more aggressive the moment he had the file in his hands.

"They should all be fired," he snapped. "Fee, Uncle John, Jill, all of them." Sullen childishness much, Robertkins?

Vivian's temper finally cracked open at the seams. "Then solve the damned case," she snarled so viciously he backed off a step. "And get the hell out of my office. All of you!"

We left. There wasn't much else we could do, though I wanted to linger and give her a piece of my mind. But you know what? It just didn't seem worth it and, from the glare she shot at me as I left, an expression that matched mine, I was right.

She threw me into the lion's pit to fight or die. I was on my own.

Not exactly. I had Dad, who stood like a towering cloud of doom next to Hugh's desk, and Jill, her arms crossed over her chest, at my father's side,

Crew and Liz already at the door, whispering to each other. Meanwhile, Geoffrey pointed at them with the smirk I was ready to permanently eliminate from his facial expression repertoire.

"If I find out you two have dug into this case further," he said, "I will ensure not only that Fleming Investigations is shut down, I will personally sue your company for, well." He shrugged and laughed. "I'll find something to sue you for." And, with that, he swept out of the entry with a nod for Robert and Rose who stood with their heads down over the file.

A moment later, before I could do the childish thing myself and snatch the papers from my cousin (the mental image of him chasing me around, whining like a brat for me to give them back, made me want to throw up and giggle in equal parts), he smiled at Rose like whatever he'd read gave him what he needed. She beamed at him before he smirked (he'd learned that from Geoffrey, clearly) at me.

"Guess you'll be known as the sheriff who lasted the shortest amount of time in the history of Reading, Fanny." He walked out, Rose trailing him, nose in the air, the snot.

Crew and Liz didn't look happy, and that didn't bode well. But, instead of filling me in on what was in the file, they left.

Seriously?

It wasn't until, glum and frustrated, I sat behind my office desk with my computer awake in front of me, prepped to do an internet search to start my own background research—too late, why hadn't I done this first? Oh, right, because I had someone doing it for me—that Dad appeared, Jill at his side.

Both of them grinning.

"I hope this means we're ahead of Robert after all." Please, I needed a bit of good news.

"Maybe," Dad said, taking the wooden seat across from me, Jill standing next to him with her thumb hooked in her gun belt. "Maybe not. But things aren't as grim as they could be. Sheriff."

Smartass father. "Out with it, then, Deputy Fleming," I shot back.

"Well, you know me and patience," he said. "I couldn't wait for you and Jill to get there, so I had Crew and Liz fill me in before you arrived."

Okay, so normally I'd be pissed because we all needed to know together. But this time?

"Awesome," I said, leaning forward. "You're forgiven, you old sneak. Tell me what Robert knows. And that he's wrong about the killer."

Dad grimaced then. "I wish I could," he said. "That's possibly the bad news, kid." He perked again. "But, on the other hand," he fished out a thumb drive from his pocket and slid it across the desk at me, "that fiancé of yours is a quick thinker. Handing over a thinned-out version of the file and giving me the full kit and caboodle the way he did."

Crew. I was going to kiss him within an inch of his life. Well, I would have anyway, but that man.

My man.

So lucky.

CHAPTER TWENTY-FIVE

I plugged the jump drive into my computer as Dad gave us the rundown on what Crew and Liz uncovered.

"According to Thea's previous parish, there was an issue with misappropriation of funds. They didn't think she was responsible, but she took the blame for it anyway." Dad sounded like he respected that decision. "That gives me reason to believe she was protecting someone she cared about." He seemed uncomfortable in his chair all of a sudden. "No idea if it's connected so we shelved it for now."

Interesting. I chose to listen first and read later, nodding for Dad to go on.

"The real point of interest is Dominic Twigg." Good to know, though he was my number one at this point, too. "He had been on my radar for years," Dad said, not even glancing at Jill when he said it. She didn't respond either, so did my father know about her connection to the choirmaster? He had to, didn't he? Or had she kept it from him? "I never made it an official investigation because no one would actually come forward." There was the side-eye I'd been expecting that told me in no uncertain terms that yes, hell yes, Dad knew everything. Not an accusation, just knowledge and the need to act curtailed into buried frustration. I was already over this job. Dad did it for more than thirty years. I had brand new respect for him, let me tell you. "And despite my suspicions, the council wouldn't listen to me, thanks to the fact he was local, and I couldn't get anyone to bring evidence against him."

"We're looking for him now," I said, "tried to talk to him earlier but he slipped out on us." I didn't say he had the chance to because I was trying to distract Jill from murdering him.

"He's always been a slippery piece of work," Dad said, his disapproval heavy in that deep voice of his. "Regardless, it's common knowledge he fraternizes with young women. Might not be illegal, since it appears they are over eighteen," he also didn't sound like that made a difference, "but still gives possible motive."

"Especially if Thea found out he and Katelyn had a thing." I nodded. "But she's twenty and it's not illegal."

"No, but it looks very bad," Jill said, speaking up

at last. "A man in his fifties with a history of such interactions might worry all it would take would be a single voice to spark an uprising that would mean his downfall." She sounded like she was a warrior princess in a fantasy novel or something, except I wasn't laughing because she was super serious.

And Dad agreed. "A man like Dominic Twigg must have worse skeletons in his closet, Fee. Possible indiscretions that could bring him a world of hurt if discovered.

I bought it. "And that's who Robert is going after?"

Dad nodded.

"How about Alfred Welling?" The jealous little weasel could have had his fill of Thea and decided to do something about her.

My father held out one hand, tilting it side to side with his palm facing the floor. "I thought about him," he said, "went back and forth, to be honest. He's been complaining about Thea since she was hired to take the job he thought he was owed." Dad's nose wrinkle told me what he thought of that opinion. In my father's world, you earned your place, yes, but no one owed you anything. "But does he have the guts to kill someone?"

I chewed my bottom lip. "And Ian Rudge?" The kid was pretty broken up over Thea's death. He claimed he owed her his life. Still, it wasn't hard to put on an act, was it? Did he protest too much?

Dad seemed to disagree. "I've looked into him, Fee," he said. "And you can check the file Crew and

Liz shared. From what I know, the kid was nearing self-destruct before he came back to Reading and as soon as Thea got her hands on him and stuffed him into her program, he turned his life around."

Okay then. Good enough for me.

"Andrew Isaac?" We had to get to forensics, the evidence now secured in the bullpen but needing to be delivered.

"I have a line on that," Dad said, "my own this time. But I don't have anything solid yet, so I'll get back to you."

Argh. I hated it when he kept secrets. Dad knew it, too, was on his feet, ready to leave, the mean-spirited old fart, so I couldn't press him further.

"Let's go talk to Katelyn again," Jill said, interrupting my opportunity to give my dad a hard time. "She wouldn't see me when we were at her father's house earlier. But I think she might open up to me if I approach her right." She glanced at Dad, sighed. "If I tell her what I know about Dominic."

My father's big hand settled on her shoulder, but that was it. He nodded to me, to Jill, his expression of sympathy all she'd accept and perfectly delivered, before he left us there, striding out of my office like it was his.

Well, had to be weird for him, too, so I cut him slack and, after a quick look through the evidence from Crew and Liz, joined Jill on another road trip.

CHAPTER TWENTY-SIX

Katelyn didn't want to let us in the front door, but a flash of two badges and Jill's booted foot across the threshold was enough to convince her we meant business.

The moment we entered the kitchen, she was on the defensive, her entire body tense, those crossed arms and that bulging chest as a result in clear evidence of her lack of enthusiasm for this confrontation.

"We need to ask you a few questions, Katelyn," I said. "First, about what happened in Montpelier at Thea's last church." She flinched instantly. "Do you know anything about why she was fired?"

The young woman's face crumpled, her lips, dark and perfectly lined with shiny lipstick, pouting a moment before she tossed her artfully curled hair over the shoulder of her low-cut t-shirt. Was I judging? Yes, I was judging, shame on me. She was allowed to wear whatever she wanted, use as much makeup as she wanted. I wasn't her mother and, honestly, even her mom had no right to tell her what to do.

But as an investigator and a busybody? Yeah, you bet I noticed how hard she was trying to stand out. For who? I had a guess.

"I have no idea." She hissed that at us, glancing over her shoulder toward the entry to the garage. "And I'll ask you to keep your voices down. Dad doesn't need that dragged up again, not now."

"And yet," I said, "it's vital to our investigation we find out the truth." Okay, I was stretching, big deal. "I'm happy to contact the church directly for the answers if you'd prefer. Though I'll have to have an official report sent to the department so I can add it to your stepmother's file." Oh, Fee. You jerk.

Worked though, didn't it? With one final flash of rebellion crossing her face, Katelyn suddenly burst into tears, covering her reaction with both hands, long fingernails separating her flat-ironed bangs.

"Please, don't." She lowered her hands, eyes huge, tears making a mess of her mascara and eyeliner. "Dad can't find out."

"That it was you who was doing the stealing?" I'd guessed as much. Katelyn nodded, misery clear. "And Thea found out and covered for you."

The young woman's arm crossing was getting

distracting, one hip cocking defiantly while she pulled herself under control. "It was a mistake. Thea took care of it." She sounded like she would have preferred jail time to owing her stepmother anything, though I highly doubted that was the case.

"Katelyn?" Andrew appeared around the corner from deeper in the house. She gasped, turned to face her father who stared with shock and disappointment. Apparently, she'd thought him still tucked away in the garage, not within earshot of our conversation. Well, as far as I was concerned it was about time this came out.

So much for not having an opinion.

Andrew confronted his daughter, his anger clear but unthreatening so I held my ground, as did Jill, and waited for the drama to unfold without our interference. We might as well have been in another state, for all the notice the pair paid us the next few minutes.

"Daddy, I'm sorry." Now she was really crying, arms at her sides, tears pouring down her cheeks, full lips quivering. "It was dumb, I shouldn't have done it. But I did and Thea found out. She covered for me." Katelyn again sounded resentful, and I wanted to shake her. The fact her stepmother chose to protect her should have been a checkmark in the woman's favor, not a source of bitterness. "She took the blame and paid the money back. That's why she was asked to leave and why we came here."

"So, the change of scenery suggestion was just an excuse." Andrew paled, face still and open, as though his whole life had been revealed as a lie and the two women in it the orchestrators of an entire performance he wasn't privy to.

Katelyn nodded, misery either an excellent act or truth. I frankly didn't give a crap which. "I didn't want to leave." There was the petulance again. "Danny and my friends were there."

Andrew snapped out of his fugue and scowled at her. "You were supposed to stop seeing Daniel Mission," he said. "That boy was trouble, Katie."

She tossed her head, all rebellion again, making me believe the crying jag was as much an act as the rest of it. "I loved him," she said. "Thea held the money thing over my head, made us move." Her lower lip jutted, anger in her flat expression that spoke volumes about her character. "I hated her for it."

Andrew shook his head, mouth open, hands extended toward his daughter. "She loved you."

"She hated me, too," Katelyn hissed then. "From the moment we got here, she tried to control my life, told me what I could do, who I could see. Why do you think she got me the job at the church?"

Her father blanched. "She wanted you to have direction, something to focus on."

"She wanted to keep an eye on me." Katelyn turned her back on her father, petty fury written on what should have been a pretty face. "And then she found out about…" She flinched then, looked at me, Jill. "Well, she ruined everything."

"About Dominic?" I finished that thought for

her.

I might as well have struck her. Katelyn gaped at me, eyes huge, horror in her gaze while Andrew blanched white as a sheet.

"What did you say?" He stared at me as if I'd pulled a rug out from under him and he suddenly had no ground to stand on.

"Dominic Twigg." That was Jill, her own anger firmly in check, tone flat and professional. "Your daughter has been having an affair with the choirmaster. We believe Thea found out and argued with him about their relationship. It's a possible motive for murder, Mr. Isaac."

The venom on Katelyn's face could have downed a small horse. "He loves me," she snapped. "Thea didn't understand, and she had no right."

Andrew grasped her arm and turned her around to face him. While I understood his upset, I wasn't willing to stand by and watch him manhandle his daughter. But she was already twisting herself out of his light grip, doing so easily, while he made no further attempt to touch her, so I let them continue.

"You're only twenty," her father said.

"Which means I'm an adult, Daddy," she said, both justifying and negating her own argument with a handful of contrasting words.

"Katelyn," I said, going for stern and capturing both of their attention, "you realize this gives you motive to murder your stepmother." There was the lower lip quiver again. Yeah, not buying it, nor the giant crocodile tears welling. "Save it," I snapped, tired of her game, and she relented, sullen once more. Her father seemed confounded as if he was only now seeing his daughter for the first time and I had a surge of empathy for him. He was in for a hell of a ride with this one. I'd been a hotheaded redhead, sure, but at least I had morals. I wasn't so sure that was true in Katelyn's case. "Not to mention we now have reason to believe Dominic might have been in on it with you."

She instantly shook her head, reaching for her father who actually brushed her off, adopting her crossed armed stance in response. Katelyn took that in a moment, and I watched her, in turn, realize she'd pushed her dad a step too far at last before she turned on me, vindictive but compliant. "Dominic threatened her," she said, pouting tone at least honest. "She was going to tell the church elders about us. It wasn't illegal or anything, but Dominic freaked when he found out." Now she seemed real, at last, a bit freaked herself, biting at that overdone lower lip. "I'm actually kind of worried. He won't talk to me, wouldn't since Thea confronted him. Says he doesn't love me anymore." Were those tears real? Who cared. Sigh. "He acted like it was a huge deal."

"It is," Andrew snarled. "I'll kill him for touching you."

"Mr. Isaac," I said, one hand up, Jill's stance shifting to defensive. "Please. I understand your anger. I share it. And if Dominic had something to do with Thea's death, I'll find out." I met Katelyn's eyes. "I always get the murderer, did you know that?

Kind of a thing with me."

She blinked quickly several times. "I swear," she said. "I took the money, I did it for Danny. And I was with Dominic, that way." She glanced at her father who quivered in anger. "But I didn't kill Thea."

Considering poison was a woman's weapon, I wasn't entirely convinced. But it would have to wait until I questioned Dominic Twigg.

That was if I got to him before Robert did.

My phone dinged, a text from Dad making me perk. I looked up from reading it and focused on Andrew who stood next to his daughter, both awkward, neither meeting one another's eyes. Well, they had their crap to sort out. Maybe this would be good for them. Not my problem, though, was it? And I now had a very serious question to ask the widow of the murder victim that pointed a guilty finger in his direction all over again.

"Tell me, Mr. Isaac," I said, handing my phone to Jill so she could see the message, catching her eyebrow arching out of the corner of my eye, "why, if you trusted your wife as much as you say, did you hire a private investigator in Montpelier to look in Thea's past?" I paused for effect. "And then lie to me about your interest in who she used to be?"

CHAPTER TWENTY-SEVEN

Katelyn appeared genuinely surprised by the reveal, so I could only imagine Andrew kept the inquiry from his daughter. He flinched before nodding slowly, clearly upset and shaken by everything falling apart around him.

"After the thefts," he said, "I started to wonder. I asked her a few things and Thea grew angry with me. Told me we'd agreed to stay out of each other's pasts. She was right, but I couldn't let it go. So, I hired a detective to look into her." His misery was as real as Katelyn's had been faked, I was positive of that. "I regret it and I had him stop even before he got started because I felt too guilty about it." He tossed his hands in my direction. "I'm sorry I didn't tell you, but I swear I never heard anything from the investigator and, as I said, I requested he drop the case." Andrew swallowed hard, his own tears trickling as he leaned back against the fridge, sagging as though only its presence kept him upright. "She had nightmares," he whispered then. "Would wake screaming at times. But she would never tell me anything." Andrew met my eyes, pleading for me to understand in that simple gaze. "I just wanted to know she really was the good person I knew."

I had more than enough of my own guilt to shoulder and couldn't offer him comfort. "We'll be in touch. For now, don't leave Reading, either one of you." I jabbed a finger at Katelyn. "And if I find out you've been warning Dominic we're looking for him, I'll arrest you and throw away the key."

She bobbed a nod. Hopefully, I got through to her. Not so comfortable leaving them there together, the wall between them growing by the second.

I couldn't save everyone.

Instead, I climbed behind the wheel, accepting my phone back from Jill, hitting a quick thanks back to my dad while we buckled in.

"Interesting," Jill said.

My favorite word. "Isn't it, though." I caught myself before I could sigh. "Let's see if we can corner our choirmaster and have a heart-to-heart. The way things stand, I'm liking him for this."

Jill grunted her agreement while I wondered if I should drop her off at the station instead of bringing her with me and opted for her having my back. She could keep herself together. Right?

Right.

The steep hill on the way to the church wound around a sharp corner. I always took that road too fast and, on habit, pumped my breaks a couple of times to slow my descent before preparing to accelerate into the turn, just like Dad taught me.

Only, when I touched the big pedal with the toe of my shoe, rather than the resistance I was used to, my foot hit the floor of the car hard as the brakes failed.

So many things flashed through my mind in the two or three seconds we had left before the corner. First, that I'd just had my car serviced a month ago and the winter tires put on so there was no way my brakes shouldn't have been in perfect order. I'd had the front discs replaced at a hefty cost, after all, damn it. Second, that I had no idea what it felt like to hit an airbag as it deployed and wondered if it hurt. And third, as was my weird brain's want to wander into the why are you even thinking that at a time like this, would it leave bruises I couldn't hide when I got married or would I have to wait until after they healed so the pictures wouldn't make me look like Crew beat me.

Yeah. Weird brain.

I didn't meep or scream or say a word. And I didn't have to. Jill seemed to assess the situation instantly, taking in what had to be a shocked and disbelieving look on my face, the rapid-fire pumping of my foot on the unresponsive pedal, and reached out, grasping the wheel in one hand. I turned to look at her in the final moment as the car entered the sharp turn, saw her grim determination and lack of fear and took that as a good sign we were going to be okay.

Not the goners I now suspected we should be.

Honestly? Thank goodness for Jill, her expert driver training and quick thinking, because I was useless in the moment it took her to ease us into the ditch on the side of the road. Well, I say ease, but it wasn't like she had much choice, but her angle and trajectory dropped the passenger wheels into the drop-off instead of the jerking motion I would have attempted that would have likely flipped the car and/or thrown us headfirst into a tree.

Instead, the passenger tires mired in snow, we spun slowly sideways, the back end of the car embedding in the bank and jerking us to a halt where we both sat, panting and, at least in my case, terrified for a long moment.

I hugged Jill a second after I had my seatbelt undone, and she hugged me back.

"Thanks," I whispered, shaking.

"Guess that advanced winter driving course came in handy," she said with her own voice trembling.

The last thing I wanted was to call Crew, though as I sat waiting for the tow truck to pull me out, the appearance of him behind the wheel of Liz's rental car, her in the passenger seat, wasn't all that surprising.

Jill looked guilty but not apologetic. "He needed to know," she said as he skidded to a halt. "Fee, that wasn't an accident and we both know it."

We hadn't even discussed it, the pair of us standing on the side of the road in mutual silence, processing our near-death experience together but individually. I could have argued but didn't because I knew in my heart, she was right.

He threw his arms around me, rocking me, not speaking as he held me tight, the warmth of him making it to me despite the thickness of his puffy jacket. I sank into his embrace, only by sheer force of will holding my tears at bay. Because I wasn't going to cry and make a big deal of this. Not now, not today when we were supposed to be married by now. Not when I had a secret I'd kept from him, that this wasn't the first attempt on my life in the last two days.

How could I possibly tell him about last night's attack now? He'd kill me himself.

Instead, I pushed back and kissed him before speaking, cutting off his ability to. "Can you please give Jill and me a ride to the office?"

Crew looked like he wanted to protest. Liz had joined us and bless her, spoke up in my defense.

"You got it, sheriff," she said, poking Crew in the ribs to get his attention. "Anything for the Reading Sheriff's Department, right, Turner?"

It was a quiet ride downtown and even though I needed to go to the church and look for Dominic, was heading in the wrong direction, I couldn't include these two in the investigation without getting blowback. Which meant picking up Crew's white pickup. No, not anymore, was it? It was mine.

When I tried to get out without talking about it, Crew grabbed my hand.

"Until we know if it was an accident," I said, low and intense so I was accessing his logical brain like a good manipulative fiancé, "I have a job to do. Okay?"

He hesitated a long moment before kissing me. "I'll be at the mechanic's," he growled. "I'll look into it personally."

Liz waved as she drove off, going with him, apparently, while I trudged up the steps and into the office. I needed to get the keys for the pickup, parked in the town hall lot just down the street, so I could finally go to the church and talk to the choirmaster and maybe solve this damned case and move on and get married and—

I looked up as I entered, catching the warning in Jill's eyes, the unhappiness on Toby's face, about a heartbeat before I spotted Robert, Rose beaming at his side, standing with one hand holding Dominic Twigg's arms, tucked behind his back.

In handcuffs.

"You're just in time," Robert said. "I'm arresting this man for the murder of Thea Isaac." He winked at me. "You lose, Fanny."

CHAPTER TWENTY-EIGHT

You know what the worst part was? Not that I again stood in Vivian's office with Geoffrey and Robert, Rose and Jill, Dad hovering in the background while my cousin took the floor. No, the very worst part was the fact that everything that came out of Robert's ugly ass mouth?

Made perfect sense. For once.

He'd even given me a few minutes to interrogate his prisoner, for all the good it did me.

Dominic's sweating, anxious face, the shiftiness of his eyes as he met Jill's gaze, the way he seemed on the verge of running at any second? Wasn't doing much for his apparent innocence despite his vocal protesting.

"I didn't kill her," he boomed in that practiced

singer's voice. I waved off his protest.

"We know about Katelyn," I said while Robert stood close as if I was going to poach his catch. Made me tired, having his nasty energy so close to me. Frankly, with the last of the adrenaline from the accident (keep telling yourself it wasn't attempted murder, Sheriff Fleming) burned out of my system and the layers of shock I was surely still dealing with taking a toll, I kind of just wanted to sit down and let my cousin have his win.

Except, well. I was a Fleming, right?

"What about her?" Dominic's face registered the fact he instantly understood he shouldn't have said a word. Especially when, once again, his gaze caught Jill's. I glanced at the deputy and was actually a bit scared for the choirmaster in that moment. If looks could kill, he'd have been so mangled and broken by her stare of doom there wouldn't have been much left of him to identify, and never mind an open casket.

"You argued with Thea about her step-daughter," I said.

"And wrote a threatening letter." Robert answered for his suspect, interrupting while Dominic's face paled to ghostly white, and I feared he might collapse in a faint. Or puke on my shoes. That would just be the best end to this entire disaster, cleaning this creep's stomach contents off my footwear.

Instead, Dominic collapsed in on himself. "I want a lawyer," he whispered.

And that was that, wasn't it?

As he broke down the case, he sounded perfectly reasonable. He reiterated everything I'd learned about Thea and the thefts, about Katelyn and Dominic's relationship. He'd even dug up old files Dad had started on the choirmaster and, as a pièce de résistance that put the apple in the sacrificial pig's mouth, handed over the letter he'd found in Thea's office, from Dominic, no less.

"Threatening her life," he explained once again as Vivian scanned it before handing it to Geoffrey who didn't even glance at it, shark grin firmly in place. "All I need now is his confession."

"How about fingerprints on the murder weapon?" I grumbled that. "Or the murder weapon itself."

Robert turned toward me, just a tilt of his body, enough I knew he was aiming his retort at me while giving Vivian his continuing focus. Since when had he learned to be political? Since that smarmy bit of ick at his side gave him lessons, I was guessing. By the way her lips practically moved every time he spoke, she'd coached him. For all I knew, he was really just a puppet robot, and she was pushing his buttons. Whatever the case, he had a case and even I knew it.

"According to forensics," he said, "the bottle of rubbing alcohol found in the church cleaning closet was the source of the poison." A bottle I discovered, thank you very much. Not that he'd acknowledge that or anything. "And while there were no fingerprints found on it matching Dominic Twigg, we did find a number of pairs of white gloves in his office, along with the set of bells he uses as part of his choir."

Damn. So, he could have used the gloves to keep his prints off the merchandise.

Vivian's face registered nothing of what she was thinking as she handed the report Robert (Rose) had assembled back to him. He accepted it while she nodded.

"Well done," she said. "But I expect an airtight case, Deputy Carlisle. Get a confession and the sheriff's job is yours."

Craptastic.

I let Rosebert leave, ignoring their smirks, their self-confidence they had their man and my job all wrapped up. I even waited until Geoffrey exited, though it took him longer to go, him lingering with his hip on Vivian's desk until her icy stare shooed him off. He grinned at me on the way by, not quite touching me but close enough I could see the stubble on his cheek in sharp relief against his skin.

Ew.

When the door finally closed, I spoke, but without hurry, and before Vivian could react. "I like Dominic for it," I said, "but there are questions about Thea's past that need to be answered. I'm not convinced he's the murderer."

Was that relief on her face? "While Robert is entertaining himself attempting to get a confession despite Dominic lawyering up, I assume you're going to continue the inquiry." Not a question.

I nodded, though my heart was heavy. "He might win this one, Viv."

She shook her head sharply, but not in denial. "If that's the case…" she looked up again, grim. "So be it."

I wasn't about to accept that outcome just yet.

We were a glum group that night, assembling like sneak thieves planning a heist already doomed to failure, huddled around Mom and Dad's dining room table while my mother served up an amazing turkey dinner—yes, with all the fixings because Mom never did anything halfway—and we quietly and, quite unable to stop ourselves, talked about the case.

No raised voices, no overt shows of anger, not from any of us. The fact Jill was part of our little last supper wasn't lost on anyone I don't think. Because that's what it felt like. The fall of an empire, the final days of our town's ability to stand up for itself, even in small ways, against the darkness that was the Pattersons and their agenda. And whatever Blackstone really represented.

We did little the first half hour but rehash everything we already knew, from the suspects and their motives to the murder weapon's confirmed source at the church, around and around until Crew finally sat back, his cutlery rattling on the edge of his plate loud enough to make me jump.

"I need to know why we care." His point-blank bluntness was met with more quiet. "I know, this is your town, John." My fiancé softened a little, nodding to Mom, even reaching out to squeeze her hand. "Lucy." When he turned to me, his blue eyes were soft around the edges, no anger in him. "Sweetheart. But." He shook his head then, taking a sip from the bottle of beer in front of him before he finished his thought. "If the residents of Reading aren't interested in being saved, who are we to force them into salvation?"

He had a point. I'd been thinking along those lines myself. Even Dad didn't argue right away, or Mom, to my surprise. They both just looked a bit sad, my mother rather lost.

Crew slipped one arm around me, tucking me into his chest, kissing my cheek. "This was supposed to be our wedding day." Again, no anger from him just resigned acceptance. "I get it. We don't have a normal life. And things don't turn out the way we expect. Especially here. Especially with this amazing woman's track record for getting herself into trouble." He winked to soften the words, but it wasn't like I could argue with him. Besides, he was completely right. What use was it choosing to be annoyed or angry over something I couldn't deny? "I'm on board with whatever you decide." Now he was talking to me, only to me, despite the fact we weren't alone. We might as well have been, for all the attention he paid the rest of the people in the room.

"I'm yours, Fee, now and forever. You want to stay here and fight? I'll be at your side, 100%, no questions asked from here on in. And." He touched the tip of my nose with one index finger, the softest caress, the contact then trailing down my cheek to my jaw. "If you decide to cut and start fresh, I'm in. You just tell me what you want. I only ever want to make you happy." He looked around the room then, a bit grim. "This isn't making any of us happy."

Dinner wrapped up shortly thereafter and I left Crew chatting with Dad and Liz, Daisy helping Mom in the kitchen, Jill departing herself quietly, claiming she had a text from Matt. Rather than hover in the gloomy air of the house, I harnessed up my pug and led her outside in the crisp air, letting her trot her way to the end of the walk to do her business.

My phone buzzed in my pocket, distracting. I checked the message, surprised to find it was from Dr. Aberstock.

Can we talk? I'm at Petunia's.

I was walking before I'd finished reading, tucking my cell away and urging Petunia along the sidewalk. It wasn't far so I didn't bother texting back, my B&B soon looming at the end of the street.

He climbed out of his car as he spotted me, parked in the lot, naturally. I joined him and, instead of going inside, led him around the house and into the yard. He didn't ask why or seem to think it was odd I avoided entering the house, and I wasn't in the mood to talk about the mess I still had to clean up.

The koi pond had frozen over but remained deep

enough the fish themselves remained safe, if dormant, for the winter. It was always weird to trust Fat Benny and his buddies would survive Vermont's intense cold, but so far, so good. No matter how many times I'd thought about relocating them for the winter, I was assured they'd be fine. Still had moments of nervousness anyway.

After all, Benny had solved Pete Wilkins's murder for me, ultimately. I was rather fond of his pudgy red self.

"I still have friends at the forensics lab." Not like the doc to dive in this way. I felt Petunia tug on her leash and unhooked her. She'd done half of what she needed to at the end of Mom's driveway, but I knew she had other business to attend to and let her go take care of things while I chatted with Dr. Aberstock. She disappeared into the dark with her cinnamon bun tail wiggling while he went on. "That's how I was able to encourage a review of Thea Isaac's autopsy."

Encourage, huh? "I take it they found something." What had Barry missed? Or, more likely, purposely left out?

"Apparently, Thea had old, massive injuries," Dr. Aberstock said, hands tucked deep into the pockets of his parka, the white fur around his face making him look... well. You know. Ho ho, and all that. "My friend was a paramedic at one point. She said it appears as if Thea was in some kind of accident, a near-death experience, in her opinion. She's seen a lot of car wrecks, Fee. That was her assessment. That

Thea had been in a crash years ago and lived to tell about it."

"Could be something to help track her history." I nodded to the doc. "Thanks. This is very helpful." I wasn't sure it meant anything, actually, but having him digging for me meant a lot considering the position Robert was in, so close to taking the sheriff's office as it happened.

Dr. Aberstock shrugged inside his heavy coat. "That was my thought," he said. "Find out about the accident, maybe about her history with drugs and alcohol. Might create a new avenue to chase down possible motive."

We seemed to have lots of motive but yes. I hated leaving stones unturned.

"I'll look into it," I said, only then realizing Petunia had been gone long enough, turning to look for her. It wasn't like her to wander too far. Usually, the little brat loved to present me with her deposit with a beaming pug grin. Besides, she hated being overly cold and it was chilly out here, enough so she should have been back at my side already.

"Petunia?" I headed in the direction she'd trotted off, Dr. Aberstock following me. It was dark, but not pitch black, enough light from the street giving my eyes illumination to make out the path ahead.

And the lump of fawn collapsed on her side, twitching violently on the flagstones.

CHAPTER TWENTY-NINE

I couldn't breathe. Didn't move. My body locked up, mind stuttering to a halt as I watched my pug seize there in front of me, thrashing her fat little body before falling still. Dr. Aberstock on the other hand?

He was already moving before Petunia's fit ended. I watched as if from a great distance as he rushed to her side, crouching and examining her before spinning on me and snapping his fingers at me to get my attention.

"Fiona!" I'd never heard him raise his voice before. That jerked me loose from the shock of the moment and dragged me as though he'd lassoed me, knees wobbling, to land at his side. Petunia was panting, her whole body heaving again while Dr.

Aberstock bent to sniff at something. While my eyes locked on what looked like the remains of a bowl of wet dog food on the side of the path.

Why was there food out here? And why was there any left? Petunia would have Hoovered up every last scrap, surely. That was her MO, no matter how full she was. What was wrong with my pug?

Yes. I knew. Deep down inside as my hand pulled free my phone and speed-dialed the vet, I understood, even as Dr. Aberstock scooped some of the food into a glove he had in his pocket (occupational hazard) and someone answered on the line.

"Fiona, tell them it's antifreeze and a large dose. Tell them to prep hydrogen peroxide. We're on our way."

Did I? Think I did, while my mind went, not so oddly, I guess, to Thea Isaacs and the parallel to her case. That the little minister didn't make it and did that mean my pug wouldn't either?

I don't remember getting her off the icy ground or carrying her to the car, though I must have. I also don't recall the drive, though Dr. Aberstock must have been behind the wheel. I have zero recollection of anything, to be honest until I came into sharp awareness in the front room at the vet's, Crew bursting in to hug me and hug me while Petunia, taken from me, that much I did recall, fought for her life somewhere past the main desk.

"Someone poisoned her," I whispered into his chest, not even able to cry just yet.

"We'll find them," his growl was deep, furious, vengeful when I couldn't be, not until I knew if she was going to live. "And we'll make them pay."

I already knew who tried to kill my pug. They'd been at my house, torn it to shreds. Destroyed my life and left my whole world in shambles. Who else had access? Who else would use poisoning just like the case we investigated as the ironic kick in the ass it was? It had to be Robert. Rose.

There'd be two more bodies to investigate before too long and I wouldn't be sorry. Not one little bit.

Dr. Aberstock emerged just as Dad and Mom hurried in, both of them hugging me, my mother weeping, even Dad with tears standing in his eyes. And then, Daisy burst into the office, the tall and gorgeous Emile Reis striding in behind her.

I embraced my bestie while she sobbed, rocking her and pulling away finally, finding my own tears in the face of her grief. "We don't know anything," I said, though I was looking at the doc when I said it.

He nodded heavily, but with the faintest of smiles. "She's not out of the woods," he said, "but she's breathing better, and we were able to get most of the antifreeze out of her system. So, if she makes it through the night, she'll be okay."

I lurched at him, hugged him tight. "You saved her life," I whispered in his ear. "I'll never forget it, not ever. Thank you for everything. For being there. I don't know what I would have done if you weren't."

He hugged me back, the sweet older doctor

patting my back with a gentle hand. "I just hope it was enough," he whispered in return. "Iris was a dear friend, Fee. And I'm rather fond of the pug in question." The doc blinked, moisture in his own eyes. He'd faced death so many times, as a doctor, as a coroner. I'd never seen any of it phase him.

But he was crying over my dog. And I joined him.

Dr. Fred Miller exited the door to the back and greeted us all with a warm smile. The sandy-haired vet had been Petunia's go-to since he'd moved here, Toby Miller's son a welcome addition to Reading, and my pug adored him. I couldn't think of anyone—aside from Dr. Aberstock, thanks—I'd trust her with more. "She's doing much better," he said, with a wave for the human doc in the room. "Thanks to Lloyd here, she's got a fighting chance. That was quick thinking and probably saved her life."

"She's going to be okay?" I hated to ask that question, especially after what Dr. Aberstock said, but Dr. Miller seemed optimistic.

"We'll see come morning," he said, pale green eyes honest behind his gold-rimmed glasses, golf shirt collar askew as if he'd barely had time to change or even get dressed before treating my pug. "But it looks good, Fee. I wouldn't say that if it wasn't true. Okay?"

I sobbed at last, nodding as I pressed both hands to my face and let out the terror of the last—how long? I had no idea how much time passed. I literally lost however long it had been to the mindless horror of the prospect of losing Petunia. There had been a time I'd wondered why my grandmother loved her farting, fat, bossy little soul. But she was mine and I was hers and if I'd lost her…

I couldn't lose her.

Dr. Aberstock finally left after another round of thankful hugs. "I'll check in on her in the morning if you don't mind, Fee?"

As if. I kissed his round cheek. "You're the best. And I'll make things right for you, I swear."

"This is the reason I'm a doctor," he said, cherub face alight with a smile and more tears. "You don't owe me anything. I'm just happy this ending isn't what I usually have to deal with."

I let him go, wanting to go back and see Petunia, but knowing I had a confession to make. I dragged Dad and Crew to one side, Liz following us, and whispered what I needed them to know.

"I'm pretty sure Rose and Robert are behind this," I said. "And it's not the first attempt they've made to hurt me." I filled them in on the first time, the car swerving to hit me before driving off. And the second, the near-accident earlier today, Jill's expert driving saving us was just another instance, in my opinion.

Dad hesitated while Crew hugged me tight as if he could protect me from all comers just by holding me. "The brake line was degraded," he said before shaking his head. "But that can be faked."

"Easily," Liz growled. "A drop or two of some kind of acid and it looks natural-like." She sounded like she had experience with such an occurrence.

"Dad." I grasped his hand. "This might be about Victor." His eyes narrowed further. "If Robert knows I remembered what happened…" Did I remember correctly? Or was my cousin just an asshat and this had nothing to do with the day Vivian's brother drowned?

No way. That darkness that ran through Robert Carlisle? That came from guilt so deep and powerful it was born of childhood trauma.

Crew's deep voice echoed hollow in my ear as he spoke. "We need proof," he said. "Damn it, I hate to admit it. I wish we could just go string up the both of them. But we need solid evidence to take them down." He pushed me away just a bit, enough to look into my eyes. "They may have just given us what we need to ruin them both."

I'd take it. "Go find proof," I said, shoving against him to set him free. "Find it, Crew. If those assholes—" I choked but when he moved in to hug me again, I brushed him off, letting anger feed me. I needed it right now or I'd be collapsing into a heap myself and would likely end up comatose sucking my thumb for comfort. So, anger it was. "Find what we need to nail those bastards to the ground once and for all."

Crew nodded, grim, as angry as I was, before kissing my forehead, the stubble on his face scraping against my skin before he spun and marched out. Dad and Liz went with him, Mom and Daisy joining me for a hug I barely accepted before pushing them away, too. I nodded to Emile rather than let them pull me into a hysterical spiral of what-ifs.

"Nice to see you again," I said. I gestured at my bestie who flushed. "Don't let her get away, okay? She's worth the fight."

He beamed a smile at me, those stunning eyes locked on Daisy. "If she'll have me," he said, deep voice soft with that lilt of old French making him dreamy all over again, broad-shouldered body leaning into her under that expensive camel coat, every inch a prince even if he wasn't officially (as far as I knew but stranger things, right?). "I will love her and care for her like the precious flower she is."

Daisy, clearly flustered, more than I'd ever seen her, waved both hands at him and giggled. While my mother swooned just a little. Nice to see them both distracted. And to feel a surge of love for my best friend and the future she hopefully would embrace with this man who clearly adored her more than life itself.

I had one of those of my own, so I knew just how precious it was, that gift.

It was harder than I thought to shoo them out, finally begging them to let me stay alone with Petunia. "I have to be here," I said to Mom, to Daisy. "I can't leave her alone. But you two should go. Emile, please." I stepped back from them, gesturing for him to guide them out. "Make sure they get home safe."

Prince Charming did just that, though my mother looked back over her shoulder the whole time as if trying to guilt me into letting her stay. Instead, I hardened my heart against her and could almost feel her sigh in my own body as she finally left, Emile holding the door for her.

I turned back when she'd gone, to nod to Dr. Miller. "It's okay if I stay?" I hadn't even asked.

He nodded instantly. "We even have a cot," he said, one hand on my back as he guided me through the doorway and into the recesses of his clinic.

I'd never been back here before, where the cages and sick animals were, where the actual medicine happened. Nothing like a regular hospital. Why was I surprised? I stopped when I spotted her, behind a cage door, at the bottom, near the floor, her fawn body silent. Another sob escaped and Dr. Miller was kind enough not to push me until I was ready.

I closed the distance at last, sitting on the tile floor next to her cage, watching her breath, her triangle ear flapped over one eye. When I looked up for permission Dr. Miller opened the cage door and let me touch her, though I did so hesitantly, smoothing back that velvet ear, fingers sliding over her shoulder, down to one little paw. I needed to trim her claws again. They were getting so long, and I'd been neglecting her.

And then, as if that thought opened a floodgate, I bent my head into my hands and wept for my poor little pug.

CHAPTER THIRTY

I woke partway through the night, not sure what made me stir. A quick check of Petunia told me she was still out cold. The place wasn't exactly quiet, a few cages housing animals in various stages of illness and/or recovery like my girl, so likely one of them make enough noise to wake me.

I'd waved off the cot, choosing to sit on the floor next to my dog and watch over her. I hadn't meant to sleep and, to keep myself awake—not that I needed to for safety, since Dr. Miller locked the place up tight before he left, leaving me secure inside—I fiddled with my phone.

And, on impulse, sent a text to the number of the private detective Dad supplied me. The one who Andrew Isaac had hired to look into Thea.

I quickly introduced myself to Orville Dunning as sheriff of Reading before asking him if it was true he'd stopped investigating after Andrew told him to. Dad hadn't said otherwise, so I assumed that was the case, but I needed something to distract me. As an afterthought, I sent him the info Dr. Aberstock gave me and asked if he'd uncovered anything about an accident.

He didn't answer, no surprise there. It was three in the morning, after all. I sighed, setting my phone aside, doing my best not to let my spinning brain have its way with me, and, holding my pug's paw in one hand, fell asleep again.

I woke when the staff started to arrive, got out of the way when Dr. Miller appeared.

"There's coffee in the staff room," he said, one of his nurses gently lifting Petunia out of the cage and carrying her toward an exam table. "I'll be right with you, okay?" I didn't want to go, hesitated, but he was still smiling. "She made it through the night, Fee," he said, pointing at where the nurse was injecting her with something. "I'm waking her up now, to check her vitals. But it's an excellent sign and I'm sure she's going to pull through."

Okay then.

I sipped a hot cup of coffee, feeling like an intruder in the staff room, though everyone was so sweet and two of the nurses stopped in to hug me, tears in their eyes.

"We just love Petunia," the smaller of the pair said, her petite body shaking with anger. "How anyone could do this to her..."

I didn't comment but thanked them both for their kindness. Restless, I finished my cup of java and headed for the entry, my coat, and outside for a breath of fresh air while pent-up fury rose in a ball of fire inside me, giving me a sudden and intense bout of heartburn.

I didn't even consider the fact that the people in my life would be yelling at me right about then if they knew I was standing outside, alone, unprotected. But it was the morning, bright and sunny and even a little warm, the kind of day that optimism was made of. Surely that meant things had to be turning in my direction, right?

The black sedan pulled up so quickly I felt panic rise, realizing then how stupid I'd been. This could be the car that tried to kill me, to run me over. Though, the moment that thought crossed my mind I knew better. Even more so when the big, tall man in the suit and black sunglasses, wire in his ear and, I was positive, pistol in his jacket, stepped out of the front and opened the back door for me.

Malcolm Murray's lead bully nodded while the man himself, his silver head poking out the door to greet me, waved for me to join him. "Get in, Fee, lass," he said.

Did he sound... excited about something?

Damn, I forgot he'd texted. An apology sat on my lips, and I almost had enough air in my lungs to let it out, even as I crouched to slide into the back seat next to my godfather when that same breath exited in a rush at the sight of the beautiful older woman sitting across from him.

And everything stopped.

"Siobhan," I managed with the last little bit of oxygen left to me.

"Oh, my darling Fiona." She leaned forward, one gloved hand pressed to my cheek, cupping my face in the soft leather, her pale green eyes glowing, white hair a wreath around her lovely face, lined by age or not. "How utterly divine to see you grown up."

Malcolm had a lake house, who knew? Dad did, I suppose. I, on the other hand, had no idea where he lived, realizing I'd assumed he perched in some kind of seedy apartment over The Orange, his bar. The stunning mix of modern and wood-accented home on the shores of Cutter Lake, however? Not at all what I'd been expecting.

Malcolm's tight grin told me he knew he'd surprised me. "Come in, please," he said, taking Siobhan's hand and guiding her steps, her small feet in black leather boots, slim body dressed well in a long, down-filled black coat with a fur collar tucked carefully around her throat. The two of them looked like the sweetest old couple ever, he in his navy pea coat and jeans, hovering next to her as though the barest breeze would knock her over while she batted at his hands and laughed a little breathlessly.

"Malcolm, my love," she said, cheeks pink from the cold, "I'm fine, sweet boy. Let an old woman be."

"Never again," he said, and yes, his voice was thick.

Oh god. I was going to start crying all over again, wasn't I? For love long lost and somehow recovered.

Because that's what this was. Love. How could anyone possibly miss the way she looked at him, how he doted on her? Like they were twenty again and had their whole lives ahead of them. Only the tragedy was they weren't and while they might have some time, could they possibly make up for all the years they'd lost?

That wasn't up to me. But didn't keep me from wanting to hug them both and cry.

Not how I'd expected to spend my morning. I did think ahead far enough to text Dad on my way to the house, to tell him I was fine, that Petunia was going to be okay and ask him to send Mom over because I had to go and—oh god, the guilt—I'd had to leave my pug before she woke up. *At least she'll have someone there she loves*, I sent.

Bad pug mom, Fee. Bad.

Malcolm helped Siobhan shed her coat, handing it to his head bully as if the man was a coat rack before guiding her deeper into the house. I relinquished mine and thanked him with a nod when he took it from me. His smile was real, genuine and not for the first time I wondered what his name was.

Me and names. I sucked.

My sock feet slipped on the polished wooden floors, the warm gold mixed with deep red and near chocolate of the multi-toned hardwood, reflective enough it picked up the sunlight streaming in the floor to ceiling windows overlooking the lake. The big open-concept kitchen welcomed me, though Malcolm was gently leading his love down the two wide, deep steps into the living room, settling her on the plush cream sofa and gesturing then for me to join them.

I did, my feet deep in the thick fur rug, my butt just hitting the seat next to Siobhan when the front door slammed open, and Dad barreled through.

Malcolm didn't have to wave off his bully, the suit stepping back and letting my father in. So they had an arrangement of their own, did they? Good to know. Regardless, Dad took one look at me and inhaled, likely to ream me a good one for going off on my own.

And froze as his gaze fell on Siobhan.

CHAPTER THIRTY-ONE

She giggled, like a girl, eyes sparkling before she met my gaze with hers. "Adorable when they are silent, aren't they, these men in our lives?" Her slow, even wink, paired with that lovely lilting Irish? Okay, I might have been overtired, but even I grinned, and I wasn't having the best week.

Dad collected himself pretty quickly. "You were to stay at the clinic," he growled. "Until someone came for you. You're not to be alone, Fee."

That got Malcolm's attention, Siobhan's face creasing into a frown.

"Why, John, what's going on?" She looked back and forth between me and Dad. "What's happened?"

Dad filled them both in while I sighed and crossed my arms over my chest, wishing he hadn't.

Because I recognized the look on Malcolm's face. Kind of a mirror to the one that Dad wore. Now that I knew the Irish crime boss was my godfather—and the woman next to me my godmother—I figured I was doubling up on the overprotectiveness that typically just came from John and Lucy Fleming at times like these.

Just what I wanted in my life right now. Another set of parents. And ones that didn't exactly think the laws of the civilized world applied to them, either.

Malcolm was on his feet, gesturing for his boy before Dad was done. "Find Robert Carlisle," he snarled, his own Irish accent thicker than ever, "and bring him to me."

Dad cut that off immediately. "We have no proof yet," he said.

"I don't need proof, John," Malcolm shot back.

"My love." Siobhan's tone was light and soft, but it carried weight. She patted my hand before speaking again. "We'll deal with this shortly. When we get John's proof. And, if no proof is to be found, well." She smiled at me, so adorable and yet so freaking deadly I shivered. "We'll still deal with it." She kissed my cheek. "Won't we, my darling Fiona?"

Oh my god. I'd been thinking about her as a lovely older woman who suffered a stroke, a grieving mother, an innocent in all this. But that was about as far from the truth as anything, wasn't it? Siobhan Doyle was no naïve girl on the outside of the mob's business.

She was one of them.

Wow. Was I happy to have her on my side.

"For now, boys, please." Siobhan gestured for them to join us and, with some reluctance, though obeying her anyway, they did. "I have something to tell you both, a secret I've shared only with my darling Fiona. It's time I told you, too." She breathed deeply, one shaking hand pressing to her forehead. Malcolm made an instant sound of concern and leaned toward her, but she shook her head then, and instead sank deeper into the sofa, pulling me back with her, holding my hand firmly in her lap. "Now, don't be like that, Malcolm Murray. I'm as fit as I'll ever be from here on in. Just a headache. They come and go, from time to time." She squeezed my hand, though she let go the pressure quickly. "I'm not as hale as I used to be," she confessed. "Though but by the grace of God, my mind has survived. For that, I will be eternally grateful."

Right, Irish. Roman Catholic. I wasn't going to argue her religion, not so sure God had anything to do with her recovery. She seemed pretty determined to me. Likely it was her, all her. And besides, what had God done to get me married, right?

Grumble, mumble. Mysterious ways, my ass.

Siobhan proceeded to tell the two men in her life who shared her grief her belief my namesake was still alive. The look on their faces, the anger that crossed their expressions, mirror images of one another. And, in that moment, as I looked back and forth between them, I saw their kinship, how alike they really were and that, despite Malcolm's background, Dad's, in a different life they would have been brothers and best friends.

More tragedy.

"Siobhan." Malcolm's anger faded into shocked disbelief and then back to anger again. "Why didn't you tell me?"

"What, that our daughter might have been alive and instead of coming home ran off somewhere, possibly with someone else's husband?" She snorted. "You would have written Fiona off after sending a pack of your bullies to punish her and we both know it."

Guilt flared on his face. "I wouldn't," he said, though he didn't sound convinced enough in his own answer to be saying so.

"You would." She jabbed a finger at him. "I needed you to find her, not blame her. And you." She spun on Dad with that same finger. "You and he were peas in a pod. What you knew, he would have known. And so, I kept the secret, hoping you would work together, find our daughter, bring her home to me."

Except they hadn't.

She seemed to know where my mind went.

"And then time went on," she said, her own regret burning in her voice, "and too much had passed for me to confess so I kept my peace and prayed, hoped, dreamed she might find her way back instead."

Again, except.

"My boys," Siobhan released me, reaching out

one hand across me to Dad, the other to Malcolm. Both men reacted instantly, taking her slim fingers in theirs, with the kind of tenderness that told me so much and left me burning with the need to rewind time and know them in the days after Fiona disappeared. Because I was getting a glimpse of the past, sitting there with their hearts bared to each other as if not one second had ticked by. And it was clear, so clear to me, that Siobhan Doyle, not Malcolm or Dad, ran this particular show.

Made me wonder what Mom thought of her. And if they were friends, too.

Siobhan's voice was soft but firm when she spoke. "I want you to let this go." She met Dad's eyes. Then Malcolm's. "Both of you." They denied it instantly, head shakes and lips parting but she was firm. So firm. I instantly admired and loved and feared her all at once. "Yes," she said. "Too many years have we let this come between us. And neglected this petal." She dropped their hands to turn to me with a smile, cupping my face in her grip, kissing me ever so gently. "I hear you're getting married. May I attend your wedding, goddaughter?"

I thought I was done crying.

Nope.

Siobhan blinked back her own tears before smiling at Dad and Malcolm. "All those years ago, I ordered you to find her. Find our Fiona. And, in doing so, Malcolm, my love," she wiped at the wetness on her cheek, "I lost you."

He was weeping openly himself, silently, while

Dad sagged back into the chair he occupied, still and quiet.

Siobhan wasn't done.

"I lost so much that day," she told me then. "My daughter. My true love. I made friends," she gestured at Dad, "and gained a goddaughter. But in my unwillingness to release Fiona, the grief of her disappearance, I wouldn't allow myself to accept the truth. That life goes on and she made her choice, my girl did." She sighed then, patted my hand. "The stroke, you see. Laid me low. But showed me, clear as a bell, what I needed to do as soon as I was able." She beamed a smile at Malcolm who smiled back, sorrow still there but love for her as strong as ever, I could only imagine. "Oh, pet," she whispered. "Can you ever forgive me?"

A low cry and an embrace later and it was pretty obvious Malcolm had no trouble whatsoever with that request.

CHAPTER THIRTY-TWO

I could tell Dad was angry on the drive back, and not just that irritated frustration he got sometimes when things didn't pan out the way he wanted. His total silence, paired with how his right hand shook just a little when he took it off the steering wheel of his pickup for a moment as he adjusted the heat in the cab, was more than enough indication.

I'd only ever seen him this level of furious once in my life. The night before I left Reading for what I thought was forever.

Instead of prodding him and making things worse, I settled back, staring out the passenger's window, watching the mountains on the other side of Cutter Lake, remembering not just the couple we'd just left, but my pause at the door, as I walked out behind Dad's storming retreat.

"I don't know your name." I'd looked up into his eyes, that man I'd always called a bully and, in that moment, he became a person to me once and for all.

"Darius," he said, in that soft tenor of his, smiling almost shyly. "Thanks for asking, Miss Fleming."

His was one name I would never, ever forget.

We were almost to town when I received a text from Vivian. *My office, now.*

"I have to go to town hall," I said to Dad.

He didn't respond, dropping me at the front door instead before peeling off again. Was he forgetting in his anger he'd just left me alone when he'd been furious with me about doing so in the first place? I sighed, tired and almost at the limit of my endurance, resigned to the fact we'd lost, though it pained me and slowed my feet to a weary drag all the way to Vivian's office.

Hugh looked appropriately hangdog when he let me in, closing the door behind me. But when I squared myself to have Vivian take my badge away, hand rising to my belt under my half-open coat to relinquish it, I was shocked instead by the sudden flurry of motion and her arms thrown around me.

Vivian shivered as she hugged me, breathing harsh, body tense and wound so tight I was sure she'd shatter if the wrong kind of pressure was applied. I hugged her back, dazed by the act of vulnerability and not sure what to do.

When she finally pulled away, I saw the terror on her face and reacted in typical Fleming fashion, guiding her to one of the plush chairs that lined the wall of her office, sitting next to her, holding her hand (thanks, Mom) while I pulled out the very last of my willpower and reserves and nodded (you too, Dad). "It's going to be okay."

She shook her head, her perfectly styled hair slipping free of the careful roll she'd created, her eyes faintly red as if she'd been crying. "It's not, Fee," she whispered, hoarse, crackling. "I'm in over my head and I have no idea what I'm going to do." She clutched at me. "Having you as sheriff was going to be my support, my backup. But if Geoffrey gets his way…" she cleared her throat but didn't seem to recover even a little bit as she sagged into the velvet seat. "I thought I was smart enough, Fee, clever. That I could convince her I was one of them, make my way into the inner circle. Uncover what I needed to find." She bit her lower lip, devoid of her trademark lipstick, slim body no longer appearing like an ice sculpture, but weak and powerless. "I was wrong, so wrong and now everything is falling apart, and I still don't have the proof I need."

"Proof of what, Vivian?" I held onto her hand as if it were the only thing keeping her with me and she returned the clutch with the same desperation. "Please, you have to trust me at last. I'm here to help you. We're on the same side."

Her huge, icy eyes blinked quickly several times before she lurched toward me, and her free hand caught the back of my neck. She pulled me in to her and whispered directly in my ear, as though what?

Fearing her office was bugged?

"I've been trying to find proof that Marie Patterson murdered my father."

I jerked away with a hiss, but she wasn't done, tugging me back toward her again.

"And I'm positive she had him killed because of what happened to Victor."

She was so alone. I saw it, now. The strong and courageous woman she'd been all along, carrying this burden in her heart, keeping everyone else out, including those who could have helped her, instead choosing to pursue the woman she believed was tied to the deaths of her brother and father.

All the old angst and dislike and judgment? Died a quick, fiery death in the face of her misery and understanding she'd miscalculated all along.

Or had she? "How do you know?" I asked that, innocuous enough, out loud.

Vivian swallowed again, leaned in, her breath tickling my ear. "I barely remember the day Victor died." She hesitated before clenching my hand tighter and rushing on. "Robert said you let him drown." That last word was a faint wail even at a whisper. "I hated you, Fee. I believed him and I spent my whole young life hating my only real friend."

Could she twist the knife of guilt and regret in any deeper? No, this wasn't on her. It was on my cousin, and, if Vivian was right, on Marie Patterson.

"I don't remember everything yet," I said. "But I do know I did everything I could." I was positive of that, guilt trying to convince me otherwise. And failing.

She flinched, nodded. "I know that now," she said. "And yet, I believed because I wanted to blame someone, and you were convenient. And then Daddy died." She inhaled slowly, while I felt her begin to pull herself together. So resilient, the Queen of Wheat.

No. I'd never call her that ever again. My friend.

"I'd always suspected something wasn't right," she went on. "Daddy and Marie had a falling out shortly after Victor's death. She'd gone into seclusion and my father went to see her." She met my eyes then. "He drowned on their dock, that day."

Wait, what? "The Patterson's private dock?" What were we even doing there?

She nodded. "Before you ask, I don't recall why we were there. Maybe with Daddy?" Vivian sat back then, spoke openly, clearly giving up on any attempt to hide from whoever might be listening. Quitting or on purpose? I had to trust she knew what she was doing.

"Vivian, why Victor?" That was the lynchpin of all of this, wasn't it? "He was just a little boy." What could he possibly have done to warrant being murdered? Or was it an accident and did Robert just freeze and panic and we were both making something of nothing?

But Vivian's face tightened like she was certain and couldn't be convinced otherwise. "Victor told me he had a secret," she said. "About Marie. But he didn't get to tell me. He loved keeping secrets." She shook her head. "Used to tease me with them, though he always told me eventually." She sniffed, tears trickling down her pale cheeks. "I used to hate him for it. That day, before we went to the lake, I told him I hated him." She broke down for real then, hands leaving mine, covering her face as she sobbed. I hugged her and rocked her a bit while she emptied out her guilt.

"He knew you loved him," I said.

She didn't respond to that, taking a firm and visible hold on her grief as she met my eyes. "Aunt Hettie had something," she said. "Papers from Daddy. I went looking for them and couldn't find them."

Wait, that rang a bell. And then I remembered. "Sadie Hatch." Vivian had asked about paperwork her aunt had hidden away while the old soothsayer had created, instead, a likeness of Victor to torment her with the help of her clever computer whiz grandson, Denver.

Vivian shrugged. "I was desperate," she said. "I knew it would never work. But I had to try. And honestly? Sadie might have been trying to bilk me out of money, but when she brought up Victor, it helped me put pieces together I hadn't considered."

"That your brother's death was tied to your father's," I said.

She nodded.

"I finally uncovered a letter from Daddy to his sister and one to me. Telling me that he suspected Marie had killed Victor and that he was trying to figure out why. But he died in the accident before he could even tell me he'd left me a letter." She wept again. "I was in Paris with Grace. I had no idea anything was wrong until Mother called to tell me Daddy was dead." Vivian seemed drained now, shrinking in on herself, as if the pink suit she wore were only a shell holding her together at the seams.

She rose on wobbling heels, went to her desk, returned with a few sheets of paper she handed me.

I took them, standing to join her, jaw tight and my determination returned even if she was in the position I'd been in when I got here, last legs be damned.

"Get your coat, Ms. Mayor," I said. "We're going on a field trip."

CHAPTER THIRTY-THREE

If Vivian expected, about ten minutes later, to be seated on Mom and Dad's sofa, sipping a hot cuppa my mother pressed into her hands, listening as I outlined to the gathering (funny how easy it was to assemble my posse and yet so heartening, at the same time) exactly what I remembered about the day Victor French died.

I relived it in an under layer of memory that revealed further truths as I spoke, flashing to the water, so cold, Victor sinking. And Victor, eyes panicked but determined, pushing Vivian into my arms, his pale gaze locked on mine, begging me to save her.

"I was going to go back in for him, too." I was. That was the seat of the guilt. That he'd made me choose, forced me to pick her over him. I knew I was crying and did nothing about it, grateful my fiancé didn't leap to my aid, that even Daisy with her penchant for tissues at times like this let me be. It all came rushing over me like the waves had that day, in a final gush of memory I couldn't control. "But by the time I had Vivian on the dock, Victor was under the water and there was nothing I could do." I had barely been able to stand, frozen by the chill. What time of year had it been? I didn't remember anything beyond the gray sky, the icy, steel-colored waves, the bare trees. "Robert stood by and did nothing, watched Victor drown." That was the worst of all, really, reliving his shadow hovering, then running off into the gray while Vivian screamed and screamed her brother's name, his pale hand sinking under the water. "The question remains, though. Did Robert let him die or was it just cowardice?"

Vivian cleared her throat. "You think he might have been part of it?" She nodded then, not waiting for me to answer. "He teased Victor constantly. Especially about his allergies."

Wait, allergies? "Dr. Aberstock said Victor was stung by a bee."

She sighed softly. "He was anaphylactic," she said, "but not just to bee stings. To a lot of things." Vivian looked out the window, one hand covering her lips, her throat working before she spoke again. "Robert loved to torment him about it."

And then, in a flash of further memory, the entire story returned, framed in sharp focus—

Robert, taunting Victor. That he had a secret to share, to show him. Victor and his secrets. I could see Victor's smiling face as he led me toward the lake. We were trespassing, not supposed to be there. It was Robert's idea and Vivian, like always, led the way as if it were her plan all along. The four of us, friends since childhood, misfits the other kids didn't like. Me because my dad was a cop, my mother a teacher. Victor, his wealth and his allergies. Vivian her attitude and that same old money. And Robert...

Robert had nasty streak.

How had he known to take us there that day? Why did we go? I don't remember, except that Victor loved secrets. More than anything. And Vivian was so easily led, while I just wanted to be with my friends.

He had to have known when he sent Victor under the edge of the pier. He must have been aware how dangerous, putting the boy with all the sensitivities so close to the wasp's nest. Not bees, after all.

I remembered. That it was dormant, that Victor was scared and then fascinated, Vivian terrified, ordering him to leave it alone, while I watched, not sure what to do, while Robert...

Poked the nest with a stick.

It only took one angry, early risen wasp, responding to the threat to its nest, to do the deed. A quick sting, Victor's face, him stumbling back, off the edge of the pier, into the water, Vivian beside him, taking his sister with him.

The lake current was strong, dragged them out so fast and I leaped, didn't think, just acted. Victor was already in trouble, face red, but he pushed her into my arms and, in doing so, shoved himself out of my reach.

Instinct, the rest of it. We barely made the pier, the ladder to the planks, while Vivian screamed. I looked up at Robert, no longer a shadow in this memory, saw the sick pleasure mixed with guilt and remorse and just the barest bit of sociopathy that colored his expression. Just before he spun and ran away while Vivian screamed at her brother, and he sank under the water—

When had Vivian stood and come to me, hugging me so tight, weeping again while I cried on her shoulder? Did I say all of what I remembered out loud? Weird, felt like I'd only lived it. But when she pulled back, nodding and wiping at her nose in the most unladylike way that made her all the more human to me, I realized I must have given the memories voice.

"He did it on purpose," Vivian said, steel in her eyes, in her tone. "Whether guided or because there is just something wrong with him, I'm not sure. But he killed Victor that day, Fee. And destroyed my family."

The "and he's going to pay for it" she implied at the end? Unspoken and unnecessary.

"There's more you need to know." I looked around at the others, caught their surprise but approval, and met Vivian's eyes. "This might be tied to the Reading hoard."

She blinked, a faint frown pulling her back from her vendetta. "What?"

That dictated the next fifteen or so minutes as I walked her through the evidence we'd collected, showing her everything from Grandmother Iris's music box to the doubloon and the map, Crew's tattoo, the book his grandfather wrote. Everything, all of it, while Vivian sat in silence with her mouth hanging open.

When I fell quiet, it took her a moment to snap out of her shock. And then she started to laugh. Soft, at first, a giggle that turned into near hysterics where she struggled to breathe and slapped her thighs with both hands while tumbling sideways into Mom who supported her until she devolved back into snickers.

"Of all the things I expected to hear today," she said around a big grin that barely hid the grief she still fought, "evidence of Captain Reading's treasure was nowhere near the list."

"Tell me about it." I sighed then, knowing this was serious but glad she was able to vent her feelings in a way that didn't have me pretending to investigate Robert's murder.

Oh, I had her back, yo. Forevs.

She patted Mom's hand, her own composure returning. "You're wondering now if the treasure could be tied to the reason Victor was killed. And my father."

It crossed my mind. "All I know is, something like the Reading treasure?" That was the sort of secret Victor would have loved. "Money is an excellent motive for murder. The kind of money we're talking about…?" Well, no one knew, did they? Reading's hoard could have been the single doubloon I had in my possession already and the remainder a wild goose chase.

Or.

Or. More gold and gems and priceless artifacts than any of us could possibly imagine.

Shiver.

"Vivian," Dad spoke up, "could Victor have uncovered something about the treasure, something the Pattersons knew and silenced him for?"

She hesitated, shook her head. "He had a secret he didn't get to share," she said. "Told me it was big-big." Vivian wrinkled her nose. "That was his code for the best kind of secrets. So, I knew it was important. But then he died, and I never found out what he wanted to tell me."

"Dad," I said, "where did the Patterson's wealth come from in the first place?" Joseph Patterson had been Captain Reading's cabin boy, not exactly known for their status and riches. But he'd been trusted by the captain, the only one of his crew, according to the legend, he'd brought with him to the Green Mountains.

Dad didn't answer right away, though when he did it was with quiet curiosity. "Not sure," he said. "They've been firmly entrenched in Reading since its founding. I assumed they'd built up their fortune over time. Are you thinking they had—and continue to have—access to the treasure?"

"Or they had access," I said, "and somehow lost it."

The whole room fell silent at that prospect.

Vivian blew out an angry breath. "If my brother and father died over a lost pirate treasure, I'm going to…" she shook her head then and laughed one more time. "Victor would have loved that, actually."

My phone buzzed at the least opportune time but when I saw who was calling, I left the group to talk and instantly took it, stepping into the kitchen for a bit of privacy.

"Mr. Dunning," I said as way of greeting for the private investigator. "Thank you for calling me back."

"Sheriff Fleming," the man's voice sounded older, a bit rough around the edges like someone who'd seen a number of years past middle age and maybe even a few too many packs of cigarettes for his own good. "Happy to help. You were asking about Thea Isaac?"

I nodded though he couldn't see me do it. "Did you uncover anything after Andrew asked you to stop?"

I could hear pages flipping, figured he was old school, though the sound of one-finger pecking on a keyboard followed. "As a matter of fact," he said, "I did. One of my contacts got back to me after I'd closed the case at Mr. Isaac's request."

What he had to tell me? Made my entire day.

"Thank you, Mr. Dunning," I said. "The town of Reading will be paying the bill. Please contact Mayor Vivian French with your invoice." I was already back in the living room, beaming at Jill, gesturing at Vivian who perked, nodded without question.

"My pleasure, Sheriff Fleming," he said and hung up while I did a little dance in the middle of the room before leaning in and jerking Jill to her feet.

She didn't resist, eyes huge, and I realized then she, like Vivian, had no idea about the treasure, was now a part of our little mystery brigade. Which made her the perfect choice for what I was about to do.

"If you'll all excuse us," I said, dragging the deputy to the door, "soon to be Sheriff Wagner and I have a murderer to arrest."

Vivian was on her feet and on our heels. "Wait for me. Your mayor would like to personally witness the criminal being brought to justice." Her blue eyes didn't seem so icy to me anymore.

I could tell Crew and Dad, Liz and Mom, even Daisy wanted to ask, but I shrugged on my way out, grinning. "Can someone please let Dr. Aberstock know he's going to be getting his job back shortly." Okay, I didn't know that for sure, but with Jill firmly in the sheriff's chair? You can bet we'd have the leverage we needed to make sure everyone benefited from our success.

The Pattersons might have thought they were making the rules, but we were winning.

Finally.

CHAPTER THIRTY-FOUR

We found him sitting at the organ, exactly where I expected to find him. He never seemed to be far from it, and when he saw the three of us coming toward him, any remaining fight went out of him.

"I did it," Ian Rudge said. "I killed her." Took me a second to register the fact he'd dropped his stutter.

Affectations. I hated them.

Jill nodded, tipping her hat while I stepped back and let her do the job she was born to do, the sheriff's badge already changed hands, Vivian agreeing when I filled them both in while Jill drove that this was for the best.

"She wasn't Thea Isaac, was she, Ian?" Jill's tone was soft, kind, but firm, too. Misery crossed his face, but he didn't crumble, just sat there while she held out her phone, the recording capturing his confession.

"No. She was Tamara Leek, once upon a time," he said. "My aunt. My father's sister."

I held my ground next to Vivian while Jill prompted him again.

"Your mother was from Reading," she said, "but your father was from out of state?"

Ian's Adam's apple bobbed as he swallowed. "Aunt Tamara was a mess," he said. "Her whole life, she was in and out of trouble. Alcohol, drugs." He shrugged. "My father did his best to keep her away from me, but I liked her." Faint disgust there, regret. "She gave me my first drink when I was fourteen. I've been an addict ever since."

Dear god. I almost spoke up, forcing myself to bite the inside of my cheek, Vivian's hand on my wrist keeping me silent.

"I was in rehab—again—when Aunt Tamara and Mom were in the accident." He wiped his nose with the back of his hand, rubbing it against the thigh of his pants. "Mom died on impact. Aunt Tamara almost did, but she made it." I watched him lose his temper at last, leaping to his feet, fists shaking at the ceiling of the church. "My mother never did anything to anyone. And you let Aunt Tamara live."

Jill let him have a moment before her level voice cut through, that perfect mix of kindness and understanding more than I could have managed and proving to me I'd made the right decision.

"You came back to Reading, Ian," she said.

"Why?"

His trembling sent him back down to the bench, as though his knees could no longer hold him. "I heard she was here. That she'd 'recreated herself.'" Hello, bitter resentment. "Some garbage about making amends as a new woman. I confronted her, told her I knew what she'd done, that she'd changed her name, got remarried. I was going to expose her. You know what she did?" He glared at us, accusing, furious. "She begged me to forgive her and then helped me get clean."

So that much was true.

"You've had this information for some time then," Jill said. "Why not turn her in?"

"I didn't know how." He slumped, leaning against the organ like only it could give him strength. "I wanted to hate her, but she saved me despite myself. She was still my Aunt Tamara. But I couldn't live with it. Not anymore. She told me…" he choked. "She told me she loved me and always had and that she was *sorry*." He put so much weight on that word it hurt to hear it. "She had the nerve to bring me my one-year pin and tell me she was *sorry*. Imagine."

"When was this, Ian?" Jill was a rock, and I was a mess inside.

"Three days ago," he said. "The night before I decided I couldn't live with it any longer."

"You could have turned her in." Jill didn't use an accusatory tone. "Why kill her?"

"Because she was sorry," he said at last after a long, painful silence. "And I couldn't forgive her for that."

So many layers of screwed up I could barely stand it. Good thing Jill remembered handcuffs.

Vivian watched her lead Ian out, still holding my wrist. "You were right," she whispered. "She's perfect. Thank you, Fee." And then she followed her new sheriff, leaving me to wonder if I was off the hook or not.

At least now I could get back to my life, to Petunia's (oh my god, Petunia!) and my wedding.

Right?

I'm not sure what was more awesome in the moment that Vivian made Jill's new job official after the deputy—now sheriff—presented her case conclusions with confession to the entire council. It was honestly a tossup between my friend's beaming smile and the furious frustration on Robert's.

You know what? I went for Jill's happiness because that's who mattered to me.

Robert still had what was coming to him pending. I'd celebrate over him soon enough.

If Geoffrey was going to protest, he made no sign of it nor showed a scrap of disquiet attached to the outcome of our particular little competition. Though he did stare at me the majority of the time, those cold eyes locked on me and that dangerous smile firmly in place, so if he was plotting behind it, I couldn't tell.

Good bet.

"Thank you, Mayor French," Jill said as Vivian handed over the sheriff's badge. My friend's voice practically vibrated with do-gooder attitude and heroic intentions. "I promise to uphold the laws of our town, to serve and protect all Reading residents, and to do so with professionalism and dedication to the badge." Had she been practicing that speech? Sounded like it. Good for her.

That meant she'd either been dreaming a long time about being sheriff herself one day or trusted me when I told her I had her back. I chose to believe the latter.

"If I could make a request?" I nodded to Jill, to Vivian. "I'd like to be officially stricken from the deputy roster."

Jill looked faintly disappointed. What, she was finally hoping for the chance to boss me around? No, of course not, that wasn't Jill. If anything, she was probably feeling a little alone right now. Because as soon as I spoke, Dad raised his hand and nodded.

"Me too, please," he said.

Vivian didn't protest, though I was sure she wanted to. But after the conversation we'd had not so long ago, she was finally trusting me, I think, as much as she wanted me to trust her. The old friendship we'd lost, destroyed through acts not under our control, that had rekindled at last, and I hoped we'd get a chance to make up for lost time.

As for Jill, I hoped she'd find a way to clean house ASAP and not be stuck for too long with

Rosebert as her only backup.

A firm round of applause followed, the council members seemingly pleased with Jill in her role, and I almost left her to her small talk and political maneuverings, knowing she could handle it when she left Terri Jacob to come to my side and shake my hand in full view of everyone.

"I'd hug you and thank you," she whispered, "but I don't want to show weakness."

I winked. "I'll take the hug later," I said. "Good luck, Jill. You know I have your back whenever you need me. For what that's worth."

She blinked, nodded, smiled. Then hugged me anyway.

Sheriff Jillian Wagner was too good-hearted for the cutest town in America.

There was only one other confrontation I wanted to have, and I considered leaving it alone until I could corner them in private. Glared at the pair of deputies who stood to one side, fuming and pathetic while all I could think about was Victor French sinking under the water, my totaled bed and breakfast and the twitching, seizing form of my fat pug on the walkway in my backyard.

Was there steam coming out of my ears? Could I kill with thoughts alone? I don't know where I found the internal strength to turn my back at last and walk out instead of losing my crap all over them.

Vengeance would be had. But on my terms and in a way that would seal their doom.

I did leave then, heading back to Petunia's at last,

to finish the cleanup. I'd extended the closure by another week, shuffling some visitors, canceling or postponing others, still not excited about the work it was going to take to restore the house but knowing it was time I tackled it. Thing was, I knew as soon as I dug in it wouldn't take long at all and I'd be back up and running in no time. But the prospect of cleaning up after Robert and Rose?

That turned my stomach.

Dad slipped one arm around my shoulders as we left the council chamber together, sighing happily.

"Got over your temper, did you?" I didn't mean it cruelly, more to tease him, and he took it that way because he grunted but through a lingering grin that surely meant he was up to something.

"Fiona Doyle is the past, kid," he said. "I'm more interested in the future."

"Meaning?" He'd been offering some of my favorite people jobs and now had two of them signed on as temporary owners of Fleming Investigations. Dad didn't like letting people go once he had a hold on them, so I could only assume, as long as they were willing, our company had grown by two permanently.

"Just happy to know possibilities have opened up for all of us." He hugged me before guiding me toward his truck. "Let me give you a lift home."

I accepted, knowing he wasn't going to let me walk anyway, and with my car still in the shop and, as far as I knew, Rosebert still trying to do me damage, it made sense not to let them have another go at me. Though, now that I wasn't sheriff, would they turn their attempts on Jill?

Yikes. I had to warn her.

Dad parked in the lot beside the house, following me inside, his head down, hands in his pockets, lips twitching. He clearly wanted to talk about things further, so why didn't he just spill? Except, as I stepped through the front door and into the bright foyer lit with the last of the day's sun, I realized it wasn't something he wanted to discuss with me that made him glow like a child with a toy he wanted to share.

Mom, Daisy and Liz beamed at me, Crew holding out a bouquet of roses, Petunia sitting at his feet, panting softly, eyes heavily lidded. As I took in her presence, I absorbed a second truth that made me burst into tears.

In the time I'd been avoiding my responsibilities, these amazing, wonderful, loving and incredible people in my life took care of things for me.

Good as new was an understatement. I let my tears fall as I smiled and turned a slow spin, at the newly painted walls, the carpet freshly cleaned, the sitting room on my left fully reassembled as though it had never been touched by defiling hands.

"We still have a bit of sorting to do," Mom said then, wringing her hands a little, glancing at Daisy who nodded with enthusiasm, brilliant smile lighting her up. "But we managed to take care of most of it."

"Thank you." I went to Crew, kissed him, kissed them all, but not before lifting my pug into my arms. Petunia grunted and snorfled my cheek before resting her chin on my shoulder and sighing a deep and contented pug exhale. I cuddled her against me, so grateful for my life and loved ones and finally feeling hopeful our wedding might actually happen before something else leaped up to get in our way.

How awesome was that?

"Fee, your dress." Daisy's turn to look at Mom, then back at me, biting her lower lip. "We couldn't salvage it."

I didn't care about that. "You gave me so much more," I said. "It's just a dress." Crew's smile matched mine. "I don't need it to make our day the most amazing of my life."

"Our lives," he whispered in my ear, pressing those delicious lips to my temple, hugging me and Petunia both.

I loved the sound of that.

CHAPTER THIRTY-FIVE

I sat in my car outside the door of a house I never expected to visit, jaw tight, body tense. I had to sneak away from the wedding prep—now set for tomorrow at last, only three days late and so what if it was a Wednesday, weddings didn't have to happen on a weekend, right?—to tackle this task I'd been sitting on for the last little while and just couldn't let go.

I really needed to just drive away and forget about it. Confrontation would get me nowhere, I was positive of that, and yet I just couldn't bring myself to leave. Instead, I tried to distract myself with deep breathing and recounting all the reasons I was happy, so happy and didn't need to do this to myself.

Jill had caught us up this morning on the wrap-up

of the case, as comfortable as sheriff as she'd been being deputy, though there was a tension around her now I could only attribute to Rosebert.

"I tried to fire them," she'd said without having to qualify who she meant. "Still working on it."

Well, we knew the council was controlled by the Pattersons, so… hardly a shocker. Still, good to know Vivian and Jill had each other. And us, even if we could only work behind the scenes from now on.

"Andrew and Katelyn are moving back to Montpelier," the sheriff told me over coffee. "Funny how chasing a new life in a new place only gets you more of what you used to have when you're not ready to do anything about who you are."

The single most profound thing I'd ever heard her say. And made me even more hopeful for our future here in Reading.

"And Dominic?" I'd already heard from the Jones sisters that Alfred Welling was throwing a conniption fit that the church had decided to, yet again, hire outside Reading. Mary's near-giggling really shouldn't have made me want to snort in return. I was a terrible person.

Jill's grim delight told me the choirmaster was finally going to get what was coming to him. "There's an inquiry," she said. "I'm dealing with it."

Good on her.

She'd left with the promise she was still on to read for the wedding, bless her. I wondered if her newfound determination might affect her current relationship with Matt and wished them both well.

She'd always been awesome? But now I had a feeling Jillian Wagner was a force to be reckoned with.

Speaking of couples, that made me think about the lovely Irish pair I still struggled to quantify in my life. Regardless of their criminal status, I'd invited Malcolm and Siobhan to the wedding, but when I tried to reach them, I could only get Darius.

"They've left town," he told me in that gentle tenor. "I know they'd love to be there, Miss Fleming, so I'll do my best to get in touch with them. They both adore you so much."

That was the most he'd spoken to me ever and I took it as a great sign. Though why I cared if an Irish mob boss's head bull—security guard liked me or not?

Yeah, I cared.

Daisy's request to have Emile added to the guest list wasn't a surprise. In fact, I made absolutely certain she knew he was welcome by hugging her as hard as I could and saying, "of course, Day," before she even had a chance to get the question out fully.

"Oh, Fee," she'd gushed. "I don't even know why he loves me." She blushed, eyes wet with unshed tears. "He's so wonderful and I'm…"

"Amazing," I said, wanting to shake her.

Her hesitation told me there was more to it and it was finally time to force that particular conversation. So, I'd dragged her downstairs with me to my apartment, poured her a glass of wine and sat there, Petunia firmly in her lap so she couldn't run away, staring at her, until she finally cracked and fessed up.

"Life is so short." She sighed, patting Petunia. The fat pug was still slower than usual, groggy yet, though Dr. Miller assured me she was going to recover fully. She'd just turned eight, though, and how long did fat little pugs with a penchant for too much food that's not good for them and three near-death experiences under her belt usually last?

Forever, Fee. The answer was forever.

"Almost losing Petunia?" Daisy met my eyes, her fingers digging into the dog's ruff. "That was the moment, Fee. When I finally decided I was worth it." She let out a soft sob but shook her head when I tried to comfort her. "I'm okay, I promise. I've had a secret for a long time, one only Rose knew about. And I let her use it against me for far too long."

I knew it.

"Just after you left town," she said, "going off to your glamourous life at college," right because it had been so glamourous I just couldn't even, "I met someone. A visitor. He wasn't here long, and I barely remember him." She blushed deeply. "But he was sweet and we, well. After he left, I found out I was pregnant."

Oh. My. God.

"Day." I stopped myself instantly while she shrugged, gray eyes haunted.

"I know, stupid, right?" She laughed, brittle and high-pitched. "Seriously, I knew better. But he was my first and I thought I loved him." A tear trickled its shining truth down her cheek. "I blame myself."

Because visitor boy had nothing to do with it,

right. Growl.

No time for protective Momma Bear instincts with Daisy rushing on now that she'd started like she couldn't keep it in a second longer.

"I had no one to turn to. My mother was passed, and Rose's mom didn't like me much. And I couldn't tell my father." Her strained relationship with her dad wasn't a secret. "I thought about Lucy, but instead, when she caught me crying, I told Rose." Daisy's jaw jumped and her hand fell still on Petunia's head. "Biggest mistake of my life, aside from getting pregnant in the first place."

Okay, scratch the shelving of the wrap my bestie in a bubble and keep her safe mode. I was all over that. Except I was way too late, wasn't I?

"I wasn't here for you." Daisy really needed my guilt layered over her story.

She grasped for my hand, hugged me. "Don't do that to yourself," she said. "This isn't your fault." She sighed deeply, looking down again, resuming her pug scratches to which Petunia groaned her joy. "Rose suggested I get an abortion. And, after thinking about it for a long time, agonizing over it, I agreed with her." She blinked at me. "Don't hate me for making that choice."

As if. "Now it's your turn to stop doing terrible things to you."

She shrugged at that. "The thing is, I didn't have to follow through. Two days before my appointment, I had a miscarriage." Fresh tears, renewed sorrow, all aimed down at the dog in her lap who absorbed it into her magical fawn fur and gave the kind of snorty, farting support that really was the best antidote to grief, in my opinion. "Didn't matter, though. Rose has held my choice, and the pregnancy, over my head my whole life. Telling me how stupid I was to make such a mistake, that I was going to go through with taking a life. She brought it up as often as she could, and I let her."

Wait, there had been a hint of this, hadn't there? There had been, when Kami Derham, the young model who had tried to blackmail Grace Fiore's ex-husband with an impossible pregnancy. Rose had made a comment about abortion and Day…

My beautiful friend had reacted. I didn't understand why at the time. But now?

Crystal clear.

Daisy nodded, with no idea where my brain had just taken me, and I wasn't about to remind her. "Just another moment Rose used to prove to me I wasn't worthy of love, of anyone, that all I'd ever be was a dumb and terrible person."

While I really wanted to murder Rose before, the intensity of my dislike ramped up so high I could barely sit still. And yet, it was Daisy's place to pull the trigger, so to speak.

"Let me know when and where," I said, "and I'll help you hide her body."

Daisy laughed at that. "You know what Emile says, Fee?" I shook my head. "He says the very best revenge against her and the way she treated me is to be happy. So happy it makes her crazy. And he's right." She beamed at me. "He makes me very happy, Fee." There was that dark cloud again. "He doesn't even care that when I had the miscarriage, I found out I can never have kids." How much weight could those beautiful shoulders of hers carry?

"I like Emile's plan a lot," I said and hugged her. "But if you change your mind? I have this idea about pulling Rose's lungs out through her nostrils."

That should have been it. Wasn't it. After our conversation Daisy seemed brighter than ever, happier than I'd seen her since I came home to Reading. And Emile clearly doted on her. I knew the guy was uber-wealthy old money, and yet he had pitched in to help with Petunia's, surely the sign of a good person with a big heart worthy of my Day.

The trouble with other people moving on and accepting things was that it didn't always apply universally. Especially when I had my own conflicts with not just Rose, but Robert. And so, as the story Daisy told me layered into the previous hurts and griefs, I realized I couldn't drop it.

I had to confront them.

Thus, me sitting in my car outside the last place I ever expected to be sitting the day before my wedding, doing my best to control my temper while figuring out the best way to make them both go away forever.

Maybe I would have just gone home eventually, except as I sat there, hands clenching the steering wheel of my newly repaired car, Robert walked past his kitchen window. The sight of him in a t-shirt too tight for his present lack of health and fitness, that 70s porn 'stashe an affront to the entirety of the male population who sported facial hair, lit a fire under me and sent me over the edge.

And out of my car.

Up the walk.

To their front door.

Where I rang the bell.

He opened it without checking to see who was there, obviously, because he was shocked by his expression, more so when I forced my way past him and into their small living room. Rose stood abruptly from the coffee table where she'd been sitting, studying something, and my eyes settled, for the briefest moment, on a piece of parchment with black lines that looked like the side of a lake on it.

And I knew.

Didn't care.

Wasn't here about the treasure.

Rose squirreled the map piece away while I confronted the two of them. "The next time you want to try to destroy my home," I jabbed a finger at him, "or run me over with your car," this jab was hers, "or cut my brake lines," double-tap, both hands at once, "or poison my dog," they were lucky I was out of appendages to wave around, "you take a long, hard thought about it. Because I'm watching you. And your days are numbered."

Robert's lips flapped before he did what I expected him to do. Lied. "You're cracked, Fanny," he snapped. "We didn't try to kill you."

Grunt. "Of course, you didn't, Robert," I hissed at him. "Tell that to Victor French."

He flinched. Like I'd punched him right in the face. And his guilt, oh his guilt. Legendary and telling and tragic all in one before the darkness flooded his expression and he jerked the door open.

"Get out," he snarled.

"Already gone, Booby," I snapped back, using his teenage nickname for the first time in years, just because I wanted to remind him of Victor one more time.

And left.

It might not have been smart to confess to my family that I'd gone to see Rosebert, but I did, at our new rehearsal dinner, with Dr. Aberstock—reinstated at the hospital and, it turned out, an ordained minister who was happy to marry us—and Bernice in attendance. Neither seemed super shocked by the treasure's reveal, though the doc was very excited to see the map and the frame.

"I don't have the piece," I said, handing a slip of paper to Dad who took it eagerly, "but this is what I remember." I'd drawn it on a scrap I'd found in the car the moment I climbed behind the wheel, letting the excitement of the hoard hunt wash away my fury.

Not that it appeared to help. When Dad fit it into the empty spot, my rendering rather a good one even if it didn't quite line up, it was clear gaining that last image did little to tell us more.

Ah, well. Didn't stop everyone from speculating and enjoying themselves while doing it.

It was late when Liz finally dragged Crew out, one final kiss for me lingering in the doorway, laughing as he left me, blue eyes a bit hazy from one too many beers but that dear, loving face the best thing I could ask for to fall asleep to.

"I can't wait to marry you." Tipsy Crew was adorable lovey-dovey Crew, and I wasn't complaining, giggling. "I love you so much." Whispered over my lips in the cool air that left a puff of white between us.

"I love you too." And then, laughing again, he was gone, one arm around his best friend and the beautiful December night leading him home.

Mom and Dad wanted to stay, but I insisted they leave. "I'm fine," I said. "Robert won't try anything. I'm not sheriff anymore."

"He now knows for sure you know about Victor," Dad fretted.

"Let him try anything," I said. "Dad. Go home. I'll see you tomorrow."

Lots of kisses, lots of goodbyes, hearts in the right places, and hope, lovely hope, carrying me at last to a final tour of Petunia's to lock the doors, to wait for my still slow pug to do her business before carrying her downstairs, to retreat to my bedroom and slip under the covers, anticipating my wedding day and the rest of my life with Crew Turner.

My mother's dress hung upstairs in the Green Room, newly tailored to me, and I couldn't wait to get married in it.

I'd hoped to sleep soundly, instead waking every

half hour or so, starting into alertness as nightmares and dreams, more vivid than I'd ever remembered before, kept interfering with my rest. Victor, of course, and the heavy body of Skip Anderson lying across my legs in the back of a carriage. The bulging eyes of Lewis Brown hanging against me on a zipline. Falling into the black water of the harbor, first to catch and rescue my pug from Robert's assault, next near death as I plummeted from Doreen Douglas's attack.

So many memories, so many bodies, so much hurt and struggle. But, so much love, too. The day we opened the annex surfaced in my mind, my first moment standing in the foyer upstairs when I'd come home to take over Petunia's. The first time I laid eyes on Crew, and the love of my parents, my friends.

This town of mine. So complicated, like my life. And I wouldn't have traded it for anything.

I finally fell asleep, hoping for the last time, jerking awake once more, groggy and frustrated, noting the clock read 4AM and hadn't I just closed my eyes a bit past one? It took me a second to realize two things. One, that Petunia wasn't beside me, her familiar warmth missing from my legs.

And two, I wasn't alone in my room. I inhaled to protest this surprise, still half asleep and struggling for focus when the light beside my bed switched on.

"Hello, Fiona," Peggy Munroe said from where she sat beside me, hovering over me, while, for the second time since I'd known her, she faced me over the barrel of a gun.

CHAPTER THIRTY-SIX

There are times when feeling like an utter idiot can outweigh fear, at least for the instant it takes to process that I'd been so blinded by my hatred (strong word, considering the expression on the face of the withered old lady pointing a gun at me) of my cousin and his vile girlfriend I'd failed to put the most logical two-and-two equation of all time together before it was too late.

Because it was too late, with Peggy sitting there next to me with her hunched, thin shoulders rounded toward me, evil shining in her eyes, her thin lips pulled back to reveal she'd lost a few teeth in prison or else misplaced her dentures.

"You tried to kill me." Of course, she had. My gaze shifted as someone else entered the room and I wasn't shocked this time to see Ruth Wilkins had joined us. Except that the big, robust and daunting nurse I'd known as Pete's intimidating sister had lost her edge, her face gaunt, her height diminished by a slouch that seemed to collapse her in on herself. The low light from the lamp wasn't doing much for her looks either, cheeks and eyes sunken, wrinkles deeply laced around her downturned mouth.

"We don't have time for this." She met my eyes, lips twisting. "We have to go."

"Hush," Peggy snapped at her. "I'm talking to Fiona right now. Aren't I, dear Fee?" She giggled and I saw the insanity inside her, witnessed its surfacing like a whale broaching for air. Would it retreat again? Didn't look like that was the case, though she was, if not completely in charge of her marbles, totally in control of that gun.

"Peggy." I cleared my throat. "You tried to kill me." I swallowed. "Twice."

"Three times, actually," she said in a sing-song voice. "You just didn't notice the third one. Ruth botched the drive-by." She glared at her grandniece who sighed and shook her head. "And the brake line fiasco was a bust." Peggy seemed far from satisfied with the quality of help she had available to her. Wow, was my brain really cracking jokes at a time like this?

Where was Petunia? That cut through my need for jocularity and my gaze roved the floor over Peggy's shoulder, noting the silent fawn body lying on her side next to the closet door. I stared at her, willing her little ribs to rise and fall and almost wept when they did.

"The third time, that was a peach, but you evaded us." Peggy shrugged like it didn't matter. "If your father hadn't arrived, you'd have gone in that lake, my dear, Malcolm Murray and his bodyguards or not."

Yikes.

"And Petunia?" I would never forgive her for that.

She winked, licking her lips. "That stupid little beast was always such an easy target. She'll eat anything, won't she, the idiotic creature." She didn't glance my pug's way, though Ruth did, looking a bit sick to her stomach.

"Killing innocent animals not your idea of a good time, Ruth?" I hadn't meant to prod the younger woman and spoke before I could censor my anger.

She flashed me a grimace but didn't speak to me again. "This is a mistake," she said, low and intense, leaning into Peggy. "We have to go."

"Not yet." The old woman spun and smacked her grandniece's hands away. "Not until Iris knows why it is I hate her so very much."

Ruth sighed then. "Fiona, Aunt Peggy."

The old woman's crazy showed up all over again. "Same thing."

"You let a psychopath out of prison," I said to Ruth. "Nice going." Why wasn't I scared? Where was my fear? Maybe reliving all of the nightmares in one go had cut off my ability to be afraid. Or perhaps I was just tired of this old woman and her nuttiness lingering in my life.

I had to get my hands on that gun.

"For what it's worth," Ruth said with grim regret, "I would have killed you quick and painless."

Wow, how big of her.

"Quick and painless is too good for you, Iris." Peggy cackled, poking me with one sharp fingernail. "I'm going to make sure you never, ever rise from the ashes."

And, in that instant, when she jabbed me and spoke at the same time I smelled it. The unmistakable scent of gasoline. Understanding was a wave of nausea that rippled through my body and left me cold and panting.

"You stole him from me," she hissed then, her lips pressing to my ear, the butt of the gun tight into my ribs. "And you'll finally pay for that."

"Daniel," I whispered back. "This is about your husband."

She jerked away from me, snarling, hand shaking on the handle, finger vibrating on the trigger. "Don't you say his name ever again!"

"I'm not Iris, Peggy," I said, but it didn't matter. She was running off on a tangent with her eyes bulging and tiny flecks of spittle flying from her lips.

"Marie told me about it, you know. She was the one who turned you in." Peggy's cackling laugh returned. "Not that it matters. She got hers. And now the Patterson matriarch has her own secrets." Peggy rocked back and forth, snorting and giggling. "She doesn't think I know, hiding on her mountain all this time. But I know. I've known all along." She leaned in suddenly then, eyes intent on mine. "I've known since it happened."

"Known what, Peggy?" Why did I care what she had to say when my death loomed? Because even if I got control of the gun, I had Ruth to deal with, too, didn't I? Panic and fear were finally coming to roost, the last of my curiosity still giving itself the leeway to ask the question.

Besides if I was going to die? I wanted to know everything first. Busybody to the end.

"Peggy." Ruth's voice came out in a growl. "Now."

The old woman spun on her, shaking the gun in her face. "When I'm ready!" She tossed her head, turning back to me, sullen and childlike in her insanity. "You'll go down with me, missy, if you don't do what I say."

Ruth swallowed, nodded. "I can't go back to prison." She held up a roll of duct tape. "I'm sorry about this, I really am."

It only took her a few minutes to truss up my hands and feet, Peggy standing to one side, watching with a mix of glee and desperate need. I didn't speak, knew begging wouldn't help, my mind lost in Crew.

My chance at happily ever after. Gone in a puff of smoke. At least, once the flames died.

They were going to burn Petunia's down.

No. It couldn't end this way.

Peggy's dissatisfaction with my silence grew on

her face until she was waving the gun at me. "Beg, Iris. Beg for mercy."

It wouldn't help to correct her or to plead. Instead, I glanced at Petunia.

"My pug," I whispered. "Save her."

To which Peggy laughed out loud and said, "Because you asked, she'll burn with you."

They left abruptly, Ruth with a final grunt over my bindings, disappearing out my bedroom door. "Peggy, finish now. We're leaving."

The old woman came to me again, bending to plant a wet kiss on my cheek. "Goodbye, Iris," she whispered. "I'll dance around your funeral pyre, my dear, and delight in your passing."

I'd expected her to linger longer, to gloat more. Hoped she'd give me time to escape. Instead, my desperate heart now pounding in my chest, I watched her go, heard her footfalls in the upstairs as she passed through the foyer, Ruth's heavier treads following.

And then, just like that, they were gone, the house silent.

No, not silent. What was that sound? Like a giant inhale? As if Petunia's held her breath?

In that moment I felt the oxygen leave the upstairs and knew, without having to see to understand, that I was out of time.

Petunia's was on fire above me and it was only a matter of minutes before I was (pardon the damned pun and my brain) toast.

CHAPTER THIRTY-SEVEN

My father taught me a long time ago not to be a quitter. Mom, too. Between the pair of them? I'd had a formidable (if couched in loving attention, for the most part, disguising the lessons) education in taking care of myself.

But it had been that most amazing of women, Jill Wagner, who'd taught me not so long ago the very important and, as it turned out in the next few seconds, vital skill of breaking free of various types of bonds and escaping.

"Thing is," she'd said as she'd wrapped the stuff around my wrists, "it's not as hard as you think to break out. And I figure, considering how many times you've been in a bad position the last few years…"

"Knowing how to free myself from bondage is a

good thing." I'd laughed at the terminology I'd used at the time, if only because I'd been thinking, not about life and death situations, but the man I was in love with, and the word bondage made me giggle like a wicked little girl.

She'd not only shown me how to cut a zip tie with a shoelace (I kid you not), and how to pick the lock on a pair of handcuffs with a rusty nail, she'd demonstrated and made me practice the rather simple and effective technique behind escaping duct tape.

I leaped to my feet, raising my hands over my head, bringing them down as hard as I could while trying to separate them and felt the lateral stress on the tape part the sticky stuff.

How cool was it when things worked under pressure just like they did when you were practicing?

Now free, precious seconds burned up (again, pardon the puns, but my weird brain, remember?), I leaped from bed and threw myself at Petunia. Yes, I'd seen her chest rising and falling, but she shouldn't have been lying on her side like that, ignoring the fact Ruth and Peggy had been present. Despite her lingering weakness from the poisoning, if she'd been hale and healthy she would have been on the bed with me instead of limp, unresponsive, unconscious at the foot of the closet door.

I lifted her into my arms and scrambled for the bedroom exit, my pug bouncing in my grasp in that boneless manner that had me choking up over her state of wellness but unable to take even a second to check and be sure she was okay. First things first. Priorities, Fleming.

Like getting our asses out of my burning house before we died. That sounded good right about then.

Instinct carried me to the steps and the door at the top but the instant I set foot on the landing I knew there would be no way out, not like this. Heat radiated through the panel between me and Petunia's foyer, a thin line of smoke curling in almost pretty patterns under the lip of the door. I stared at it, fascinated horror controlling me for far too long.

The handle started to glow. Time to go, Fee.

Petunia twitched in my arms, groaned, shaking me out of my frozen reverie. Right, self-preservation was a thing. I raced back down the stairs, my pajama pants too long, tripping me a little as I stumbled on the hems. Normally I liked the fact they hung over my toes, used the excess to tuck around my feet when I sat and watched TV so I didn't have to wear slippers. The perfect arrangement. And Crew seemed to appreciate the fact my feet weren't freezing against his legs in bed, so… win-win.

That was until I tried to run in them, down carpeted steps and across a slippery tile floor to the other side of the apartment with the dead (worst choice of words ever) weight of my pug in my arms and panic driving me with a crackling whip toward the window over the sofa and (hopefully) safety.

It had to be locked, right? As the ceiling above me groaned the deeply wounded sound of a dying house, the rushing noise of accelerating flames devouring everything so loud I couldn't slow my heartbeat. I banged on the window, on the half-circle latch, until it opened at last, slow, so slow. It took me another five precious seconds of swearing and fury, forced to set Petunia on the back of the couch so I could use both hands, to pry the screen from the window. Icy air washed over me while I panted sobs and harassed myself internally for not taking the damned screen out when summer ended. Such a simple detail, so small, that meant, in that moment, the difference between lots of time to get to safety and, well, maybe not.

I wasn't taking that as an option.

Something crackled overhead, the sound of wood breaking a booming death cry. Ceiling tiles caved in behind me, dropping embers to the tile floor while smoke and fire wicked out with seeking fingers, crawling across the ceiling above me like a living thing looking for more to devour, destroy. I took one second to note the pale blue of the fingers, trailing with yellow and orange, and the ball of black smoke that oozed after them and, bending with desperate determination, grasped my pug, wrapped her firmly in the throw blanket I kept on the sofa and shoved her bodily out into the snow on the other side of the window.

Snow piled up against said window. Her body created a plow for mine, pushing back the soft stuff, meeting crust but no match for my determined shoving, until she was clear with one last grunting effort that sent her tumbling, over and over but still bundled in the blanket, thankfully, into the yard and clear of the house.

My turn. Slow-motion never felt so real as it did those next few heartbeats. Thank goodness for the height of the sofa. The fact it sat right under the window. That I could stand on the back and heave myself out the opening, my stomach on the ledge, wriggling myself out into the snow after my pug.

When the hem of my pants caught on the latch, I almost screamed in frustration at the same instant the interior of my apartment disappeared in a cascading gush of fire and first-floor detritus, falling through the ceiling and shaking the window, the entire house. I half turned, looked up. And caught my breath, lying beneath the furious heat and tumbling fall of embers, at the fiery tower above me.

Surreal, that moment, staring into death's beckoning flames, the searing heat barely registering, nor the icy cold of the ground beneath me. Something hit my foot, sizzling and I kicked hard, tearing the hem of my pants, free at last.

Just in time. Smoke poured out of the window I escaped, slamming me with its acrid heat and I choked, coughed on a lung full while I flipped over on my stomach once again, pulling myself through the snow to Petunia. I reached her, gathered her into my arms, forced myself to my feet, toes going numb in the snow as I ran, not feeling the cold, deeper into the yard toward the Carriage House and safety.

Turning back only once I felt we were far enough to watch, tears now rising and falling freely, as

Petunia's burned.

Sirens in the distance. Time started up again, flashing lights appearing on the far side of the flames. Far too late, I was sure of that. The roof was already gone, and I'd experienced the collapse of the first floor almost too personally. The yard flooded with people, neighbors, faces I knew, guests from the annex, local volunteer firefighters whose masks and helmets and heavy suits hid their identities from me. But I knew them, too. Almost told them not to bother.

Petunia's was lost.

Until I realized they weren't here for my beloved bed and breakfast, but to save the other houses in the area. No bitterness there, and fair enough. I stood with my back to the Carriage House, accepting someone's offer of a blanket to stand on, only then noticing the fact I couldn't feel my feet.

Another blanket descended around my shoulders, my pug silent but breathing in my arms while I stared, unable to stop, at the flaming, smoking beauty of my home. It felt like it would never end, that the fire would go on and on forever while I was forced to stand there, like some terrible nightmare, and watch as she died endlessly.

I should have taken better care of her. Loved her more. It was like a part of me was dying with her, that noble house and her history. I know I was crying, probably sobbing. I'd lived through enough shock in my lifetime it was hardly a surprise. At least I wasn't in a puddle on the ground. Or dead.

Or *dead*.

Was it my mind playing tricks on me I saw Robert watching? That he stood there, near the parking lot, for just ages, staring in my direction? It felt that way, especially when, superimposed over the image of him, was his shadow against the fire, tied to the shadow he was that day Victor French drowned.

Someone said my name, catching my attention, turning my head. Jill was running toward me, horror on her face. I turned back again, but Robert's shade was gone, and I let it and him go in favor of my friend's firm hung.

"Fee." She turned to look up, to watch the fire with me, both of us locked in our fascinated horror. "I'm so sorry. Are you okay?" She looked me up and down, hissed at the sight of my bare feet on the blanket. "Fee, what happened?"

No questions, not yet, I couldn't do it. I shook my head at her, biting my lower lip to keep from sobbing all over again. And couldn't help it when, out of the smoke and mist from the water now pouring over the flames, the man I loved more than life itself appeared to engulf me in his arms and hold me and Petunia so tight I heard her chuff a protest, finally awake.

Not just him, then, but Mom and Dad, Liz and Daisy with Emile at her side, Dr. Aberstock and Bernice moments later. Vivian French, for the first time since I could remember free of makeup, her hair in a messy ponytail, nightgown under her long coat, grasping me from Crew's arms to hug me and hug me and hug me.

And then, in silence because there was really nothing to say, the people I cared about most in the world stood by me, taking turns holding me and each other, and watched in group solidarity for her old faithfulness as Petunia's burned to the ground.

CHAPTER THIRTY-EIGHT

My reflection told me I'd lost weight, just like the bridal magazines ordered, only I doubted they'd recommend my particular method of loss as something conducive to mental health or a long, happy marriage.

Good thing I wasn't your typical bride then, huh?

I'd felt pretty guilty over losing, not just my dress to Rosebert's attentions, but Mom's as well, the gown burned up with my bed and breakfast.

"The last of my worries, sweetie," she'd said as I'd tried to apologize yesterday morning, the sun rising on the still smoking ruin of Petunia's. I could see the thin black cloud in the distance from her kitchen windows and couldn't help but stare at it in sick fascination while Mom did her best to distract me.

When Daisy appeared with a garment bag and a giant smile on her face, Vivian French in tow, I had forced myself into a happier state and found it turn to real pleasure at the sight of the gorgeous dress they showed me.

"Grace sends her love," Vivian said like it was no big deal a world-famous designer was my friend. Our friend. "She heard about the fire and wanted you to have this."

This. Yeah, not the word I'd use to describe the stunningly simple and yet utterly divine slip of a silken gown of perfection that, when draped by its dainty spaghetti straps seeded with endless pale pearls and empired at my ribcage with another two-inch row of matching multi-hued gorgeousness made me look like a redheaded goddess.

Yesterday morning. I glanced down at my toes, the dainty shoes Daisy lent me perfectly skimming the skin beside the burn on the top of my foot, keeping pressure off the bandage. Something borrowed, she'd said.

I glanced at the bed, toward the fawn pug watching me with her big, brown eyes, head in her paws. She perked when I looked her way, black velvet ears rising, a mewing yawn escaping her as her cinnamon bun tail wiggled.

"What do you think, pug?" I turned slowly to get a good look at myself in the full-length, tri-fold mirror next to the tall window overlooking the backyard of the annex.

Daisy hadn't hesitated to evict guests. I had no idea what she did with them, clearing the honeymoon suite for me. I hadn't even argued, not like me. Felt so weird to be here, to glance out the window and see the now tarped-over corpse of my home pretending to be a pending construction site waiting for the backhoes and the bulldozers and the dump trucks to unearth what remained of her bones and carry her away forever.

"If you cry," Mom said, appearing from behind me where she'd been sorting out my jewelry choices, "I'll seriously smack you, Fiona Fleming."

I laughed, couldn't help it, caught in a flood of emotion while she laughed in return and hugged me, her own eyes brimming.

"Sorry, Mom," I whispered, choked up. "I'll try not to ruin my makeup before the pictures."

She sighed, shook her head. "Oh, Fee," she said. "I just want you to be happy." And burst into her own weeping.

I hugged her, held her, or tried to. But she pulled away as the door opened, Daisy rushing through. Mom dashed at her tears while my bestie froze, her flowing crimson dress stunning on her voluptuous figure.

"I'll be right back." Mom hurried from the room with a kiss for Day's cheek while my best friend let her go.

"She'll be okay," Daisy said, sounding way more mature than I felt in that moment. "We're all just..." she glanced out the window, blushed, sighed. "No one knows that better than you."

"At least Mom's getting her wish," I said with a lip twist and not a hint of bitterness. "We're having the wedding in the annex like she wanted all along."

Daisy's soft smile was a clear precursor to her own tears. "I'd have rathered Petunia's." And then she started crying on me.

Seriously. We had to get a grip already or this wedding was going to turn into something that felt more akin to a funeral.

I went to the window and very firmly pulled the curtains, taking one last moment to look out over the fresh snow, the blue tarps, the empty skyline that had once been filled with a big, white house.

"I can't wait to get married," I said, feeling my heart soften, my whole being shift. "Life goes on, Day. In the most amazing and unexpected ways."

She hugged me in turn, and we rocked a bit, not letting each other go, whispering things that we'd meant to say for ages and ages and never had the chance. Things about love and acceptance and best friendness that would never die, never let us go or put distance between us again. No, I don't remember everything I said. But the intimacy and the heartfelt connection?

That I would cherish for the rest of my (very long) life.

"The Christmas decorations are going to look perfect," Daisy said. "The best time of year for a wedding."

I couldn't have agreed more. Because marrying

Crew? Any time was the best time.

And then it hit me.

I was marrying Crew today.

Imagine that.

I knew he fretted. There had been no sign of Peggy and Ruth, not since they tried to kill me. But I wasn't worried, not anymore. I had so many people watching over me, over Petunia, even. The little pug had fully recovered from her second bout with the horrible women I'd have a reckoning with down the road. She'd been struck, knocked out, but again the dear Dr. Miller told me she'd be fine, and she seemed so, as farty and snorty and sweet as ever.

The door opened again, Vivian sweeping in. As she did, I caught sight of the towering form of Darius just outside in the hall. He nodded to me, hands clasped behind his back, wire in his ear and I caught myself grinning and shaking my head.

Crew hadn't been too happy about his appearance at the annex this morning. How the big bodyguard informed me—while ignoring Crew completely—that Malcolm had sent him to protect me at all costs and that for the duration of said employment his life would end before I was ever put in harm's way again.

Well now. How about them apples?

I had put my foot down when he'd tried to guard me from inside the honeymoon suite, however. While I felt a bit guilty about making him stand in the hall, he seemed happy to be there, so I did my best to get used to the fact my godparents were as protective as my real ones.

Could I blame them?

"Here, let me." Vivian was at my side, adjusting one of my straps that had started to slide for the fifteenth time since I put the dress on. She circled behind me, a pin in her hand, and while I stood there and tried not to breathe, she did something that I'm sure was a model's secret and, a moment later the strap was behaving perfectly.

"Thank you," I said.

Vivian's hands settled briefly, gently on my shoulders, her blue eyes clear and open. We hadn't talked about the morning of the fire, of her hug and her terror and our reconnection. We didn't have to, not yet. But we would.

"Fee," she said. "You're welcome."

Daisy didn't seem jealous, bless her, and it wasn't about that. I hoped she knew. Instead, she squealed at the sight of the shoes. "They fit!"

"Day, they're perfect." I smiled at them both. "It's all perfect. I couldn't have asked for a more amazing everything."

Vivian winked. "Including that delicious fiancé of yours." She laughed then, the first time I'd heard her laugh in a long time, and never with me. Like she'd let go of some great weight holding her back and was suddenly the woman she'd always meant to be. "You know, I was so damned mad at you when you moved home." She booped my nose. "I knew the second Crew set eyes on you I didn't stand a chance."

Whoa. "What?" She was gorgeous. Always had

been. She was a freaking *model*.

But Vivian shrugged her delicate shoulders inside her pale green Grace Fiore and leaned in to kiss my cheek.

"Not a chance," she said. "He's perfect for you, Fee. I'm so happy you found each other."

Lingering sorrow. And determination to make sure Vivian found her own happily ever after.

Vivian glanced at the drawn curtains, faint frown soft and sad. "Will you rebuild?" She looked shocked at herself then, shook her head as if to stop me from thinking about Petunia's, but I smiled, feeling better myself for all.

"I don't know," I said, recalling that self-same conversation I had with Crew last night, in his living room, cuddled on the couch while Liz texted every ten minutes to remind us I had to leave before midnight. The brat. "We'll see." It felt... wrong to replace the house. And we still had the annex, the Carriage House. Who knew what the future had in store? "Maybe a fresh start is a better idea." Like letting Mom and Daisy have this place while I chose to follow the path I'd always wanted.

Fiona Fleming, private eye. Had a fun ring to it.

Vivian left then with another hug for me, whispered thanks though I had no idea what she was thanking me for. Inviting her to the wedding? Maybe. But it felt like more than that.

She and I were due for a heart-to-heart, and I actually couldn't wait.

Daisy beamed at me, squeezing me hard before

letting me go, her gray eyes sparkling.

"Everything is ready," she said. "Emile even had some of his favorite champagne flown in just for the dinner. And he had some chocolates sent, too. Your mother loves them." She laughed then, fluttering her hands at me. "I'm sorry, I'm thinking about him far too much."

"No such thing." I kissed her softly. "You deserve to be happy, Day."

Tears again. Sheesh. Both of us, this time. Mom was going to kill me.

My phone chimed and I took the distraction with gratitude, dabbing at the corner of my eyes with a tissue. The tears dried instantly, further shock at the source of the email making me gape and, in a surge of relief, absorb the message with eager excitement.

Sorry to be absent, Pamela Shard wrote. *I left voluntarily, to hang out with my favorite brother.* Wait a second. She hated her brother. Sarah Shard's father and Pamela weren't friends, they were estranged. Which told me that this was, in fact, Pamela writing to me and that she wanted me to know it was her. Big sigh of relief as I read on. *Don't worry about me. I've dealt with worse. Though I'm digging and I'll be in touch. It's a deeper chasm than I expected, Fee, and I've given up more than I expected to see this through.* Did that mean she'd broken up with Aundrea? I'd had zero contact with Alicia, Jared or his mother in simply ages. The only way I'd known Pamela was missing was thanks to Sarah back in September. Months without word. I should have been angry, but I just nodded at the phone instead and finished the email. *I'll be in touch when I have what I need. Closer than ever. Take care, happy wedding day and be safe. I honestly believe they'll stop at nothing to protect themselves over whatever it is she's hiding.*

Pamela signed off on it, and that was all. I glanced up at Daisy while the door opened and Dad entered, looking pretty darned amazing in his tuxedo and small red rose in the buttonhole of his jacket.

"Ladies," he said in that deep, gravel voice I knew so well. "If you don't mind, Day, I'd like a minute with Fee before we go downstairs."

My bestie crossed immediately to Dad and kissed his cheek before waving at me and leaving, closing the door softly behind her, leaving me alone with my father.

CHAPTER THIRTY-NINE

Weird how we both stood there a long moment in awkward silence, him just staring at me, while I reached for something to say, before landing on the obvious.

"Pamela," I blurted, holding up my phone. "She's okay."

I was expecting some small acknowledgment but the wave of relief that passed over his face surprised me. Dad joined me, read the email, handed back the phone with a grin.

"Leave it to Pam," he said. And tossed the cell to the bed beside Petunia who sniffed it like it didn't matter one little bit to her.

And, I guess, in that moment, it didn't.

Dad sat down on one side of her, pushing my

phone away, pulling me down on the other side, holding my hands in his. He was silent a long moment, cleared his throat, tried to speak. Stopped. Tried again. All the while not meeting my eyes, his face turning red, throat working.

I finally leaned in and hugged him, and he embraced me back, the familiar comfort of his arms enough to make me cry.

Sorry, Mom.

When Dad gently detached himself, he wiped at tears on his face, accepting the tissue I handed him. "I love you, kid," he managed. "So much. And that man of yours. You really are perfect for each other. I knew it the moment I met him, that the two of you would be together someday. Wanted to knock your heads on occasion for being so stubborn. But it's made you stronger, the time you took, the way you stood up to him, and him to you." Dad nodded while I sat still and listened. "Your mother and I are so proud of you, Fiona. Of everything you've ever done. You are as strong and beautiful and amazing as we could ever have dreamed of, and I hope you know how important you are to us."

Dad and emotional outbursts? Yeah, this was a very special occasion. Before I could say anything, make a comment, ruin the moment, he reached into the inside pocket of his tux and drew out a small something he handed to me.

"Your Grandmother Iris would have loved for you to have this," he said. "Considering you already have two more. I spotted them in the music box when you showed us the evidence." He shrugged as I opened my hand and looked down at the butterfly hairpin there. "She always wore them. I kept this one from the funeral, couldn't bear to bury it with her."

I'd thought the pieces were costume when I'd first examined them. The one I'd found in the box from the nursing home had been a bit tarnished, seen better days. And the other in the music box I'd never really taken a close look at. But with the bright light of day, I realized the tiny gems in the hairpiece were real. Diamonds and sapphires in the wings of butterflies.

So beautiful.

I went to the music box, sitting on the side table, and gathered the other two, joining Dad again and handing them to him. "Would you help me?"

He swallowed, hands shaking, but nodded and proceeded to thread the hairpins into my updo, gentle and slow, and when I stood to look at the finished result, the three butterflies in a triangle near my right temple, I smiled.

"Something old," I said.

The dress was my something new, of course. And now, in the hairclips, I also had my blue.

I turned back to Dad and held out my hands, the weird awkwardness between us vanished. He stood, took my fingers in his firm grasp and bent to kiss my cheek.

"Are you ready, kid?" His eyes glistened with more tears, but he looked happy.

I nodded, reaching up to cup his cheek in one

hand before linking my arm through his offered elbow. "So ready."

Mom appeared as if summoned, her makeup pristine, to give me the once over and assure herself all was well. I laughed, light-hearted, felt like I was floating when she finally let me leave the room, gliding past Darius who smiled and blushed and waved a little when I patted his cheek on the way by. I might as well have been suspended on some kind of cloud for all the control gravity had over me, the steps under my feet barely registering, Dad guiding me at a slow and measured pace I settled into, knowing I was beaming.

Petunia hopped down beside me, grunting when she reached the floor, the pretty red tutu Daisy had made for her wiggling around her little waist in a frilly circle of ridiculousness. Made me laugh all over again, catching the attention of the gathering in the main sitting room, including the stunning man at the far end, standing next to Dr. Aberstock.

And then the music started, right? I think. Maybe? Because Daisy was walking down the aisle with flowers in her hands, and Petunia followed her and people were smiling and taking pictures, but I don't remember really because the floating feeling continued and I think, without Mom on one side and Dad on the other I might actually have drifted away.

It took forever and no time at all to reach him. When I was pulled to a halt I almost protested before Dr. Aberstock laughed and asked some question I'm sure was important to the ceremony but was just keeping me from those blue eyes and that amazing smile and those broad shoulders. His lips and hands and the arms that could embrace me and make everything go away.

So, here's how the rest of that went. Whirlwind, yada, question, nodding, more questions, say something, Fee, love.

Vows. I wrote them. Fumbled through them. While his made my heart ache and sing and want to leap out of me and land at his feet for him, forever.

"Fiona Fleming," he said, simply and with adoration and the kind of love that never ends, "I wouldn't change a thing."

And then, the best part. "Fiona Marie Fleming," Dr. Aberstock said with points of pink on his cherub cheeks and a massive smile splitting his Santa beard. "Will you take Crew Michael Turner to be your husband?"

I didn't need to think, to breathe, to hesitate even a moment.

"I do."

Reading United
Methodist Church
Uniting Reading's Faithful!
(213)555-1969

READING
UNITED
METHODIST
CHURCH

ALL PAWS
Pharmacy Clinic
All Paws
Welcome!

ALL PAWS
Because all paws are
always welcome!
(213) 555-1111

The Reading
Reader Gazette

VOLUME 1   ISSUE 1   DECEMBER 15TH, 2020   WWW.RRGAZETTE.COM

News Briefs

1. **Santa Claus is coming to town!**: With many thanks to our own Dr. Lloyd Aberstock. Photo hours Saturday and Sunday all December from 10-12PM and 2-4PM with story time courtesy of Mrs. Claus (thanks, Bernice!) Santa helper volunteers still wanted.

2. **Parking Violations:** Your town council would like to remind you that parking restrictions continue year round. Any Reading resident caught street parking will be reprimanded and their car impounded. While we realize parking has become a major issue for our town, the sheriff's department is authorized to remove your car without notice. They ask you to please park responsibly and with our town's continuing prosperity in mind. Let's keep Reading's streets safe!

3. **Stolen Gingerbread House:** Could anyone with information please come forward regarding the missing Gingerbread House supplied to town hall courtesy of French's Handmade Bakery. While we realize it's delicious, it's meant for our whole town, not just your enjoyment. Thank you.

4. **Statue Pranks:** We do understand your creative talents have improved over the years and are considering a retrospective on your current phallic artwork. Perhaps if you'd like to come and chat with us we can discuss some sort of art scholarship as it is clear your skills are improving with time.

Just kidding. Please stop.

Winner of this week's Fire Hall 50/50 draw: Dr. Fred Miller. Congratulations, Dr. Miller!

Please send any pending community notices to: chris@rrgazette.com before 4PM.

Organist Angst Ends Minister

Ian Rudge, 24, of Reading, Vermont, has confessed to the murder of United Methodist Minister Thea Isaac, 50.

Addiction Leads to Lies, Deception and Death

By Christopher Jenkins

The sudden death of local minister, Thea Isaac, left Reading residents stunned early Friday afternoon during the wedding rehearsal of local bed and breakfast owner, Fiona Fleming and former sheriff Crew Turner. Her untimely end came at the hands of her nephew, Ian Rudge, whose grudge against his aunt ties to the accident she caused that killed his mother five years ago.

As a cruel twist of irony, Rudge chose to poison the woman he knew as Tamara Rudge with rubbing alcohol, the recovering alcoholic and drug addict turned minister known for her support of young people in Reading and surrounds, helping them to say no to addiction.

"Not to speak ill of the dead," says junior minister Alfred Welling. "But I can only hope that God himself can forgive her for her deception, since she lied to get the job she held. Reading's faithful population deserve only the best spiritual care."

With the release of former sheriff Turner, the subsequent stepping aside of short-term Sheriff Fiona Fleming and the newly appointed leader of our local law enforcement now in place in the person of former deputy Jillian Wagner, this reporter wonders if the mayorship of Vivian French won't be a short one after all.

It is interesting to note that, during the course of this investigation, now Sheriff Wagner has chosen to pursue legal action against choir master Dominic Twigg and we await word on that case and will report in full when information becomes available.

Let us take a moment to express our condolences to Fiona Fleming and, indeed, all of Reading, for the loss of Petunia's Bed and Breakfast to a terrible fire. The landmark location, originally opened by her grandmother, Iris Fleming, has stood as a cornerstone in Reading's business community for many years. The loss will no doubt mean hardship for Miss Fleming as well as the guests she will no longer be able to house.

Don't despair! The final book in the **Fiona Fleming Cozy Mysteries** is available now! Grab your copy of *Pirate Gold and Murder* and find out how the series ends!

AUTHOR NOTES

My very dear reader:

It's not my fault. Please, please don't send me hate mail about Petunia's. This is not my fault. I repeat: this is NOT my fault.

Blame Fee. It's been all her all along. I know, there are those of you who don't believe me. But it's the truth and even though I argued with her, pleaded at one point, to save Petunia's, that's not how the story goes.

So. No hate mail. Thank you.

We have one book left in this series and I started outlining it months ago, piecing together all the threads and trails and mysteries Fee's been dropping on me since I met her. From the mystery box in her garden left by her Grandmother Iris to the broken music box at the bank to the doubloon, the map pieces, Siobhan and Malcolm, Fiona Doyle, Blackstone and the Pattersons. The death of Victor French.

The hairpins…

Oh, dear. Foreshadowing. Or not. We'll see.

I'm excited to finish this series. It's been a little over two years in the making, book one published in January of 2017. And while I had a bit of a slow year last year, I've stayed tied to Fee all along and I can't wait to share with you the final installment in this, her first series.

Yes, her first, in case you missed it. The second

(titled for now **Fleming Investigations)** will be likely next year as I have two new projects I'll be working on in the coming months. One is a cozy paranormal series about a young mortician turned coroner who discovers she's the heir to a supernatural gate called the **Covenant of All Hallow**. And the other, still in the cozy genre, based on our very own Alice Moore and Denver Hatch from none other than the cutest town in America, as they wander the continent debunking paranormal events and stumble on murders of their own. Which means a few guest appearances from characters you know and love.

Look for book one of the **Alice Moore Paranormal Cozy Mysteries** coming this spring.

For now, Fee wants to thank you for your patience and is delighted you could attend her wedding.

Best,
Patti

ABOUT THE AUTHOR

EVERYTHING YOU NEED TO know about me is in this one statement: I've wanted to be a writer since I was a little girl, and now I'm doing it. How cool is that, being able to follow your dream and make it reality? I've tried everything from university to college, graduating the second with a journalism diploma (I sucked at telling real stories), am an enthusiastic member of an all-girl improv troupe (if you've never tried it, I highly recommend making things up as you go along as often as possible) and I get to teach and perform with an amazing group of women I adore. I've even been in a Celtic girl band (some of our stuff is on YouTube!) and was an independent film maker (go check out the Lovely Witches Club at www.lovelywitchesclub.com). My life has been one creative thing after another—all leading me here, to writing books for a living.

Now with multiple series in happy publication, I live on beautiful and magical Prince Edward Island (I know you've heard of Anne of Green Gables) with my multitude of pets.

I love-love-love hearing from you! You can reach me (and I promise I'll message back) at patti@pattilarsen.com. And if you're eager for your next dose of Patti Larsen books (usually about one release a month) come join my mailing list! All the best up and coming, giveaways, contests and, of course, my observations on the world (aren't you just dying to know what I think about everything?) all in one place: https://bit.ly/PattiLarsenEmail.

Last—but not least!—I hope you enjoyed what you read! Your happiness is my happiness. And I'd love to hear just what you thought. A review where you found this book would mean the world to me—reviews feed writers more than you will ever know. So, loved it (or not so much), your honest review would make my day. Thank you!

Made in United States
North Haven, CT
29 August 2024

56676181R00173